HIS LORDSHIP'S RETURN

Book Three of His Lordship's Mysteries

Samantha SoRelle

Balcarres Books LLC

ISBN-13: 978-1-952789-09-0
ISBN-10: 1-952789-09-5

Cover design by: Samantha SoRelle
Printed in the United States of America

Patior ergo pateris

CONTENTS

CHAPTER 1

Balcarres House, Scotland
March 1819

At first, Alfie didn't know what had awoken him. It might have been the chill in Dominick's room as the last embers burned low in the grate. Or it might have been the lightening of the sky outside the curtains, the sun rising over the distant Scottish coast in a mottled grey that might promise a day of fog, rain, brilliantly clear skies, or a bit of each in turn. Or it might have been the wound in his leg, long since scarred over, but still twinging with pain when he least suspected it.

Most likely, however, it was the mouth around his cock.

"M'Nick?" he murmured groggily, trying to see anything in the pre-dawn light.

He received an affirmative hum in answer that sent shivers running through him. He threw his head back against the pillows as Dominick's tongue laved against the underside of his cock, tracing the vein there.

Alfie wasn't even fully hard yet, barely awake and unaware which way was up or down. He gripped the sheets, digging into the mattress as the rich fabric twisted between his fingers.

"Ah, ah, a moment! Give me a moment!" he gasped.

Dominick exhaled heavily through his nose in either a laugh or a sigh. The hot gust of breath against Alfie's groin had the opposite of a calming effect. Dominick pulled back tortuously slowly, keeping up a light suction all the while, until Alfie nearly ordered him to get back to it just to stop the maddening contradiction of sensations.

Before he could gather the words to say anything, Dominick released him with a wet pop. Alfie breathed a sigh of relief, only to gasp again when he felt the press of lips against his leg, a series of kisses dappled across the sensitive skin one by one. Then that sinful tongue began to trace shapes against his inner thigh. D...o...m...

Finally untangling his hands from the sheets, Alfie lifted the covers. Dominick looked up at him like an animal exposed in its den. Blinking, he pressed a kiss to Alfie's leg, dotting the "i".

"Good morning," Dominick said, his voice deliciously rough. "Did you sleep well?"

"I did until someone rudely awoke me."

"Rude, was it? Bold words from a man completely at my mercy."

Alfie didn't even try to pretend those words didn't flare something deep inside of him. Still, it wasn't good to let Dominick have his way too easily. He was cocky enough already, no reason to add fuel to the fire.

"At your mercy, am I?" Alfie countered, letting the covers fall around Dominick's shoulders. It took most of his composure to affect a sceptical air as he reclined back decadently. "From my vantage point, things look rather different."

"Oh, really?" Dominick flexed his fingers. It was only

then that Alfie realised Dominick's arms were wound under and around him, his fingers digging into the tops of Alfie's buttocks. Coiled around him like that, Dominick had him firmly ensnared and they both knew it. Still, Alfie couldn't help but notice that he was being careful not to rest any of his weight on Alfie's injured leg.

"Really. To me it looks like you're exactly where you belong." The realisation gave more fondness to Alfie's tone than he intended. He waved a hand loftily. "Now that I'm awake enough to enjoy it, feel free to return to sucking me off at your leisure."

The words came more steadily than they would have a year ago, but a year ago he didn't have Dominick. He didn't know then what it was to be so in love and be loved in return. Back then he'd never imagined he could feel a tenth of the joy, the contentment, the *pleasure* that Dominick made him feel. And if one of the secondary effects of all that was a filthier vocabulary, then so be it.

Dominick shook his head and Alfie watched for the moment when he decided which way he wanted things to go. Was he going to give in to Alfie's command or try to punish him for his boldness? It might be... *invigorating* to wrestle for control. Alfie would never win in a fair fight against him, but Dominick wasn't the only one with tricks.

Alfie's prick twitched as he waited to see which it would be.

Then with a saucy wink more suited to the musical hall than the bedroom, Dominick leaned down and that glorious mouth was on him once again.

The sensation was exquisite. The hot, wet drag of lips up and down his length, interspersed with licks and kisses whose unpredictability seemed purposefully calculated to drive him mad. He buried a hand in Dominick's golden hair, needing something to hold onto before he flew apart. His chest heaved as he struggled to breathe under the onslaught of pleasure, the cold air raising bumps on his bare skin.

"Up, up," he panted after only a few minutes, tugging Dominick's hair. "I want more of you."

Once again, Dominick reluctantly released him, making Alfie question his own sanity. What kind of man wakes to find his gorgeous lover in the process of bringing him to climax and interrupts him not once, but twice?

Then with a final squeeze, Dominick unwrapped his arms from around Alfie's legs and dragged himself up the bed with the sinuous grace of a jungle cat, rubbing every inch of his naked body against Alfie's as he did so. He planted his elbows on either side of Alfie's head and leaned down to kiss him.

The taste of his own pre-spend was rich in Dominick's mouth and Alfie's hips jerked involuntarily, held firmly down by Dominick's own. It seemed he wasn't the only one who was hard.

"Was something the matter?" Dominick breathed against his lips when he finally pulled away. "Or were you just cold?"

"Bit of both. You were too far away and I'm afraid my nightshirt is..." Alfie tore his gaze away from the man above him and squinted at the room. Dominick took the opportunity to bite gently against his jaw. "Elsewhere."

Dominick chuckled. "That's your own fault. I'd have happily fucked you in it last night if you weren't such a damned prissy little lordling."

Prissy little lordling. Even though he knew Dominick didn't mean anything by them, something about those words made Alfie's stomach squirm in a way that was not entirely pleasant. But he couldn't put his finger on what exactly bothered him, so he pushed the feeling aside. He had more important things to focus on.

"I see no reason for doing things by halves," he sniffed. "If I'm going to dedicate myself to the sybaritic pleasures of being a catamite, I'm going to commit to them fully, with no layers of fabric to impede the process."

Dominick's head dropped against his shoulder. "I'm not awake enough for that kind of language. Just tell me how you want to fuck."

Alfie gave that question the consideration it was due, even as his entire body screamed at him to pick something, *anything.* He twisted his fingers in Dominick's hair until his lover made some truly indecent noises, then ran his other hand down the great planes of his back.

He couldn't quite reach Dominick's arse, the angle being too awkward and there being quite a lot of broad shoulders and heavy muscle in the way. His fingers brushed the dimples at the base of Dominick's spine. If he really reached, he could just barely feel the delicious swell of his buttocks below. Dominick arched his back, pressing up against Alfie's hand, the "Is this what you want?" as clear as if he'd spoken the words aloud.

As tempting a thought as that was, the urgent throbbing of his cock made the decision for him.

"I think I would prefer to be the literal definition of catamite once again."

Dominick pulled back just enough to blink at him.

"That means I want *you* to fuck *me*."

"You could've just said," Dominick grumbled.

He let Dominick pull away to fetch the little bottle of oil they'd used the night before.

"I wouldn't last long enough to get you ready," Alfie responded, wrapping a hand around himself as he waited, missing the feel of Dominick already. "I should still be mostly prepared from last night."

He let his hand drift lower, feeling his entrance. A bit tender, but nothing he didn't think he could handle, and still relaxed. He slid two fingers inside himself, wrinkling his nose at the sensation. He'd definitely need more oil before he was ready for Dominick's cock.

"Christ, look at you. Fuck, Alfie, you're so gorgeous I can't bear it sometimes." Dominick sat heavily on the bed, bottle in hand.

"Then stop looking and do something about it," Alfie said, cheeks flushing at his own brazenness.

The next few minutes were something of a blur as Dominick slicked his fingers and replaced Alfie's with his own, kissing and licking and biting Alfie's chest and throat all the while, mixing praise with obscenities. He shouldered his way between Alfie's legs as he worked, forcing them apart, and it was all Alfie could do to bite his wrist to keep from screaming the manor down.

"You fucking beauty," Dominick whispered. "Look how easily you spread yourself for me. Christ, you really want it, don't you?"

"Want *you*, Nick." Alfie panted.

His injured leg took that exact moment to protest, a

sharp pain radiating out from his wound causing Alfie to kick out involuntarily and gasp.

How Dominick realised it was a gasp of pain and not pleasure Alfie had no idea, but he immediately stopped his madding strokes inside him, three fingers by now. It took effort, but Alfie kept Dominick locked in place with his good leg, even as his left leg felt like it was being stabbed with knives.

"Shh, shh, it's all right, love," Dominick said. "I've got you."

Alfie rolled his head back against the pillows. No, it fucking wasn't all right. He wanted Dominick to fuck him, not be his fucking nursemaid.

"It's fine," he gritted out. "Keep going."

Dominick scoffed. "I'm aiming for a bit better than 'fine'. Only you would be so persnickety about having your cock sucked, only to then try to ignore a gunshot wound."

He lowered Alfie's leg to the mattress and Alfie wanted to cry at the gentleness of it.

"Don't stop," he begged. "Please."

"I'm not doing anything of the sort," Dominick said—the liar—even as he pulled his fingers from Alfie's body. "Just changing directions. Roll over for me."

Alfie did, his injured leg immediately relaxing as it rested against the bed and was no longer being forced into the air. The pain still lingered, but was nothing compared to the need thrumming through Alfie's body, now heightened to a fever pitch. The sun had risen fully and they didn't have long before the rest of the household began to stir.

He watched over his shoulder as Dominick fussed with

the pillows until he found one he deemed adequate, sliding it under Alfie's hips. This angle was even better, taking more pressure off his leg, even as it put him fully on display like an unrepentant wanton. He buried his face in the remaining pillows so Dominick couldn't see his blush.

"Better?" Dominick asked, carefully nudging Alfie's legs apart just enough to kneel between them but no further.

"Better." Alfie admitted.

"Good."

He twitched as Dominick's hands came to rest on his hips and braced himself for the coming onslaught. But Dominick only rubbed his thumbs in small, firm circles right over the joints that hurt when Alfie walked for too long. With every stroke, a bit more of his constant tension left him.

"Thank you," he murmured into the pillows. "You're too good to me."

"I'm exactly as good as you deserve," Dominick said. Alfie felt the brush of a kiss behind his ear. "But love, you've been tormenting me long enough. I really would like to fuck you now."

"Well," Alfie said, turning his head so he could look at Dominick with one eye. "Perhaps you should do that. After all, I am completely at your mercy."

They both groaned when Dominick lined up his cock and slowly sunk into him inch by inch. It seemed like it would never end. Alfie had perhaps been too cavalier in assuming he was ready to be penetrated again so soon after the night before.

The angle allowed Dominick to push deep inside and for an overwhelming moment, discomfort sparked along his nerves as Dominick pressed in, feeling larger than ever. The ring he wore on a chain around his neck dug into Alfie's back, the metal already warmed by their bodies.

Alfie couldn't breathe. Dominick was in him, around him, above him. The smell of his sweat filled Alfie's lungs and when he tried to exhale, Dominick was twisting over him, parting Alfie's lips with his tongue, claiming him yet another way.

The moment passed, leaving only lust in its wake. Alfie surged upwards, rocking his hips back against Dominick and deepening the kiss, sucking Dominick's tongue further into his mouth and lapping at it with his own. Beneath the lingering traces of himself, he could taste the slight sourness of morning breath and the barest hint of cloves from Dominick's tooth powder the night before. Somehow the mundane domesticity of that taste dissolved all his fears and discomfort, mixing what remained into a heady blend that drove his desire even higher. Dominick wasn't some perfect storybook prince. He was better than that—he was real, he was here, and he was all Alfie's.

Everything that had happened since Alfie awoke hit him all at once and he bucked his hips, driving himself back onto Dominick again and again.

"Shh, you'll hurt yourself," Dominick said, voice filled with the strain of holding back.

"Don't. Care."

Alfie nearly cried out when his frantic thrusts were stilled by one of Dominick's heavy hands forcing him down into the mattress, as unforgiving and immovable as stone.

"Well, I do. Now stop squirming and let me do this properly, you rattlebrained idiot."

Finally, *finally,* Dominick began to move, long slow thrusts that belied the harshness of his words. Nearly every one hit that spot inside Alfie that made lights explode at the corners of his eyes. Beyond all movement or speech in the face of such overwhelming pleasure, he let the sensations wash over him. He felt like he was floating above the bed, held to Earth only by Dominick's hand between his shoulder blades. His leg didn't hurt anymore. Indeed, he hardly knew he had limbs at all as he sunk bonelessly into the mattress.

The only downside was that he couldn't properly see Dominick from this position. He could feel him—*God could he feel him!* Alfie could hear his harsh breaths above him too, so he focused on those, closing his eyes as he imagined how Dominick must look driving into him, every muscle in his powerful body taut as he kept his strength leashed just enough to keep from hurting Alfie as he lay spread out like a sacrifice before him. The first rays of morning light would be making Dominick shine, glittering against the ring on its chain as well as the sweat that trickled past it through his chest hair and down his belly before dripping onto Alfie. If he could look back, would he be able to see steam curling off Dominick's body like a horse run too hard on too cold a day?

Alfie barely had the presence of mind to sneak a hand under himself, not even getting his fingers fully around his prick before he was coming—a shocking, sudden climax that stole all control from his body. He let out a strangled shout as the pleasure throttled him in its intensity, leading him from one peak to the next. Distantly, he heard Dominick swear and felt the pulse of hot liquid inside him.

When he eventually came back to himself, Dominick was no longer on top of him, but tucked up against his side, one heavy arm still thrown over Alfie's back.

"My God."

Finding it too much effort to lift his head, Alfie merely cracked open an eye. He was rewarded with a vaguely stunned Dominick looking back at him.

"That was…" Dominick started but trailed off.

Alfie completely agreed. "It was."

He rolled his shoulders to see if the rest of his body had returned to him yet. Not quite, but he could feel the imprint of Dominick's hand between his shoulders, marking him like a brand.

"You're all right?" Dominick asked. His hand ran over Alfie's back, frowning as he checked him over. His fingers didn't linger anywhere in particular, so he must not have left any visible marks, but Alfie could still feel every glorious touch. When Dominick's hand delved into the cleft between his buttocks however, Alfie mustered up enough strength to bat him away.

"I'm better than all right. Just be with me for a minute."

That turned Dominick's frown to a soft smile and he obediently drew close, shifting his body towards Alfie's rather than using his strength to pull Alfie against him. *Ridiculous man.*

Dominick dropped a light kiss against the bridge of his nose and rested their foreheads together. Alfie could happily stay like this for hours, but the dawn was ticking steadily into morning and the great clockwork that was Balcarres House would be ringing in the new day any minute.

"I'll get you a washcloth," murmured Dominick, but the way he carefully edged a leg between Alfie's suggested no such move was imminent.

Alfie yawned. "Don't bother. I'll have to head back to my room to get dressed in a minute. I'll clean up there."

"If you insist."

They lay there a few more minutes before Dominick rolled over with a sigh. "Go on then. Before I refuse to let you go at all."

Sitting up was more of an endeavour than expected. There was a pang in his backside that suggested he'd be aching all day. Slipping into his robe and slippers—his nightshirt was still nowhere to be seen, but Dominick would be sure to find it before Jarrett arrived to light the fire—Alfie was almost glad he had the excuse of his cane to lean on.

As he walked—he refused to use the word "hobbled"—to the door between their rooms, he heard Dominick call out.

"Alfie?"

He turned to see Dominick lying on his back, sheets kicked to the end of the bed, one arm over his eyes.

"Next time I wake you up like that, please just let me finish sucking you off. Christ, I can't do that every morning."

"But Nick," Alfie replied, pressing a hand to his chest in over-exaggerated surprise. "Why are you blaming me? After all, I was completely at your mercy!"

CHAPTER 2

Dominick couldn't hide his self-satisfied grin as Alfie stepped gingerly into the breakfast room and took his seat with a small wince.

"Wipe that smirk off your face, you look like a melodrama villain." Alfie hissed, rapping Dominick's ankle with his cane.

Dominick grinned wider and picked up the teapot to pour Alfie a cup. "Why should I? It's a beautiful morning. Can't a man smile at such a lovely start to the day?"

Alfie mumbled something about him never getting a lovely anything ever again, but Dominick stirred plenty of cream and sugar into the tea before sliding the cup over and that placated him.

In truth, aside from Alfie's beautiful performance in bed, the morning truly was a ghastly one. Dominick didn't think there was anything as miserable as a Scottish winter, but it was possible a Scottish spring was even worse. While the winter had been an unending grey, the spring rain was nearly as cold as it had been in January, but pelted down like an overturned bucket, soaking through even the thickest wools.

The Scottish weather was made worse by the few brief moments when the clouds parted and the sun shone down on the landscape. Then, the sodden earth shone with a metallic intensity and the flowers of gorse bushes that ran rampant hurt the eyes with the brilliance of their yellow blooms after so much grey. There was something not quite real about such a place, and Dominick's breath would catch in his throat, all the stories of fair folk seeming so real he could almost hear a faint laughter rolling up from under the hills. Then the rain would start again, and the world was wretched and gloomy once more.

He'd had a lifetime to get used to the cruelty of a London winter. Years of permanently damp shoes and frozen toes, blankets that were always too thin, the endless cough that came of sitting too close to smoking black hearths for months on end, never escaping the reek of coal and tallow that meant you'd kept warm enough to live through another night. He'd been lucky to survive his childhood, Alfie even more so, the two of them curling together on a grimy workhouse mattress, packed as close as two rats in a nest to keep what little warmth they had between them. Dominick could still remember the icy blocks of Alfie's feet pressed between his knees, and praying to whoever would listen that the smaller boy would keep shivering, because it would be worse if he stopped.

How wonderful it was now to be able to curl up with Alfie under thick blankets and heavy down, free to hold each other close not because it meant the difference between life and death, but because they wanted to. Because the feeling of Alfie in his arms, warm and soft and *safe* was the greatest joy Dominick had ever known.

Although the little blighter still wedged his icy feet between Dominick's shins.

He glanced over at where Alfie was cradling his teacup under his nose, eyes closed in contentment as he breathed in the aromatic steam.

Well, perhaps the world isn't quite so wretched after all.

Dominick gave Alfie's shoulder a brief squeeze as he rose to view the offerings on the buffet table. It was silly to have a whole buffet just for the two of them, but unfortunately Dominick's Christmas gift to Janie had had an unintended effect. He'd hoped the cookbook would help the maid-turned-cook produce something edible, but instead of improving her efforts, it had only emboldened them. As a result, the usual eggs, rolls, and sausages were today accompanied by thick slices of what was hopefully pork, an unrecognisable and unappealing jam, and a haggis so undercooked it could still bleat.

"You do know you're an earl," he said as he picked through the least-burned slices of toast and added two to Alfie's plate. "You could have any chef in Scotland, or even most of Europe if you wanted. You've had plenty of time to find a new one."

"I know," replied Alfie, looking slightly abashed. "But Janie tries so hard. I'm sure it's only a matter of time before she comes into her own in the kitchen. Besides, if I can't have Mrs. Hirkins' cooking, then what's the point? My God, did she ever make you Bath buns while we were in London? I would do ungodly things for just one more of those."

Dominick noted that for future reference. Aside from the fact he'd happily eaten them all, he couldn't remember any particular treats from Mrs. Hirkins' kitchen. Alfie's kitchen really, although it'd been destroyed along with almost everything else when the Bedford Street townhouse had gone up in flames. He tried to think about that terrible night as little as possible and any memories he had of meals prepared by Alfie's cook were flavoured with a rightful fear of the formidable woman and her rolling pin.

He gave the pork a sniff and added a slice to both plates. "So be it, but you'd best remember you said that when you're casting up your—"

Whatever Alfie might be casting up was interrupted by a quick knock at the door, followed immediately by Jarrett, the young valet's eyes bright as he gave Dominick a quick once over. The idiot flirted as easily as he breathed, but that wasn't what had Dominick so annoyed.

"Oi, what was that?" he demanded, handing Alfie his breakfast.

"What?" asked Jarrett with his usual lack of decorum. "I knocked, didn't I?"

"And did you hear a 'Come in, Jarrett.' or a 'Sod off, Jarrett.'? You've got to wait for a reply."

Jarrett rolled his eyes.

"And show some respect to His Lordship while you're at it."

Jarrett rolled his eyes again, then added a cheeky, "Sir."

Alfie snorted into his tea.

"Much better," Dominick said. By Jarrett's standards, it actually was. "And what can we do for you this morning?"

"Brought the post, sir."

"Thank you. Hand it over and help yourself to something if you haven't eaten yet."

Jarrett set the few letters down on a small tray within Alfie's reach designed for just that purpose.

"I've eaten already, sir. Thank you," the valet said, with

his best attempt at manners. He immediately ruined the image of the respectful servant by dipping a finger in the jam and looking up at Dominick through his eyelashes. "Although, I do love a bit of sweet in the morning."

Before Dominick could warn him, Jarrett popped his finger in his mouth. His attempt at a sultry look immediately turned to one of revulsion before he began to hack and cough.

"Ah, we've finally found the batch of preserves Janie made with salt rather than sugar," Alfie said, reaching for the letter opener without looking up. "Thank you, Jarrett, for testing it so Dominick and I didn't have to. Your loyalty to the household's continued well-being will be reflected in next quarter's wages."

Still spluttering, Jarrett exited without waiting to be properly dismissed or even giving a bow. But under the circumstances, Dominick could forgive him.

"You could replace him too, you know," he muttered as he tucked into his breakfast at last.

"Nonsense," said Alfie. "You like him too much."

Dominick dropped his fork. Before he could put into words the many, *many* ways Alfie was grossly wrong to even suggest such a thing, Alfie interrupted him with an unconcerned wave of his hand.

"I'm not jealous. It's good for you to have a friend. Besides, as long as he's making cow eyes at you, he's not getting into worse trouble by flinging himself at the wrong man."

"Blatant little trollop's going to get his head kicked in if he's not careful."

"Precisely." Alfie flipped over another letter. "Which is

why it's good he has you to keep that from happening. Why do you care so much about his manners anyway? You act like a cat held over a bath every time I try to teach you any."

That was only partially true. Dominick had become much more interested in proper etiquette once Alfie added cocksucking as a reward for lessons learned.

But that was not an approach he was willing to suggest to Jarrett, no matter how effective it would probably be.

"Do I really need to explain why us having some warning is important when we're alone in a room together?"

Alfie nodded his head, silently ceding the point.

"And besides, it's just... we'd been practising, is all," Dominick said, feeling his ears grow distinctly red. "We've got all the dishes down now; him which plate to take after each course and me which forks to use to eat off 'em. I thought he'd want to show off what he'd learned, not be a contrary nag."

Alfie's lips twisted in a small, sure smile. "I can't imagine where he picked that up," he murmured. Then his smile grew broader. "Speak of the Devil and *she* shall appear! We've a letter from Mrs. Hirkins!"

Alfie swiftly tore the letter open and scanned the first few lines. His eyebrows shot up before dropping into a frown. He glanced through the few pages, then let out a laugh.

"I think this page is meant for you," he said, handing over the paper. "She's not usually quite so... direct in her letters to me."

Dominick took the letter.

Damned cully! Why waste money sending me that blasted

shawl? You forget we have those in London already? I'll wear it because it's warm and the colours are fine enough. But if I knew you were going to bleed away Master Alfie's coin, I would've thrown you out on your ear. Thank you for asking over Daisy, the damned dog is useless as always. She's with my son's family now and better behaved than half his whelps...

"I knew she'd like the shawl." Dominick grinned.

Alfie hummed distractedly and when Dominick looked over, his brow was furrowed.

"What's wrong?"

"She says her husband is still unwell." Alfie turned over the page he held and began reading the back. "He often takes a chill in early winter, but he was still abed when she sent this."

Dominick didn't like the sound of that. "What's the postmark?"

"Late-February."

"That's a long time for an early winter chill to linger."

I know, that's why I'm worried. She doesn't outright say it, but it sounds like she's worried too."

Dominick skimmed over the rest of his own letter. "She doesn't mention anything in mine."

Alfie shook his head. "She wouldn't unless you specifically asked. Mrs. Hirkins is happy to tell the whole world their business, but shuts up tighter than a clam about her own."

Dominick remembered her telling him the story of her lost childhood love and was even more honoured to have been taken into her confidences than before.

"How can we help?" he asked.

Alfie set the letter down. "I don't know. I sent plenty of

money for medicine with her Christmas gifts. She spends half a page berating me for the unnecessary expense, although in slightly more polite language than she sent you."

"Slightly?"

"Well, she crossed out the obscenities after committing them to paper. It's the thought that counts."

Alfie tapped the table, a quick, nervous tattoo. "It does seem like there should be something else to be done. I could write a letter to a doctor in London, send it post-haste. But the only doctor I really knew was Doctor Barlowe."

The sour feeling in Dominick's gut at the mention of the man's name matched the look on Alfie's face.

"And by the time I send a letter asking an acquaintance to find someone..."

"Even if you do, any fancy Harley Street doctor they come up with isn't going to take the health of a housekeeper's husband seriously. Certainly not enough to do anything before his winter chill turns into a summer one."

Dominick didn't have to ask Alfie why this was so important to him. Mrs. Hirkins had been the only one to give a damn about Alfie after he'd been secretly adopted by the former Lord and Lady Crawford. Whether he realised it or not, the woman was the closest thing he'd ever had to a mother. If the incredibly generous pension he'd given her didn't make that clear, the glowing warmth in his voice whenever he spoke of her certainly did.

Alfie sighed. "If only I wasn't so far away."

Dominick looked down at the mangled and charred

crusts on his plate. Mrs. Hirkins' bread had tasted like a slice of heaven itself, served every morning with honey butter alongside fried sausages, plump and juicy, whose skin gave with a mouthwatering crispness to each bite. On further reflection, the crusts on his plate might actually be the remains of Janie's attempt at sausages. They certainly had the same sooty taste.

"We could go back to London," he offered, as much out of the desires of his belly as the goodness of his heart.

"What?" said Alfie.

"Not forever, of course." Dominick began to warm to the idea. "You're entirely wrong about Jarrett being anything other than a damned nuisance, but despite him, Balcarres House does have its charms. I like the horses and the countryside is pretty enough to look at if it ever stopped raining. It's a nice little set-up with our connecting rooms too. I have found a use for that a time or two."

Alfie shook his head again, this time fondly, and Dominick congratulated himself on bringing a smile back to his love's face.

"But that doesn't mean we can't flit off down to London now and then. Go and send your letters ahead to as many of those acquaintances as you have addresses for and we'll follow them down. Let's see if those doctors don't find their feet moving a bit faster with an earl breathing down their necks!"

"Do you really mean it?" Alfie's voice was choked, but for the life of him, Dominick couldn't understand why.

"Sure. If all those lovebirds in novels can fly up to Gretna Green for a hasty marriage, I see no reason why we can't fly back down."

Dominick stopped as one reason sprang to mind. "Unless the journey would be too hard on you. I could go by myself. I'm no earl, but what I lack in a title I make up for in a stiff right hook."

Alfie laughed. "Let's subdue your 'persuasive demeanour' when we meet the doctors. I can't have you threatening half of Harley Street. And my leg's fine. It won't be a problem."

Dominick couldn't keep the look of disbelief off his face. Seeing Alfie get shot was one of the worst things that had ever happened to him. He wasn't likely to forget it any time soon, no matter how much Alfie attempted to dismiss the severity of his injury. The fact that at first Alfie avoided doing any of the recommended exercises hadn't helped it to heal, nor had his endless running after ghosts and murderers once they'd arrived at Balcarres. The gymnasium Dominick put together in one of the spare rooms had helped, although not as much as Alfie's realisation that getting strong enough to ride again could apply to more than just horses. After that, he'd been all but dragging Dominick to the gymnasium to help him work up a lather.

They even managed to stick to the prescribed regimen. Mostly. Dominick dared anyone faced with a flushed and shirtless Alfie covered with a fine sheen of sweat and glowing with pride to not think up ways in which his increased flexibility could be put to the test.

Even though he still wasn't fully healed, their hard work had seen results outside of the bedroom—and gymnasium floor, abandoned tool shed, secluded corners of the gardens—as well. They'd taken a few short rides together around the grounds, Alfie grinning in the pale spring sun, puffs of breath hovering like clouds around him as he laughed and pushed his horse to a trot. He wasn't strong enough to canter yet, and the day after any ride saw him limping around the manor as heavily as before, fingers white-knuckled around his cane. If a short horse ride could do that much damage, how much worse would untold days in a carriage be?

Dominick tapped his foot pointedly against the gold-handled cane leaning against the breakfast table. "The fact you still need this says to me your leg might not be up to the trip."

"Really?" Alfie snatched up the cane and rose. "I mostly keep this around for the look of the thing, you know. Quite fashionable. And the sword within has come in handy, I admit."

He did a lap around the perimeter of the room, pointedly keeping the cane off the ground at all times. Despite his claims, Alfie's gait was markedly uneven and by the time he returned to his seat, the toll the unaided walk had taken was clear in the pained lines around his mouth.

"Don't give me that look." Alfie snapped. "You know perfectly well I don't always need it. I can usually walk just fine when I haven't been subjected to *someone's* oversized appendage first thing in the morning."

That startled a laugh out of Dominick. "I'd best keep it to myself then. For the sake of your health."

"Don't you dare." Alfie glowered, then his expression softened as he went back to Mrs. Hirkins' letter, reading it through again. "I think," he said softly, "for her I can do it."

The look on his face—worried and fierce all at once—

was more than Dominick could bear.

"All right," he said, touching Alfie's wrist gently. "But you change your mind at any point, I'll be happy to dump you at a coaching inn and go on alone."

Alfie shook his head. "No, you wouldn't. You're a damned mother hen. If I so much as have an itch on the back of my knee you'll be telling the driver to pull over so you can lay damp flannels across my brow and carry me back to the manor in your arms like an overcome damsel."

"Been thinking about that a lot, have you?"

Alfie didn't dignify that with a reply. "Look at it this way: the sooner we get on the road to London, the sooner we can find a doctor to take Mr. Hirkins' illness seriously. And the sooner Mrs. Hirkins can repay our kindness in sweet rolls."

Dominick had his chair pushed back before Alfie had even finished speaking. When he put it that way, there wasn't any time to waste.

CHAPTER 3

The trip back to London was, in a word, hell.

Alfie groaned as the hack pulled to halt in front of the famous Grillion's Hotel in Mayfair. Despite their determination to get away, it'd taken several days to ensure Balcarres would run smoothly in their absence. Gil had been a tremendous help as always and it was he who'd suggested that since time was of the essence, they take a personal carriage only as far as Edinburgh then catch the mail coach from there. This suggestion had led to Dominick cursing the man's name aloud every time the speeding coach hit another bump in the road to London, sending them flying up off their poorly-sprung seats, heads knocking against the low ceiling before crashing back down. Alfie gritted his teeth against the waves of pain the unpredictable jostling caused, but couldn't bite back a whimper each time the coach sped past a cosy looking pub without the least sign of stopping.

Battered, bruised, and with only a few hours of snatched sleep the entire journey in coaching inns with walls so thin Alfie was surprised they didn't dissolve in the rain, they eventually reached London. Although Alfie was in no state to enjoy the return to the city in which he'd spent most of his life. It was all he could do to pry himself out of the mail coach then back into a hackney.

"Slowly please," he gasped to the driver. "And as smoothly as you can."

The man gave him an odd look at the request, no doubt used to being barked at to get everywhere on the double, but Alfie wasn't entirely uncertain that a single jolt from a missing cobblestone wouldn't kill him. His teeth felt nearly rattled out of his head and his entire leg throbbed in constant agony. The gunshot wound itself felt like an imp had stuck a hot poker through it and was slowly twisting.

"Damned hard-headed sod," Dominick grumbled as he waved off the liveried footmen and helped Alfie up Grillion's marble stairs himself. "I told you I could've bloody well come by myself. Now look at you. Christ, sit here while I get everything sorted."

Alfie dropped, partially at Dominick's command, but mostly from sheer fatigue and was pleasantly surprised to find himself on a velvet divan in Grillion's lobby.

"I've written ahead, while we were still at Balcarres," he said weakly. "And there'll be letters from my man of business, correspondence about suitable doctors..."

"I know all about your fucking letters," Dominick replied gruffly.

His hands twitched, as if he wanted to make Alfie more comfortable but only at the last minute remembered they were in public and such things between two male acquaintances, even those who claimed to be cousins, would be frowned upon, if not worse.

"If there's any doctors available, they'll be seeing you first. Mr. Hirkins can wait his turn. In fact... Oy, you!"

Dominick pointed at one of the footmen who wasn't carrying their limited luggage in from the hack. "This is the bloody Earl of Crawford. He needs a doctor, a room, and a hot bath. Quick now!"

Alfie smiled through the pain. Softly so only Dominick could hear, he said, "So commanding. I'll make a nobleman of you yet."

"Shut up or I'll finish what that damned mail coach started and beat you to death right here in this fancy hotel in front of all these other toffs."

"It's not too late for the damsel carrying and damp flannels."

"Don't tempt me." Dominick turned his direction back to the footman. "And don't forget his damned correspondence!"

❋ ❋ ❋

An indeterminate amount of time later found Alfie housed, bathed, and in possession of a number of tinctures and tonics pressed upon him by the hotel doctor. He rolled one of the small bottles back and forth between his palms.

"What do you think the odds are of being poisoned by two murderous London doctors in a row?"

"Less than the odds of me tying you to the bed and forcing that down your throat if you don't take it yourself."

"Perhaps another night," Alfie said, leaning back against his bed's many pillows. Not that Dominick would ever *force* him to do—or take—anything that Alfie didn't want, and there were few things that Alfie *didn't* want when it came to him. But Dominick really was so very strong. If he wanted to, he could. Especially if Alfie was tied up…

His cock gave a valiant twitch at the idea, but he was in no state to do anything about it.

Dominick exited their private bathing room rubbing a towel over his hair. He was naked save for his necklace but had a look on his face that said that even if Alfie was in a state to want it, he wasn't in any mood to give it to him.

A shame too, the crowded mail coach had lacked both space and privacy for anything more than a bit of surreptitious hand holding. Their suite offered more than enough of both. It wasn't as comfortably familiar as their rooms in Balcarres, but it made up for the lack in sheer opulence.

Grillion's was considered one of the few hotels in London suitable for nobility and even occasionally royalty. Gleaming white and black marble ran from the floor up to the three separate fireplaces in their set of rooms alone. Every flat surface large enough to hold a vase had been ornamented with fresh flowers whose scent worked wonders to keep the ever-present smell of the London streets at bay. The curtains hung around the windows were of a rich peacock blue that matched both the wallpaper and the exotic rugs that covered nearly every inch of the floor.

The exotic rugs that Dominick was currently dripping on. Even by Alfie's standards the place was exorbitant, but either Dominick had become more inured to wealth during the last year or he'd been too focused on finally getting a chance to wash off the road dust to notice.

"Well, what are you waiting for?" Dominick said. "Take your medicine already, it hurts to look at you."

Dominick disappeared to rummage through the clothes that had already been put away by the hotel staff.

It'd been all the two of them could do to shoo away the complimentary valet. They could easily manage between them for their short stay and the fewer persons inclined to pop into their suite, the better.

"Perhaps later," Alfie replied. "I can smell the poppies coming off this one through the bottle. It's barely past noon and once I take laudanum, I'm going to be useless for the rest of the day. Honestly, the hot bath did more for me than a dozen patent medicines. I'll be all right until we can get a doctor sorted for Mr. Hirkins. Where did you put those letters?"

Dominick, now dressed in shirtsleeves and trousers, came over to where Alfie was propped up in bed, letters in hand. "Are you sure? One more day won't hurt if you need to rest."

"For God's sake!" Alfie snapped, pain giving his words a sharpness he didn't intend. "I'm not an invalid. I'm a bit sore, not coughing up blood. Stop hovering and just give me the fucking letters!"

Wordlessly, Dominick handed them over. Then he turned his back on Alfie and went back to dressing.

Alfie sighed, setting the letters down in his lap. As soon as they were in his hand, shame had risen up, choking his throat and burning his eyes. Dominick was only trying to help and he was right, Alfie was in pain. The whole trip had been a terrible idea. What point was there in coming to help in person if he was too hurt to leave the bed. It'd been his damned pride that had put him in that coach, nothing more. He'd wanted to prove that he was strong and capable and he'd done just the opposite.

As strong and capable as Dominick? A dark voice

whispered. Alfie did his best to push it to the back of his mind. Of course, he wasn't as strong as Dominick. That was fine. He didn't need to be. He was just so tired of his damned leg slowing him down, that was all. It'd been a mistake to assume it was more healed than it was without consulting a doctor, but there was nothing he could do about that now.

If only Dominick didn't look at him that way when his leg was especially bad, like Alfie was something small and delicate and in need of protection. Like a pampered pet rabbit too vulnerable to survive in the wild.

"I'm sorry," Alfie called out. "I shouldn't have snapped."

"You shouldn't," Dominick said, returning to the room. He was mostly dressed now, save for an undone cravat. "But I'll forgive you because I feel like I've been rolled all the way here in a barrel and I *don't* have a hole in my leg."

He set a small object into Alfie's lap, then pulled a chair up beside the bed. Alfie fished around in the blankets and came up with a letter opener. It was gilt, of course. Slicing open the first letter, he skimmed the contents before tossing it aside and reaching for the next.

"Lady Warriston sends her regards and rejoices in my return to the ton but has no idea where to find a doctor willing to travel to that part of town. However, she will be throwing a lovely soiree..."

"You'd think we were asking them to go to the Devil's Acre, not Canonbury."

The next letter was much the same, although more overt in mentioning Sir Burford's most accomplished —and unattached—daughter. Several other letters were equally unhelpful, so he tossed the unopened remainder aside one by one until he came across one addressed in a plain, bold hand instead of one so needlessly decorative as to be illegible.

"Any luck?" asked Dominick.

"I think this is from my solicitors." Alfie tore open the letter. "Thank God. A Doctor Geddes was dispatched—what's the date?—yesterday. There should be a letter with his findings."

" 'Geddes' you said?" Dominick bent down to pick up the discarded letters that had slid off the bed to the floor.

"Yes, why? Do you see it?"

"I think so. Handwriting's a bit messy, but not the way the others are."

Alfie extended the letter opener handle-first, but Dominick just broke the seal with a finger. He read slowly, lips moving as he went.

"Well, what does it say?"

Dominick was silent for a long moment. Then he cleared his throat.

" 'I regret to inform you that by the time I arrived, the patient was beyond treatment. Preparations are currently underway for his burial, the details of which I have listed below if you are interested in attendance. His widow asked me to pass along her thanks for your concern.' I'm so sorry, Alfie."

The hot agony he'd endured since he left Balcarres chilled into numbness. All this way for nothing. If he'd responded faster, or thought to send doctors to check before he'd gotten Mrs. Hirkins' letter, knowing her husband's annual illness, would it have made a difference? Would Mr. Hirkins still be alive if Alfie had done something

—anything?

He reached for the medicine bottle as Dominick read off the details for the funeral to take place in two days' time. That was a small blessing at least. Alfie had plenty of time for the laudanum to do its work and ease his pain.

At the moment, he couldn't think of anything he wanted more than to not feel for a while.

CHAPTER 4

Alfie didn't have much to say the next two days and Dominick tried not to let that worry him. He should be pleased Alfie was actually listening to doctor's orders for once, resting his leg and taking his medicine. However, he knew there was a problem when he suggested Alfie do his leg stretches and Alfie actually did so without complaint.

"Did you know him well?" Dominick asked.

They were on a rug in the suite's sitting room, Alfie's leg extended in a straight line before him, Dominick's hands wrapped around his foot. He applied pressure and Alfie hissed as he pushed as hard as he could, trying to point his toes while Dominick forced them back.

"Did I know who?"

"Mr. Hirkins, the man whose funeral we're attending this afternoon." Dominick let his grip slacken and watched the tendons in Alfie's leg relax.

"No," Alfie finally replied. "I only met him a handful of times. I do feel terrible for Mrs. Hirkins though."

Dominick nodded and pressed against his foot again. "She's a strong woman."

"I know," Alfie said, voice tight with strain. "But she shouldn't have to be."

Dominick couldn't argue with that. They repeated the exercise a dozen times more, then ran through a few stretches. Finally, he extended a hand to help Alfie to his feet.

"I don't know who's in charge of cleaning these rooms," Dominick grumbled as he dusted off his trousers, "but they're doing a piss poor job of it."

Alfie laughed. "You're sounding more like a real aristocrat every day! 'Dismiss Jarrett! These eggs are undercooked! I can't see my reflection in the washbasin!' Next thing I know, you'll be complaining that the linens aren't properly pressed and the pillows are under-stuffed!"

Dominick flashed a glance guiltily towards his bedroom. Fortunately, a maid had already come by, so the pillow he'd folded in half in the middle of the night had been returned to its proper place and couldn't be used to prove Alfie right.

"I'm just saying," he grumbled, "with all the money you lot throw around, you think there'd be a little more to show for it."

Alfie shook his head. "*Our* lot. You're worth as much as I am now, Nick. You've done marvellously learning all the silly rules that come with wealth. Remember, I know how hard it is to adjust to it all too. It doesn't make you soft to want nice things now that you can have them."

Dominick didn't have a response to that. Time was, he would've envied a woman who had a steady job as a maid in a place like this, even if it meant putting up with the rich swells who thought they deserved whatever they wanted just because they had money. It was hard to believe he was now one of those rich swells and was behaving just as badly. He pushed down the rising shame.

"Don't forget to touch your toes," he grumbled. "Then

we'd best get dressed for the funeral."

Alfie sneered in an unhappy but silent response.

* * *

Some time later, they found themselves trundling along the streets of London in a carriage provided courtesy of the hotel. Dominick would've been happy to hail a hack, but instead they'd been obliged to wait as the concierge summoned the single most gaudy monstrosity ever set upon wheels. If it was meant to be an advertisement for the opulence of the hotel, it was all that and then some.

The body of the carriage was a lacquered peacock blue that glimmered like the shell of an insect suspended above pristine white wheels that looked far too delicate to support its bloated body. Dominick didn't envy the boy whose job it was to keep those wheels clean of the London filth, not to mention whoever had to shine all the unnecessary flourishes on the many brass fittings. The metal decorated every conceivable edge of the carriage in delicate scrollwork that must be the devil to polish. As the carriage pulled to a stop, a footman dressed like he'd hopped out of a portrait of Alfie's ancestors, powdered wig and all, held open a carriage door adorned with the Grillion's crest in gilt paint.

At least the footman himself wasn't as perfectly shined as the carriage. Dominick couldn't help but notice that his wig was slightly askew and his stockings hung limp over his skinny calves. The young man then unfolded a little step so they could go straight from the hotel's marble steps into the carriage's carpeted interior.

"He'd better not take my hand to help me in," Dominick muttered under his breath.

"Then don't offer it," replied Alfie with an ungentlemanly snort of laughter.

Only a year's worth of exposure to the life of an earl kept Dominick from groaning when he discovered the inside of the carriage was possibly even more overdone than the outside. The lining was all done in blue velvet, the same shade as the curtains in their suite, and seat cushions were stuffed within an inch of their lives. He wouldn't complain about that at least, his arse could still feel every rut in the road from Edinburgh to London.

As they rode along, Alfie sat across from him with his leg propped up beside Dominick's hip, his still-pristine shoe not even leaving a smudge of dust on the cushion. He looked as fine as ever. The funereal suit his usual London tailor, Mr. Bonheur, had provided at great speed—and even greater expense—was a pure black that contrasted beautifully with Alfie's creamy complexion.

He'd slicked his hair back in a way that Dominick hadn't seen him do in months. No reason to, with no one to impress in their tucked away corner of Scotland, but seeing his abundant curls beaten and tamed reminded Dominick once again that he was sharing a carriage with a bloody *earl* now. Alfie wasn't the boy who'd cried when his hands were pricked raw from the oakum ropes they'd had to pick apart at the workhouse. Or he wasn't *just* that boy. It was easier to forget at Balcarres, but seeing Alfie back in London, back in his element, gave Dominick an odd feeling he couldn't put into words.

His own expensive suit suddenly felt damnably ill-fitting.

"Penny for your thoughts?" Alfie asked.

"Just wondering if I shouldn't have stayed back at the hotel."

"Nonsense, it will mean a lot to Mrs. Hirkins that you came."

"Right, but how are you going to explain me to everyone else? Sure, she knows I'm both Dominick Trent, your fancy man, *and* Nick Tripner the bare-knuckle-boxer-and-worse, but I imagine someone's going to ask, and I doubt the truth will be taken well."

They probably should have discussed this less than three minutes from the chapel. Alfie took up another whole minute in thought before he answered.

"First of all, you're not my fancy man, you're a well-turned-out gentleman in his own right. The fact you're mine is an entirely separate matter. Secondly, we'll stick to the story that you're my cousin. It would be odder for Nick Tripner to turn up in a fine carriage than the cousin of a lord who just happens to look a bit like him. And no one will recognise you in those clothes. Mrs. Hirkins is a shrewd woman. We don't have to worry about her giving the game away. Besides, they'll all be far more focused on their own grief than us."

As the carriage pulled up in front of a whitewashed chapel, Dominick knew Alfie was terribly, terribly wrong. The small crowd gathered in the courtyard all looked up at their arrival. Most weren't in black, just the nicest clothes they owned in sombre colours, sturdy wools in a dozen shades of brown and grey. The few black suits and dresses he spotted had the worn look of many washings.

He and Alfie were as conspicuous as two great bloody ravens in a flock of sparrows. And that was without the liveried footman hopping around the bloody carriage like a robin. Dominick got out first to block the view if Alfie stumbled, but Alfie made it out with apparent ease, passing Dominick and heading towards the chapel gates with his head held high and his—Oh, Christ—gold-handled, ebony sword cane tapping along beside him.

To Alfie's credit, he hung back a discreet distance from the burial and the attention of the crowd soon turned back to the rector as he carried on, Mrs. Hirkins planted resolutely beside him. A young woman stood on her other side, their arms linked in support. She was whispering in Mrs. Hirkins' ear, likely something comforting, but from the look on Mrs. Hirkins' face, she hadn't heard a word. She was staring at the coffin as it was lowered into the grave, but Dominick had no idea what she was really seeing.

The rector seemed in no rush to hurry things along, extolling the dead man's virtues at length and listing the rewards that were now his in the kingdom of God. To Dominick's surprise, the man's words seemed genuinely heartfelt and the faces of the fellow mourners held only grief, no trace at all of impatience to get on with their day. The few funerals Dominick had attended had been more because it was the right thing to do rather than for any actual feeling for the deceased, but the people around him were genuine in their sorrow.

He wondered what it must be like to have so many people care for you that they genuinely mourned your passing. The score or so gathered in the churchyard were hardly the crowds that turned out for the death of a royal, but their grief was all the more meaningful for its honesty.

He reflected on the few times he'd met Mr. Hirkins the year before, when he'd helped the couple move into the modest home Alfie had gifted Mrs. Hirkins upon her begrudging retirement. The man had seemed a decent sort, a pleasant enough gaffer to share a pint with by the fire. Given the choice between being remembered that way by a choice few or as a king with a thousand indifferent soldiers marching behind his coffin, Dominick knew which he'd choose.

When the ceremony finished, they waited while the other mourners offered Mrs. Hirkins their condolences. The young woman hovered near her, taking condolences of her own from some of the mourners while sharing nods of mutual sympathy with others. Finally, when the crowd had thinned to just the last few stragglers, Alfie made his way over to her, Dominick trailing behind him.

"Mrs. Hirkins, I'm so sorry—"

"Oh, Master Alfie! I thought that was you!" cried Mrs. Hirkins. Her eyes were dry for now, but her voice was distinctly watery. "Well, of course, who else would it have been? And what were you about, skulking around in the bushes! You come in here, cutting up the peace in some flashy cart, then stick to the shadows like a villain? Cock and pie! My mister's passing will be on every gossip's tongue for a month!"

At this she let out a single sob, barely managing to muffle it behind her handkerchief. The woman beside her patted her arm.

"Er, I'm sorry?" Alfie said again, clearly off his stride. He looked over at Dominick for help, but Dominick had about as much experience in dealing with distraught women as he did. Christ, what if she started crying?

Some of his alarm must have been clear on his face, because Alfie rallied. "My *cousin*, Mr. Trent and I wanted to express…"

Mrs. Hirkins snorted into her handkerchief. "*Cousin* is he now? Well, he's better than the last cousin you had. God rest his soul. And I suppose if it's good enough for the Regent to marry his cousin, then you can certainly—"

Dominick moved forward as Alfie let out a strangled noise. Mrs. Hirkins might not be crying, but she had a wildness about the eyes of a person who'd had the ground pulled out from under her and didn't know which way to turn. He'd seen the look in his own reflection before. Even if he wasn't sure how to handle female emotions, he'd best do *something* before she said anything they'd all regret later.

"Mrs. Hirkins," he said, stepping forward and taking both her hands in his. "It's wonderful to see you again. I must say, widowhood suits you."

The young woman gasped and the awfulness of his own words echoed in Dominick's ears. Mrs. Hirkins froze in place, the only movement the slight quivering of her hands. Dominick braced himself for a well-deserved slap.

Then she threw her head back and laughed. And laughed. And laughed. Her voice began in her usual steady tone, but the longer it went on, the higher and more hysterical it became.

Dominick was beginning to worry for her sanity when, just as quickly as it had begun, the laughter turned to tears. Before he knew it, she'd cast the younger woman off and

Dominick had an armful of sobbing retired housekeeper in his arms. He looked up at Alfie in a panic, only to receive a mouthed "What did you expect?" in return. The other woman was no help either, watching the scene with a pursed mouth and reddened eyes.

Finally, Mrs. Hirkins collected herself enough to take a step back. Immediately, the other woman was at her elbow again.

"Oh, Mr. Tr-Trent. The nerve of you, saying that to a woman at her husband's funeral! What a charmer you are, eh? Christ alive, I needed that. Since it happened, everyone else's been acting like I'm made of glass."

"Glass? Fine crystal, more like." Dominick said, *feeling* his Spitalfields accent thicken as much as hearing it.

She shook her head. "What nonsense you talk."

"It was nice to meet you both," said the young woman, her voice clearly conveying that it was not. Dominick had to admire her boldness. The little thing couldn't have been more than seventeen and her dark grey dress, though perfectly neat and clean, had clearly been passed down from a larger woman, perhaps a sister or cousin. Her oversized black shawl and cap added to the effect, making her look even smaller. But from the way she glared up at them from beneath escaped wisps of mousy brown hair, she was clearly related to Mrs. Hirkins.

Her next words only confirmed it. "I'm sure it would have meant a lot to my grandfather that you were here. Now if you'll excuse us, we must be getting along. There is to be a *private* supper for the family."

"Agnes," said Mrs. Hirkins sharply. "Stop being such a cross patch. Master Alfie and Mr. Trent will be joining us, of course."

"We couldn't possibly," Alfie protested, but Dominick didn't think she was asking.

"If you're sure," he said. "We don't mean to intrude. We could come back tomorrow or some other more convenient time."

"Nonsense," said Mrs. Hirkins dismissively. "It's rude to turn down a woman in mourning."

Agnes looked as if she'd eaten a raw onion, but if her grandmother noticed, she didn't show it. Dominick had the feeling it wasn't the first time since her husband's death that Mrs. Hirkins had used that line to get her way. Nor would it be the last.

Mrs. Hirkins' gaze went over their shoulders and her eyes, though still watery, shone with mischief. "Supper's at my home, the one Master Alfie got me when he cast me aside. Do you remember it, or does your man in the silk britches over there need directions?"

Alfie had hardly cast her aside, her pension being more than generous—quite a lot more than generous, in fact —and the home was a nice one. It wasn't a city palace in Mayfair, but it was a perfectly respectable home in a perfectly respectable neighbourhood—quiet, modest, and all the other virtues Mrs. Hirkins pretended to have herself.

Although the idea of taking the hotel's carriage down the tidy lane that led to her door made him uncomfortable. They were conspicuous enough here with it parked on a public road in front of the chapel. Heads would be hanging out of every window if they were to leave it in front of Mrs. Hirkins' home. If it was only him, he'd have walked the distance in a matter of minutes, but with Alfie's leg the way it was...

"I think the driver can manage the direction well enough," Alfie said. "But you must ride with us. It wouldn't be right for us to ride and leave an ol—a woman in mourning to walk."

"I could walk with her," suggested Dominick in desperation.

"Don't you dare," Mrs. Hirkins hissed. She extracted her arm from Agnes' grip and offered it to Alfie. "I suppose, since you're no longer my employer, it would be all right for you to escort me home."

"I'd be honoured, ma'am. Despite the circumstances, it really is wonderful to see you. You must tell me everything I've missed on the way."

"Oh, because you're suddenly yearning for society life, now are you? It used to be that I couldn't pry you out of that townhouse for weeks on end."

"Then it's a good thing it burned down, isn't it?"

As the two strolled slowly out of the courtyard towards the carriage, Mrs. Hirkins on Alfie's left, allowing him to still use his cane freely—surely no accident—Dominick realised he'd been left alone with Agnes.

"I am sorry for your loss. And for intruding."

Agnes frowned even harder, deepening the family resemblance. Christ, were Hirkins women born with the ability to terrify men twice their size or was that a secret they passed down the generations?

"I don't need to tell you that what Nan wants, she gets. I've not heard her speak of you before, but I know who 'Master Alfie' is. An earl at the supper table. Lord, can you imagine? I won't be able to hold my head up in church!"

Dominick grinned. "Most people would brag about it."

"Yes, well, most people don't have a rector who takes the odds of a rich man entering heaven and a camel passing through the eye of the needle seriously."

She stepped away and walked back to the gravesite. "Goodbye, Grandad. I hope there's darts in heaven."

She turned to Dominick. "Best go and warn your coachman. And if there's a flask hidden somewhere in those fancy togs, you might want to empty it now."

"Your family don't drink?" Dominick asked with some surprise.

"Don't be daft. But you're about to face the lot of them at once. Even I don't do that sober!"

Dominick nodded but felt awkward leaving her alone beside the grave. He looked around. The churchyard had already emptied, save for a pair of surly looking gravediggers eyeing them impatiently.

"Do you have someone to walk you home?" asked Dominick.

Agnes' chin tilted up defiantly. "Not that I need anyone, but my fiancé will be along at any moment."

Dominick took another look around the churchyard, but before he could think of a way to tactfully ask Agnes if she was sure, she spoke again. For the first time, her voice was uncertain.

"He was supposed to be here already. Larry said he had to work a half day this morning, but he'd be here in time."

"I'm sure it's not his fault," Dominick offered. "Something must've come up. Why don't you let me walk you home? Or no, that might raise eyebrows. We could ride in the carriage with your nan?"

At her horrified look, he pointedly directed his gaze over to where Mrs. Hirkins was climbing into the carriage by herself, slapping away the hand of the astonished footman.

"It can hardly be worse than it already is," he pointed out.

Agnes sighed. "She's become a proper terror since her 'Master Alfie' left. I think there wasn't a reason for her to hold her tongue and be respectful anymore, aside from maybe making sure Grandad weren't too embarrassed to show his face at the pub. Lord knows what she'll be like now."

"You're saying the way she used to be was her being *respectful*?"

In answer, Agnes started grimly towards the carriage.

The footman was clearly wary of offering his hand a second time, but Agnes took it and ascended as gracefully as any lady. Dominick took a moment to confirm the driver knew their direction and warn him they'd be staying for supper, something Alfie had doubtless forgotten to mention.

The matter settled, he climbed into the carriage himself and they were off.

"Your Larry never showed," Mrs. Hirkins said, having quickly gotten over the astonishment of riding in luxury.

"Nan!" Agnes hissed.

Mrs. Hirkins shrugged. "All I'm saying is, if he's got a girl in a delicate condition, the least he can do is be there to show a bit of respect for her family. Your grandad let him into our home so to save money for the coming babe, and this is how he repays him?"

Dominick and Alfie shared a horrified look. Suddenly Agnes' oversized dress made more sense. And now they were all trapped in the carriage for this conversation. Christ, what had they gotten themselves into?

"M-Mrs. Hirkins," Alfie stammered. "You never told me; did you ever find out who was responsible for the butcher cancelling your order?"

"Don't think you can distract me so easily, young man. Come autumn I'll be a *great*-grandmother, what do you think of that? But as a matter of fact, I did find out. Now, I'm not one to gossip…"

Fortunately, she spent the remaining carriage ride doing exactly that and by the time they pulled up in front of her door, even Agnes seemed to have forgotten the earlier awkwardness, leaning forward in her seat to catch every word of the tale.

"…well, of course, I told him he was mad if he thought I'd believe any such thing and furthermore—Why's the door open?"

It took Dominick a moment to realise her question wasn't a part of the story. He looked out the window and sure enough, the whitewashed door was ajar, revealing the first few inches of the home within.

"Are you sure you didn't forget to lock it?" asked Alfie, suddenly serious. "It's been a very distressing day for you. Your mind might have been on other things."

Mrs. Hirkins shook her head. "No, because I'd been thinking when I locked it about how us getting robbed would be the last thing I'd need today."

Her voice held a note of fear Dominick had never heard there before, not even after she'd awoken from being clubbed over the head then dragged from a burning building. He didn't want to hear it again.

His eyes met Alfie's.

"I'm certain it's nothing," Alfie said. "Perhaps someone with a key made it back from the funeral before we did and decided to be helpful. One of your children, perhaps? Or other grandchildren?"

"That'll be it," Dominick chimed in. "Why don't you all stay in the carriage while I make sure whoever it is hasn't gotten into your best whisky before I could?"

Stepping out of the carriage before any of them could respond, he paused on the front step, dismayed but unsurprised to hear behind him the distinctive *click* of Alfie releasing the sword from within his cane. He'd hoped Alfie would take the hint and stay where it was safe, but Dominick had known him most of his life and could hardly be surprised when he didn't. Besides, when it came down to it, there was no one he'd rather have at his back, regardless of the situation.

The fact Alfie was armed was a nice benefit as well.

Dominick pushed the door open just far enough to let himself in. He waited a moment for his eyes to adjust to the dim interior before stepping inside. The curtains were all drawn, but enough light filtered through the thin material to illuminate the outlines of a cosy sitting room with two chairs sat before a still-smouldering fire, a large basket of knitting beside one of them.

In the other chair sat a man, his head tucked down against his chest. He wore a black jacket and trousers, and must have been wearing a black waistcoat as well, because Dominick nearly missed him in the dark without the tell-tale white of his shirt to give him away.

"Oy," said Dominick. "Who said you could be in here?"

When the man didn't respond, Dominick bit back a curse. The damned cove *had* broken in and been at the whisky. How dare he take advantage of a household's grief like that? Even worse, how dare he take advantage of Mrs. Hirkins like that?

"I'm talking to you," growled Dominick, stalking across the room towards the man and hoisting him up by the lapels.

"Nick!" Alfie warned, but it was too late. Dominick shook the man, whose head lolled from side-to-side with the movement, then tilted back at an impossible angle.

The man's neck opened in a gaping wound like a second mouth yawning wide, the flesh cut so deep that Dominick could see the white of bone. With a shout, Dominick dropped him. He crumpled in a heap at Dominick's feet. Through his horror, Dominick became aware of a tacky wetness on his hands. He looked down at them, knowing already what he would see. The man hadn't been wearing a waistcoat at all. In the dark, the red of blood looked so very much like black. And there was so very much of it.

"Alfie," he whispered. "Get back. Get outside. Now!"

"No!" shrieked a voice too high to be Alfie's.

Dominick turned, hands still raised. The door had been flung wide and in the light his hands glistened a terrible crimson. Agnes was in the doorway, clutching the frame with both hands. She cried out again. Her eyes weren't on Dominick, but on the man at his feet who stared sightlessly back.

"Oh God!" she howled. "Oh God, no! It's Larry!"

CHAPTER 5

By now, Alfie should have been used to the sight of Dominick with blood on his hands. But the childhood terror of seeing Dominick hurt had been a part of him for too long and had only strengthened with time. The immobilising panic was not a feeling he could quickly shake off. However, Agnes' screams were enough to do the trick.

He spun, barely remembering to sheath his blade back into his cane before another tragedy could occur. Dropping the cane entirely, he gathered Agnes in his arms and dragged her, still shrieking, from the house.

Mrs. Hirkins still had one hand on the carriage, bewilderment writ clear on her face.

"Agnes? Agnes? What is it, dear? What's happened?"

"He's dead! Nan, he's dead!"

At this, Agnes broke down in tears, louder and wilder than any Mrs. Hirkins had shed.

Mrs. Hirkins knelt beside the girl, taking her from Alfie in a comforting but firm embrace. "Who, dearie? Not your grandad?"

Agnes shook her head minutely, burying her face in Mrs. Hirkins' neck, but was unable to say anything more.

"She said the name 'Larry'," said Alfie softly. "That's her fiancé, is it not?"

That set off another round of shrieks, confirmation enough in themselves. The carriage horses tossed their heads uneasily at the sound and Alfie saw more than one door open along the street.

"Is he…" Mrs. Hirkins didn't have to ask the rest.

"I couldn't see much," said Alfie, thinking of the glimpses of wet shadows, the wide-eyed body staring from the hearth rug, the fear in Dominick's voice when he'd told him to get out.

The blood on his hands.

He nodded.

"Right," Mrs. Hirkins said. She squared her shoulders and before his eyes, she transformed into the ruler of the Bedford Street house she'd once been: wielder of rolling pins and guardian of urchins disguised as earls.

"Master Alfie, can I trust you to handle whatever's… inside?"

"Of course," said Alfie, feeling like the words land in his heart like a promise. He hadn't done enough to help Mrs. Hirkins' husband, but if taking care of this latest tragedy could ease even a fraction of her pain, he swore he wouldn't fail her this time.

"Good. Mrs. Channing, is that you?" she called out to one of the neighbours who'd come to gawk. "Help me get this girl into your house. She's had quite a shock. Yes, yes, your condolences can wait. Right now, what we need is a warm blanket and a strong drink. Come along now, Agnes, let's get you sorted."

Between them, they got Agnes to her feet and stumbling in the direction of the neighbour's home, still crying all the while. When he knew she could stand on her own, Alfie released her into Mrs. Hirkins' care, then took a moment to catch his breath. He'd hardly expected to deal with a second tragedy today. But then, did anyone? For God's sake, he hadn't been back in London a week and already he was surrounded by death. Images of those last terrifying moments with Baz and Doctor Barlowe came thundering back along with all the horrors he'd witnessed in Scotland, but with effort he pushed them aside.

Now was not the time. He had a murder to deal with. And it had been a murder, hadn't it? All he'd seen was the blood. It was possible the man had taken his own life, but it seemed an odd time and place to go about it.

Something within him rebelled against the idea that it was a suicide, but that wasn't for him to decide. Best to press on assuming a crime had been committed until proven otherwise.

"You!" he shouted, addressing the carriage driver. "Go find a constable. And a magistrate. Hell, grab up half of Bow Street if you can. Tell them there's been a murder and they're needed urgently. And you," he said to the footman, "keep these people back, I don't want any of them getting more of a look than they should. Understand?"

The pair nodded, faces nearly as pale as their cravats.

"My lord," the driver said diffidently, "usually a coroner's the one who looks into murders in the city. Shall I get one of them too?"

"Fetch anyone you think may be useful."

Just before the driver could snap the reins, Alfie stopped him.

"Wait!" He gritted his teeth, aware of the eyes of the neighbourhood upon him, but if ever there was a time to play this card, it was now. "Tell them they're needed urgently by The Right Honourable Alfred Pennington the Earl of Crawford."

The driver nodded his head, and then he was off. The carriage tore along the lane faster than was safe, but Alfie had more important concerns.

Dominick.

Walking back into the house was like stepping into the past. No longer was he in the sitting room of Mrs. Hirkins' comfortable home in Canonbury, but instead he was in Dominick's draughty old rooms in Spitalfields—cold and dark, and reeking with the iron tang of blood. It was all the same. The body on the floor, Dominick—standing this time, thank God—but was he injured? Alfie rushed forward.

"I'm fine. I'm fine." Dominick said before he could reach him. "Stay back, the floor's... rather wet. No, don't look down. You know why."

Alfie let out a sigh of relief. "Come here then. You swear you're all right?"

"I swear. You've called for a constable?"

"Yes, as many as will come. Coroners, magistrates and Bow Street Runners as well."

Dominick shrugged, crouching down beside the corpse, but careful not to kneel in what Alfie could now see was a prodigious pool of blood. "Not as good a fee for catching a murderer as for a debtor, but you might get one or two to show up."

"I used my full title."

"Two or three then."

Dominick's hands hovered over the dead man for a

moment, then he grimaced and rolled him over. Alfie bit back his many questions as Dominick started going through the man's pockets. He'd seen Dominick do this back when they'd found a body at Balcarres House, but the sight still turned his stomach.

Eventually, Dominick let out a satisfied grunt and sat back on his heels. To Alfie's surprise, he gave the dead man —Larry—a pat on the shoulder, then with two fingertips, closed his eyes for the last time.

He stood and held out a closed hand to Alfie. "You have something I could put these in? I'll have enough trouble explaining the blood on me."

"Here." Alfie pulled a snow-white handkerchief from an inner pocket and sacrificed it to the cause. "What did you find? Anything useful, like a suicide note?"

"Weren't a suicide," Dominick said. Alfie was taken aback at how much thicker his accent had gotten. It was as if Dominick had shaken it loose in the months they'd been away, but now the city was seeping its way back in. "*Wasn't* a suicide, I mean."

"How do you know?"

"His throat's cut, for one."

"You read about men slitting their own throats all the time in novels and such. When they've lost a fortune or been jilted by a lover. There must be some basis in fact."

"Maybe," Dominick said. "But they don't slit them like that. Trust me, I had a closer look that I wanted. If the bloke who did it had been any stronger, we'd have found him in two pieces."

Alfie didn't care for that image at all.

"Besides," Dominick continued, "say he did do himself

in, where's the knife? I doubt he had time to stroll down to some convenient trash pit after he'd done this."

Alfie frowned. "You checked everywhere?"

"That's what I was doing while you were dealing with the rest outside. It's nowhere he could've gotten to. Not even the fireplace, though I singed my fingers trying to look. Buy Mrs. Hirkins a longer poker."

Alfie shook his head slowly. "She wouldn't have left a fire burning unattended. He must have lit it himself. And if he did do himself in, it's an odd place to choose, don't you think? To cut your own throat in the home of your fiancée's grandmother. But if he came here to kill himself while everyone was out at the funeral, why light a fire? It wasn't like he'd need it."

"That's what I thought. Not proof enough of murder on its own, but taken with the rest?"

"All right, you've convinced me. What *did* you find?" Alfie opened the handkerchief and spread it over his open palms for Dominick to drop the items into.

"Just a few bits." Dominick poured the coins into the handkerchief, leaving red circles on the fabric. Without wanting to take a longer look, Alfie winced and folded the handkerchief over them several times.

"And you picked the pocket of a dead man, why?" Alfie asked, gingerly tucking the handkerchief away in his coat pocket and praying the blood wouldn't seep through.

Dominick's eyes fixed on his, wide in the dim light, but solemn as well. When he spoke, his voice was knowing. "Things go missing from corpses all the time. Better they go to the poor girl than to some greedy constable or undertaker."

"After we've cleaned them," said Alfie, more steadily than he felt. "Speaking of, let's find a pitcher. You look ghastly."

* * *

It took some time—and more than one basin of water —to get Dominick's hands cleaned to Alfie's satisfaction. There had been some flecks of blood on his shirt as well, but there was little they could do about that other than button his jacket to the highest button. Still, Alfie was worried.

He wasn't sure what was going to happen with the magistrate, or Mrs. Hirkins' granddaughter, or even Mrs. Hirkins herself, but this at least was something he could do. He picked up the rag from the kitchen counter and took Dominick's hand. Before he could start scrubbing again, Dominick trapped Alfie's hands between both of his own.

"Love, you scrub any harder and it will be my blood you're trying to get out."

"That's not funny."

"It's true though."

Alfie sighed, and with a glance towards the front door, leaned in and gave Dominick a kiss. Just a light one, more a request for comfort than out of desire. How could it be, with a body just feet away? Dominick gave him all he needed and more, squeezing Alfie's hands tightly. When he broke the kiss, he rested his forehead against Alfie's, the simple touch as soothing as a balm over Alfie's battered nerves. They stood like that for several minutes, just breathing in each other's presence until the sound of hoofbeats filtered in from outside heralding the return of the carriage, and hopefully, a magistrate.

Alfie gave Dominick's knuckles a quick kiss, confident in his handiwork. Then straightened himself and headed towards the door.

"I'll stay in here unless you really need me."

Alfie turned back and looked into the shadows of the kitchen. The strong and comforting Dominick was gone. This Dominick wouldn't meet his gaze, his arms crossed over his chest and shoulders folded in on himself as much as his jacket would allow.

"I'd rather not see any London constables. Or rather, have them see me. Just in case."

He didn't need to say anything else. In the years without Alfie, Dominick had been a boxer, but he'd also been a thief and a prostitute. Of course, he would want as little to do with the official policing forces as possible, even if they'd never recognise the polished man he was now as the scraping wreck he'd been a year ago.

Alfie nodded. "You're Dominick Trent now, don't forget. They've nothing on you."

Dominick gave him the dregs of a smile, but there wasn't time for Alfie to say any more. Instead, he merely picked up his cane, checked to confirm the blade was once more hidden safely within, and rapping its gold handle on the wall once for luck, went to meet the assembled forces of justice as the earl he was.

The assembly was underwhelming.

Although more than just the two or three Dominick had predicted, the half dozen men crowded on the stoop looked more likely to nab a winning ticket at the dog pits than apprehend a killer. The coachman stood at the front of the group while the footman struggled to keep back the curious crowd that had gathered, resorting to threats that would be decidedly frowned upon if the concierge of Grillion's heard about them.

"I beg your pardon, my lord," said the coachman, his powdered wig held between his hands like a cap. Alfie hadn't much cause to look at him before, but beneath the white wig his dark hair was just beginning to grey, although the exact colour was difficult to tell due to the sweat that matted it to his scalp, no doubt from wearing the ridiculous wig all day. He was of average height with a rounded figure that no doubt made being knocked against a hard bench all day slightly more comfortable. His keen brown eyes that had likely seen every street in London were apologetic.

"I tried to find as many on the list as I could, my lord, but the local magistrate wasn't in, getting over to Bow Street and back would've kept you waiting for hours, and the coroner at the local office wasn't interested, even when I mentioned Your Lordship by name. As I had already given the address, I'm not sure if he believed me. I found a few constables though, and some watchmen. Shall I go find more? Or there's private thief takers for hire. I know the addresses of one or two."

Alfie barely contained a sigh. It wasn't the coachman's fault, although he would absolutely be taking the name of the coroner for later.

"No, this will do, thank you. Please go help the footman keep back spectators. Actually, before you do, the lady of the house, Mrs. Hirkins, and her granddaughter are with one of the neighbours. A Mrs. Channing, I believe. If you would please check on them, I would appreciate it."

"I'll relieve Martin, that's my footman, sir, and send him over instead if that's all right. It seems like he's had the worst of it."

"You can have him direct any other members of the Hirkins family over there as well. I imagine a good number of that mob were at the funeral."

At the driver's bow, Alfie waved an appropriately lordly hand to dismiss him and turned to the collection of constables. "Who is the most senior here?"

"That'd be me, my lord. Turnbridge, they call me," said a voice from the back of the group.

When the constable in question elbowed his way to the front, Alfie's heart sank. It wasn't right to judge a man based on appearances alone, but Turnbridge's waistcoat was a full two buttons out of alignment. Hardly the fine observer of minute detail Alfie had been hoping for.

"Very well, Mr. Turnbridge. Why don't you all come inside and I'll tell you what I know."

* * *

By the time Alfie had finished walking Turnbridge through the events of the day, including the finding of the body and "his" observations on how it was unlikely to be a suicide due to the wound, the fire, and the lack of either knife or note, his hopes in the constable had dropped even more. At least he'd pretended to listen to Alfie, the other constables too busy crowding around the corpse, gawking and discussing where it ranked against other grisly scenes they'd witnessed.

When he caught one of the men surreptitiously swiping a hand into the dead man's pocket, only to pull it out with a disappointed scowl, he'd had enough. He slammed his cane on the floor loud enough to make all of them jump.

"If you gentlemen have nothing relevant to add, your presence is no longer required."

It took them a minute to parse through his words, but when they did, they filed out with little more than indifferent shrugs, likely off to earn a few pennies describing what they'd witnessed to those in the crowd outside interested enough to pay.

Turnbridge chuckled. "A bit harsh, wouldn't you say?"

Alfie fixed him with a glare. "Would you?"

To his credit, Turnbridge blanched, then gave a stilted half bow. "Beggin' your pardon, sir. Of course not. If you don't mind me saying though, I'm afraid you're wrong about this being a murder."

The constable apparently took Alfie's stunned silence as permission to continue. "You see, this is a nice neighbourhood and that sort of thing just doesn't happen here. You add to that this Larry bloke having a girl in trouble as you said and well... Not to mention the Mr. Hirkins who'd just died. Maybe he was fond of the gaffer and with that on top of everything else, it seemed like the best way out."

"But the knife!" Alfie spluttered. "And the wound itself! And the fire in the grate!"

"With all due respect, my lord, I've been at this a far sight longer than you. The fire means nothing; I don't see why you'd think it would. As for the wound, when men get pushed to a certain point, they're capable of all kinds of things. Like men who get a leg blown off in battle and don't realise 'til after the fighting's done.

"Probably how he got rid of the knife too. Tossed it out the window after he'd done the deed and some child snatched it up, thinking it was a prize. It'll turn up in a day or two when they realise what they've got. Mark my words, this was a suicide. Tragic for the family, of course, but nothing more."

"So, you're saying you won't investigate?"

"What I'm saying, sir, is that there's nothing *to* investigate."

Alfie grasped for anything he could think of. "What about witnesses? There's half the borough out there, why don't you interview them?"

Turnbridge gave him a look that started out withering until he remembered who he was speaking to and added just enough respect that Alfie only wanted to hit him in the face, rather than beat him to death with his cane.

"Oh, we had a score of witnesses already before you opened the door. All of them with a different story. A suspicious man. A queer woman. Slim, fat, tall, short, light, dark, runnin' left, runnin' right, take your pick."

The constable's voice softened. "I respect you're tryin' to do right by the family, sir. If you want me to tell them it was an accident, I'd be happy to do that. But even if it was a murder—and I'm not saying it was—you said yourself there's no knife, no good witnesses, and nothing else that would lead to a conviction. No coroner would even bother with an inquest. Better to just let the family move on."

Alfie had no idea what to say. He looked towards the kitchen, wanting to call on Dominick as if there was anything he could do to help.

Then two heavy knocks came from the front door. In the open doorway stood a man, his fist resting on the frame.

"Fist" indeed. Alfie had been served ham shanks that were smaller. The man himself resembled one of the heavy wooden bookcases that filled the library at Balcarres House —imposing, the same width from top to bottom, and likely to crush a person if pushed the wrong way. He wore no jacket, but a striped waistcoat whose buttons appeared to be in imminent danger of popping off from strain. Instead of a cravat, he wore a belcher around his neck, the garish red and yellow handkerchief tied in the style common to sailors. If everything else about him wasn't enough to suggest he was a dangerous man, the crumpled pair of boxer's ears confirmed it.

Having gotten their attention, the man walked into the house and stepped aside, revealing a second man who'd been completely hidden behind his bulk. This second man was vastly different to his companion. Quite a few years older, he was narrow with a slight paunch that was mostly concealed by the apron tied around his waist and held up by the top button of his waistcoat. He had the rosy complexion that suggested either a joyful life, a fondness for drink, or a bit of both. Unlike the brooding giant who came in before him, he beamed with a bonhomie quite inappropriate for the occasion.

"Sorry for intruding," he said. "But if you're both done, we're here for Mr. Lawrence Brennan."

"I'm sorry. Mister... who?"

"Larry," said the bookcase with a roll of his eyes. "Him on the floor there."

"You're the undertakers?" Alfie asked, more than a little surprised.

"Hardly," said Constable Turnbridge. "I don't know him in the doorway, but the big oaf is Jack Murdoch. We've met before, haven't we, Jack?"

From the looks on both their faces, it hadn't been a pleasant encounter.

"George Brine," said the man in the apron. He transferred a large bundle of cloth from his right arm to his left and held his hand out for them to shake. "Owner of The Rose of Normandy. One of the finest pubs in East London, I don't mind saying. Mr. Murdoch here is my employee. Keeps him out of trouble."

He gave Turnbridge a nod as he shook his hand, then turned to Alfie. "I'd be happy to stand you both a round if you ever find yourself in the area, Mister...?"

"Lord Crawford," said Alfie stiffly, feeling the situation spinning wildly out of control and falling back on proper etiquette to give himself some sense of control.

"Oh, my apologies, my lord," said Brine, retracting his hand. He gave a half a salute with it before catching himself and tucking it back under the cloth. "Well, the offer stands all the same, but I won't be expecting you to take me up on it."

Alfie had the beginnings of a headache. "I'm sorry, did I miss something? Why is a publican and his... employee here for Lar-Mr. Brennan? Did you have an appointment?"

Brine let out a hearty laugh, no doubt frequently heard

over a mug of ale. "Only the Lord Himself knows the times for these appointments, eh? No, I'm the head of the local box club. Mr. Brennan was a member, and we're here to ensure he gets what he paid for."

Alfie didn't want to appear ignorant, but things were already so far out of hand it hardly mattered. "Box club?"

"It's a sort of amicable society for them who can't afford the Amicable Society, sir," said Turnbridge. "A burial club, they're also called. You put a bit of money in the box each week and when your time comes, they see that you're not just tossed in a pit somewhere."

"And the rest of the club attends your funeral to ensure you have the proper sendoff you deserve surrounded by friends," Brine chimed in. "We're really more of a social organisation."

"I see," Alfie said. "You certainly got here quickly."

"Bad news travels fast, I'm afraid," replied Brine. "And I hate to rush you both, but if we could, we'd like to get him on his way as soon as possible. Much to organise, you understand, and we want to make sure we get him to the undertaker's before they close for the day."

If it wasn't for Mrs. Hirkins, Alfie would've tossed up his hands right there and left the whole mess behind him. Instead, he glanced towards the kitchen, but if Dominick had anything to add to this latest development, he was certainly taking his bloody time with it.

Alfie bit his lip. That wasn't fair. With as quickly as Turnbridge recognised Murdoch, he could see why Dominick didn't want the constable to get a look at him.

"Is there nothing I can say to convince you this was a murder?" he asked Turnbridge under his breath.

Both Brine and Murdoch's eyebrows rose at this, but the constable was unmoved.

"I'm sorry, my lord. But I can't find a killer who doesn't exist."

Alfie sighed. "Very well. Go ahead."

He watched disconsolately as Brine wafted out the bundle of cloth into a large sheet. He and Murdoch arranged Larry's body on it, rolling him up with both the utmost care and an ease clearly born of practice. Within a few minutes, Murdoch had the shrouded body hefted over his shoulder like a longshoreman unloading sacks of grain. Constable Turnbridge followed the two men as they carried their gruesome cargo out the door.

Alfie watched as they carried away his promise to Mrs. Hirkins with them.

CHAPTER 6

It was Alfie's second funeral in a week and he hated every minute of it. This time, the weather was truly rotten. A cold rain poured down in a constant stream that seemed bent on finding its way into the eyes and down the backs of shirt collars. The rain drowned out the vicar's words—rushed and mumbled as they were, as if the man of God was more interested in getting to his tea by the fire than in doing his duty to the departing soul. The few mourners fortunate enough to have umbrellas huddled under them while the rest pulled their hats low and drew their shawls more tightly around them.

It was Mrs. Hirkins' turn to comfort Agnes. The poor girl had started crying the moment she entered the churchyard and hadn't stopped since. Alfie thought he vaguely remembered some of the people around her from Mr. Hirkins' funeral. Other members of the Hirkins clan, no doubt. They looked with more sorrow at Agnes than at the grave and Alfie wondered which of them they were truly here to honour. But then there were the other mourners...

"How much longer you think we're stuck 'ere for?" He heard someone mutter behind him.

He turned to give the speaker a sharp look but it went ignored.

"Better not be long," another man grumbled. "I think I froze a bollock off already."

"There's a few bits o'muslin here who'd take care of that for you, for a price," said the first man. The two started laughing until Dominick turned around, his look far more effective than Alfie's.

That was something else that disquieted Alfie about this funeral. The turnout was larger than it was for Mr. Hirkins'. He'd assumed that a kind old man with children and grand-children and who'd spent his entire life in the community would have more mourners than some young buck who Mrs. Hirkins, at least, hadn't liked.

Perhaps it was the scandal. Constable Turnbridge had announced to the crowd outside the Hirkins' home that the death had been a tragic accident, but Alfie had heard the whispers of "suicide".

Fortunately, those whispers hadn't reached this vicar's ears. Half to Alfie's surprise, the two men who'd carried away Larry's body had been true to their word, finding both churchyard and vicar to bury him, although neither was quite up to the standard that Mr. Hirkins had. Alfie wasn't familiar with the area, but from the look of the buildings around them and the way he'd seen the driver rest a truncheon obviously across his knees when they exited the carriage, it was clear this was not nearly as respectable an area to be buried in either. Dominick had frowned out the window as they'd driven the last mile, but had kept his thoughts to himself.

Alfie forced his attention back to the vicar, but instead of standing at the head of the grave, the vicar was halfway across the churchyard, headed either towards the vicarage, a pub, or both. Apparently, the funeral was over. He caught Mrs. Hirkins' look of fury at the retreating man. It seemed Alfie wasn't the only one unimpressed with his performance.

"Fucking finally," said a woman to his left.

Alfie's mouth dropped open in shock, then fell even further as she pulled out a bottle of gin and passed it to the woman beside her. Who were these people? Were they the box club members Brine had spoken of? So much for giving the deceased the proper sendoff he deserved surrounded by friends! Alfie hadn't seen a single one of them mingle with the Hirkins or offer their condolences, something he was now very much thankful for. Lord knows what they might have said.

"Shut your mouth," said an old man to the woman. "And show some damned respect. You'll want the same when your time comes."

The woman gave a snort, but took the bottle back and hid it amongst her clothes once more. Most of the mourners had already streamed away in the same direction as the vicar and she was quick to follow. The old man and a few others stood beside the grave a moment more, then silently went their own ways. Not a single one approached Agnes.

Alfie turned to comment on the vulgar turnout to Dominick, but he was watching one of the departing mourners with a frown. Alfie wasn't sure if it was one of the ones who'd been so rude earlier, but the last thing this wretched day needed was Dominick starting a fight in a churchyard.

"Come on," he said, shaking Dominick's sleeve to get his

attention. "Let's go see if there's any good we can do."

His cane sank deep into the mud as they walked around the grave, careful of their footing. Dominick had suggested that they not dress quite so well for this funeral. At the time it'd sounded disrespectful, but he'd been right. While the idea had been to blend in better with the other mourners, even their more modestly priced outfits marked them as targets in a neighbourhood like this. And his trousers were going to be thoroughly ruined.

As they approached Mrs. Hirkins and Agnes, Alfie was struck by how tragically similar both women were. Two women, grandmother and granddaughter, who both seemed so strong, now leaned against each other for support having suffered a similar terrible loss within a matter of days.

Similar, but not identical. He knew Mrs. Hirkins had lost her real love, Jenny, a lifetime ago, but she'd been fond of her husband and built a life with him. Agnes hadn't had a chance to build anything with Larry. Alfie didn't know if they'd been in love or just found themselves in a situation and decided to make the best of it, but either way, they'd never had the opportunity to find out.

He didn't know what to say when they finally reached them, but Dominick solved that problem for him.

"We're taking you home," Dominick said, in a voice that brooked no argument.

For the first time since they'd known each other, Mrs. Hirkins didn't argue with him.

"Come on, dearie," she said, pulling Agnes away from the grave. "It's pissing it down, and there's been enough death lately without you catching a chill. Your Larry will understand."

At Dominick's insistence, Alfie had asked the hotel to provide a less ostentatious carriage for today—a request that hadn't even warranted a single lifted brow from the concierge—but perhaps he should've been more specific. The black coach they received was staffed by the same driver and footman as before, both in full livery.

"I'm sorry for your loss, ma'am," said the footman as he helped Agnes into the coach.

She nodded in thanks, but said nothing to him, nor to the rest of them on the drive back to Mrs. Hirkins' home. When they arrived, Alfie and Dominick escorted the two women to the door, then as one, hesitated on the stoop.

"Come in before you drown." Mrs. Hirkins sighed, hanging up her shawl beside the door. "We've things to discuss. Best to get it all over with."

As Mrs. Hirkins lit the lamps and got the fire going, Alfie escorted Agnes to the single chair that now sat alone in front of the fire. He took a moment to look around the sitting room. It appeared the same as it had a few days previous, although not only was the chair in which they'd found Larry's body missing, but the blood-soaked rug was gone as well. Still, it felt rather ghoulish to place Agnes in a chair with her feet resting only inches from where her fiancé's body had so recently lain.

"Is there anywhere else you can stay?" Alfie asked her gently.

"And where else is she meant to go?" Mrs. Hirkins snapped, answering in the girl's place. "Did you see Larry's family at the funeral? No, you did not. They're all probably off nursing their sore heads from his wake, if they remembered to have one. The whole lot of them are even more useless than he was."

"Nan," Agnes protested weakly.

"Not to speak ill of the dead," Mrs. Hirkins added, although it was clear she had plenty more words on that subject.

Dominick carried in two chairs from the kitchen and offered one to Mrs. Hirkins. "Other Hirkins family she could stay with, then?"

"Her mam died giving birth to her, God rest her, and as for her father…" Mrs. Hirkins looked like she'd spit if it wouldn't be onto her own floorboards. "My son better hope whatever ship he's on stays in the Indies or Australia or wherever it is for a long while yet. Better for the rest of us that way too. And none of my other children have the room. Besides, you wouldn't leave a poor old woman in mourning by herself would you?"

"Of course not," said Alfie, nodding thankfully at Dominick for the other chair.

"We're just worried, is all," Dominick said, crossing his arms and leaning against the hearth.

"That's because you're silly boys. You're not built to handle death like women are. Now then, tell us what you've found out."

Alfie glanced over at Agnes. "I'm not sure now's the best time."

She lifted her chin, but Alfie could see the way she twisted her handkerchief between white knuckles. "The sooner you start, the sooner I'll know who killed Larry. No reason for your coachmen to sit out in the rain any longer than they have to. In fact…"

She got up and with surprising quickness, pulled her shawl up over her head and dashed out the door. By the time the rest of them made up their minds about whether they should follow, she'd returned, leading the thoroughly bedraggled footman behind her.

He bowed awkwardly. "Frank said he'd stay out with the horses, but I haven't a coat."

Mrs. Hirkins gave the footman a sour look. "Well, shut the door behind you then, stop letting in all the rain. There's bread and cheese in the kitchen. You can warm yourself there, but don't interrupt."

"Be sure to get some for your friend too," Agnes added.

"Yes, ma'am," he said, bowing to her, then perhaps realising his mistake, bowed to Mrs. Hirkins as well. "Thank you, ma'ams."

Red cheeked from more than just the cold, he disappeared into the kitchen.

Agnes settled back into her chair. "There, now we can take all the time we need."

"I hate to disappoint you," Alfie said, "But I'm afraid it won't take long at all."

"Before we get into that," said Dominick, "we have these for you."

He reached into his pocket and pulled out a small box. Alfie had no idea what their maid thought of the bloody wash water, but they'd spent the entire evening after they'd found the body scrubbing the coins Dominick had retrieved from Larry's pocket until they shone, and added a few more of their own to the collection. Not enough to make her suspicious, but enough to help at least a little. The box had been his idea, although it had been a challenge to find one that looked plain enough that they hopefully wouldn't realise how much it could be pawned for until after he and Dominick left.

"These were Larry's," Alfie explained. "He had some coins on him when he died and we wanted to make sure you got them."

Agnes took the box without opening it.

"He had this as well," Dominick added. "Do you recognise it?"

They'd argued about what to do with this other item. Dominick had been all for throwing it in the box with the rest, saying it was likely a memento of some sort from Agnes and she'd want it back, but Alfie thought it might be a clue and wanted to keep it at least until they figured out what was going on. They'd settled on offering it to Agnes and then keeping it if she couldn't explain it. Likely they were both wrong and it was just an interesting piece of trash Larry had picked up somewhere, but Alfie still found himself holding his breath while he waited for her reaction.

Dominick pulled out the item from his pocket and knelt down in front of Agnes, holding it in his palm for her to see.

It was a flat piece of metal, roughly circular in shape, about the same size as the other coins, so it wasn't until they'd washed the blood off that they'd realised this was something else. The edges of the strange token were ragged, as if they'd been sheared by hand and there was a hole punched out of the middle. It resembled the foreign coins some men wore on their watchchains, but the only markings on it were a set of notches taken out of the side.

Agnes looked at the token briefly, then shook her head. "If it was something of his, I don't remember it."

"Is it all right if we keep it then, just for now?" Dominick asked.

Agnes' eyes went wide. "Do you think it's important?"

"We're not sure," Alfie admitted.

"Do the magistrates think it's important?" As ever, Mrs. Hirkins cut right to the heart of the matter.

And this had been the part Alfie was ashamed to tell her.

"We-we tried."

And they had. They'd spent two days visiting every magistrate, coroner, and private thief taker they could find—Dominick waiting in the carriage so as to avoid the chance of recognition, Alfie with full lordly pomp on display. And every single response had been the same. They'd all been delighted to have an earl's attention, politely invited him into their offices, politely listened, then politely declined to do anything. Well, the coroners declined to do anything, deciding on the spot that Larry's death had been a suicide and not a matter of "disturbing the King's Peace". One had admitted that even if Larry had been murdered, without any witnesses there would be no point in an inquest, so it would be better if Alfie didn't waste any more of his precious lordly time.

The magistrates and thief takers had been worse. After a bit of hemming and hawing about how it wasn't really their jurisdiction, the magistrates were happy to look into the case. After all, with the reward an earl could offer, surely *some* guilty party could be found. The thief takers had said the same but more directly, simply asking Alfie who he wanted arrested and how much he was willing to pay for it to happen.

"And you should've seen him try. You could hear him shouting for justice all the way into the street!" Dominick was exaggerating, but only just. Alfie's frustrations had gotten the better of him by the end.

"But those magistrates, you know what they said? They said they were shite at their jobs."

Alfie pinched the bridge of his nose. "Nick…"

"All right, not in quite those words. But they may as well have. Bloody hell, you can get away with murder in this city as long as you're not standing there when the constables show up with a weapon in one hand and confession in the other. Either that, or if someone could turn a profit from your hanging. That'd work too. But to actually do their damned jobs? You'd think Alfie was asking them to drink the Thames up through a sieve rather than just get off their arses."

"*Nick.*"

"If you'll pardon my language."

"Are you sure," Agnes' voice was barely more than a whisper. "Are you sure it was a murder? It wasn't… That is, he didn't…"

Dominick was still kneeling in front of Agnes, but now he covered her hand with both of his.

"We're sure. I know what's being said, but try to ignore it if you can. Larry didn't do this to himself. It wasn't his choice to leave you. Don't ask how we know, there's some things you don't want to have to think about, but there was plenty to prove someone else did it. Besides, Alfie's about the smartest man I know, and me, I'm never wrong. So, of course we're sure."

Agnes looked dangerously close to tears again, but she gave a small smile.

"I know you both tried your best," Mrs. Hirkins said with a sigh. "Sometimes there's just no justice in the world."

The resignation in her voice hit Alfie like a blow. She'd lost her husband because Alfie hadn't ensured he had a doctor, hadn't acted in time when he knew something was wrong, and now her granddaughter had to live with knowing her fiancé's killer was still out there. All because Alfie couldn't even convince a single fucking constable to take him seriously. He'd failed Mrs. Hirkins unforgivably, and now he'd failed Agnes too.

"I have to keep trying."

He hadn't meant to say the words aloud, but from the looks on the others' faces, he had.

Dominick recovered first. "We both do. It only takes one honest magistrate. Surely we can find that." He gave Agnes' hand another squeeze. "In the meantime—"

"In the meantime," said Mrs. Hirkins, getting to her feet. "We won't expect any promises. Thank you for doing what you can, but we know not all questions get answered. We'll make do."

For the first time, Alfie wasn't sure he believed her. Mrs. Hirkins had always been such a titan in his life. He still saw her the way he had when he'd first arrived at the townhouse as a scrawny child, scared and alone. She'd towered over him then, but now she looked old.

It was a ridiculous thought, she was old, he knew. But she *looked* it now, old in body and old in spirit, like some part of her had finally worn out. He hated it, but he didn't know how to fix it. If it even could be fixed. He couldn't bring her husband back, and for all Dominick's optimism, the chances of finding Larry's killer weren't much better.

Then the image vanished. Mrs. Hirkins gave herself a shake and Alfie could almost convince himself he hadn't seen the way she'd been a moment before.

"I think we've had quite enough men muddying up our floors for one day," she said. "Best you two get on your way, and take that footman with you. It's been too quiet in that kitchen. I remember what you were like at his age, Master Alfie. If he's eaten me out of house and home, I'll be sending you the bill!"

✳ ✳ ✳

Alfie made them go by two more magistrates' offices before he finally let Frank turn the coach back towards the hotel. He hadn't had any luck at either, but being soaked to the skin probably hadn't helped.

Dominick sat beside him on the coach bench, the shades drawn so he could run his fingers through Alfie's hair to ease the headache that had come on full force. It felt wonderful, even as the rest of Alfie felt miserable.

"Do you think we'll find the killer?" he asked.

Dominick hummed. "I think we'll try. I think you'll run yourself ragged trying to try, if you're not careful."

"That's not an answer."

"It's true."

"That's not an answer either."

Dominick sighed. "Probably not."

"And you're never wrong, eh?" Alfie said bitterly, echoing Dominick's words to Agnes earlier in the day.

"Hey now, I also said you're the smartest man I know, so you already know I'm willing to lie to a woman. You can add that to my list of sins."

Alfie whacked him on the leg, then left his hand there.

"Truth is, Alfie, I don't know. I'm willing to do everything I can to try though."

"Me too."

"Oh, that was clear enough already. Nearly had to go get one of those suits of armour from up at Balcarres and find you a white horse to ride in on."

Alfie whacked him again.

"Of course, Mrs. Hirkins isn't exactly a comely maiden in need of rescue, though don't ever let her know I said that. Agnes is pretty enough I suppose, but certainly no maiden if she's carrying Larry's child."

"You're a beast!" Alfie couldn't help but laugh. When he tried to whack Dominick's leg a third time, Dominick caught his hand and held it. They rode like that for a little while, then Alfie remembered something he'd been meaning to ask.

"How do they know?"

"What?"

"How do they know she's with child?" He held up his free hand to forestall whatever vulgar thing Dominick was going to say. "I know how they know she *might* be in a family way. But surely it can't happen every time, or women would never get anything done."

"Well..." Dominick said slowly. "They get bigger, you know. In the belly."

"I've seen a pregnant woman before, Nick, I'm not a complete recluse. But you saw, Agnes doesn't have a belly like that."

Now it was Dominick's turn to whack him—on his uninjured leg, of course.

"I wasn't looking! That dress was plastered to her in the rain, don't pretend otherwise. I'm just asking, because it's not exactly something I was taught. The former earl just told me not to make any bastards. Oh, and to be sure to produce several heirs so I didn't end up in his position, bringing a cuckoo to the nest to keep it out of my cousin's hands. But he never said how to know when I'd been successful at it! I figured you might know what with..."

Alfie freed his trapped hand in order to use both to gesture.

"What in God's name are you doing?"

"With!" Alfie lowered his voice. "Knowing other prostitutes. Female ones."

"Christ, I don't want to know what part of it that was supposed to be!"

"Well, do you know or not? I'm rather short of experience in that area. If it's escaped your notice, I'm unlikely to have to worry about bastards or heirs anytime soon."

"You'd better not," Dominick grumbled. "I don't know. They'd chat to each other about ways to prevent getting in a family way and who to go to if they were, but they always told me I didn't want to know the rest of it. Said I was lucky to be a man and left it at that. And by the things they *were* willing to say around me, I wasn't going to press."

"Mrs. Hirkins said she'd be a grandmother by autumn,

so Agnes must be at least a few months along. Maybe it's a womanly ability? They can just somehow tell?"

Alfie shrugged. It made as much sense as anything else. He heard Frank call out from the driver's seat and the coach began to slow. They were back at Grillion's at last. It'd been a deplorable day, but as long as he could spend the rest of it —and the night—with Dominick, it wouldn't be a complete waste.

"About the prostitutes though…" Dominick trailed off.

"Yes?"

Dominick shook his head. "I don't know if it's anything, but I've been wondering all day if we've been going about this backwards."

"I don't follow."

"Just a thought I had. I want to see something, but it's a bit hard to explain. Do you trust me?"

"Of course, I do," Alfie immediately replied. "You'll be careful?"

"I promise."

"I've heard that before."

"I promise." Dominick grinned, then sealed his words with a kiss.

Before Alfie could respond properly, the coach stopped and they had to pull apart. Shivering as he left the confines of the coach, he climbed the steps of the hotel. After the first few he stopped, not hearing Dominick behind him.

He turned back. Dominick was standing by the side of the road as the coach pulled away.

He gave Alfie a wink. "Don't wait up for me."

With that, he turned up the collar on his coat as he walked away and vanished in the gloom.

CHAPTER 7

Emerging from the pawnbroker's, Dominick felt as if he'd stepped back in time. The clothes he'd been wearing, even if they were plain by Alfie's standards, were far too costly for where he was going. He tried to stretch his shoulders. The coat fit all right in the shop, but now he felt trapped in it, like he couldn't move, couldn't breathe.

"That's all in your head," he muttered to himself. "You're just nervy. Focus."

At least the shoes pinched less than he'd expected and the trousers were surprisingly soft, but he'd rather not think about how many owners they must have gone through to get that way.

It was hard to believe that less than a year ago, buying all these at once, even second and third-hand, would've been an impossible dream. A full suit of clothes with few stains that nearly fit, what a luxury!

As he walked down streets he'd tried to forget, he caught a glimpse of himself in a shop window. Only the man who looked back wasn't Dominick Trent, gentleman of means and lover to an earl. It was Nick Tripner, sometimes boxer, sometimes prostitute.

He looked away.

He'd first gotten the idea at the funeral that morning. The area the churchyard was in was worse than he'd expected, far worse too, than Alfie likely realised. Dominick had seen the driver, Frank, place his truncheon where anyone thinking of making trouble could see it and had given the man a knowing nod. He'd been furious that the Hirkins women were forced to come to such a terrible part of London. Because he'd known exactly where they were.

He'd been there often enough and recognised the church immediately. It was Christ Church, directly across from Dorset Street, well-known as the worst rookery in London, and right in the heart of Spitalfields, his home.

He shook his head. His home was with Alfie now.

That thought was enough to give him the strength he needed to wade further into the labyrinth of streets and alleys, each narrower and filthier than the last. He looked down them with a new perspective. How much dirtier it all seemed and how much worse the smell was now that he'd been free of it for so long.

He caught himself thinking, *This mud, if that's what it is, would be impossible to get out of silk.* He wasn't sure how he felt about knowing that now. Nick Tripner had never so much as touched silk.

At least he didn't have to think about where his feet were taking him. It was a path he knew well and with every step, the man he used to be wrapped tighter around him, as itchy and constricting as the coat, but far better fitting.

He only hoped that even if Mrs. Hirkins realised what an awful spot Larry Brennan was buried in, Agnes never would. His muscles had been strung taut, ready to fight, until they'd all gotten out of there.

And the first thing he'd done was come back.

His hands curled instinctively into fists and he forced himself to flex them. If he'd told Alfie where he was going, he'd have tried to stop him. Or worse, he'd have insisted on coming with him. It was easy to forget that Alfie had been born in this stew when he wore the clothes of an earl so well. But even as a child, he'd never belonged. That was why Dominick had gotten him out, and why he wouldn't let him come back.

It'd taken everything he had to keep the smile on his face when he'd left Alfie back at the hotel. Only the lingering feel of Alfie's lips on his and the knowledge that he was waiting for him in a place where he was safe and warm kept him going.

Finally, his feet stopped. The building in front of him was no different than any other along the street save for the wooden sign hanging above the door, darkened by weather and time. It depicted a long, flat-bottomed boat, barely rising above the crests of carved waves.

The Barge. Jimmy's pub.

He stepped inside, and it was like no time at all had passed. The sour-sweet smell of spilled ale and stale sweat hit him first and he found himself smiling despite himself. All the tables still stood exactly where they'd been a year ago. Exactly where they'd always stood ever since Jimmy had decided he was getting too old to be a cracksman and bought the place with his life's earnings.

It was late afternoon and the pub was quiet with only a couple of regulars pulled up beside the fire and a dark-skinned man behind the bar, facing away from him.

At the sound of the front door closing, the man asked without looking up, "What'll you be wanting?"

"None of what you're serving. Some of Maeve's stew, if there's any. Or has she finally smartened up and left you?"

The man whirled around. Jimmy was also exactly as Dominick remembered him, although it was possible his beard held a few more streaks of grey.

"Hell and damnation! Nick, is that you? I thought you were dead!"

Jimmy rounded the bar and enveloped Dominick in a fierce hug that left his ribs creaking.

"I told you before I left that I'd found work!"

"You told me that rich toff you'd been working for hired you on for good, then you disappeared. Not before leaving behind a very interesting souvenir in your rooms too. I figured you'd been used as bait in a bear pit or whatever it is that lot do for sport, then dumped in a river somewhere. I had the boys keeping an eye out for you for months!"

Dominick lowered his voice so the men beside the fire couldn't hear. "You'd have let Maeve's brothers sell me off?"

"Let's not make me find out," said Jimmy, more seriously than Dominick would've liked.

Jimmy's wife, Maeve, was a wonderful woman, all Irish freckles and red curls, but her brothers were some of the most prolific resurrectionists in the city. They each knew a dozen different ways to get paid for a corpse, depending on its freshness and whether it had any relatives in medical school likely to recognise it. That was what the "souvenir" he'd left in his rooms had been, the body of a man who tried to kill him, and whose life Alfie had taken instead.

"Let's get you something to drink," said Jimmy, moving back towards the bar. "Maeve'll be out in a minute and I want to see her face when she sees you."

Dominick pulled up a stool. "You'll protect me, won't you?"

"The Nick 'The Terror' Tripner I knew wouldn't need protecting." Jimmy raised his hands in a boxer's stance. "You been keeping up with your practice?"

"Not as much as I should," Dominick admitted. The gymnasium he'd built for Alfie as a Christmas present kept him in fine shape, but it was nothing like facing another man in the ring, fists at the ready, and the sound of the bell ringing in your ears.

Still, he got hit in the face a lot less, so he couldn't say he missed it.

"I suppose working for that sort keeps you busy," Jimmy said, with a barman's uninterested drawl that was anything but.

Christ, Dominick had missed him. He raised an eyebrow. "Are you asking?"

"No," said Jimmy, passing him a pint and raising one of his own. "I know when not to ask questions. But you're happy?"

Dominick smiled. "I am."

They touched their mugs in salute, but he'd barely tasted the surprisingly decent brew when there was a shriek like a demon escaping from hell. The next thing he knew, he had a face full of ginger curls.

"Hello, Maeve," he said, trying to keep his balance on the stool as she gave him an even more crushing hug than her husband. "How've you been?"

"Nick Tripner, as I live and breathe. You're a sight for sore eyes." She pulled back, then slapped him hard across the face. "And that's for leaving without even saying a proper goodbye. Did he tell you he had my brothers watching for your bloated body to float up?"

"I told him," said Jimmy, eyes twinkling. "He'd like some of your stew."

"I'm sure he would."

Dominick couldn't help but grin as he took her in and it wasn't long before she was smiling back.

"Ah, all right then, but you'd best come to the kitchen to get it. I left two of the wains in there on their own. Christ knows if there'll still be two of them when I get back."

Unlike Agnes, it was easy to tell Maeve was pregnant. Dominick tried to remember, but he thought this was child number six. Perhaps seven. By some miracle, all of them were still living too. He briefly considered asking her the question they'd pondered over in the coach ride, but he decided he liked his bollocks where they were.

"Actually, Maeve," Dominick glanced back over to the men by the fire, "happy as I am to see you both, I was wondering if your brothers were around. I have something I need to talk to them about."

"You're in luck, Hugh's about somewhere. I'll send one of the girls to find him while you have your stew." She leaned over to give her husband a kiss across the bar. "You're fine out here?"

"I'll give you a shout when the dinner rush starts. And you..." Jimmy said, pointing at Dominick. "Don't think you're getting out of here without finishing that pint with me."

Dominick knocked his knuckles against the mug. "After five minutes with her brothers, I'll need more than one."

❋ ❋ ❋

"You're not dead then."

"Good to see you too, Hugh."

When Dominick had known them, Hugh O'Donnell had been as identical to his sister Maeve as it was possible for a man and woman to be. Same height, same hair, same freckles. Her features were too broad for a woman and his were too fine for a man. Put her in trousers or Hugh in a frock and Dominick wasn't sure he'd be able to tell who was who. Hopefully Jimmy could. Sometime in the last year though, it appeared Hugh had decided to grow himself a moustache. It didn't exactly improve his features, but it certainly made them easier to tell apart.

Hugh gave a shrug. He set down his own bowl of stew and sat across the table from Dominick. They were in one of the back rooms the pub had for those wanting to drink in peace or have discussions that were best not overheard.

"I hate to miss out on a business opportunity, is all. Although since you left that gift for me in your rooms before you went away, I suppose I can forgive you. Thanks for that, although try not to fill the next one with holes. Makes it a bit harder to explain where they came from. Not that it was a problem for a professional like myself, of course. You see there' all sorts of markets for—"

"I've told you before, I don't want to hear about it." Hugh's business in the trade of dead bodies didn't offend Dominick particularly. After the things he'd done to make a living, he couldn't really judge how any man kept food on the table. But that didn't mean he wanted to hear the grisly details while he was eating. "I just want to know if you've found anything interesting lately."

"Well, I don't know," said Hugh, taking another spoonful of stew. "Jimmy says you're working for some *wealthy* cove now. I'd hate to think of you *spending* your time asking questions, even if I may be *rich* with answers."

"Christ, laying it on thick, aren't you?" Dominick pulled a few coins from his pocket. "Next time just ask for the money outright and don't embarrass us both."

Hugh laughed and plucked the coins off the table. "Go on then, what kind of 'interesting' do you mean? I found a boot with a foot still in it the other day. That was interesting. Hard to sell a single foot on its own, but the boot was a find. Just the right size for this one-legged gent I know. Foot wasn't his though. Wouldn't it have been a laugh if it was!"

Dominick pushed his bowl aside, no longer hungry.

"Oh, or Finn—he's off trying to act respectable for his sweetheart's family now, he'll be sorry he missed you— he happened to find himself in this churchyard the other night, just out for a stroll of course, and you'll never believe what he saw just sticking up out of the ground!"

Dominick wasn't sorry Maeve's other brother wasn't around. Of the two of them, Hugh was actually the less repugnant.

"I mean interesting like, 'Do you know what this is?' " Dominick pushed the token he'd found in Larry's pocket over to Hugh.

Hugh only gave it the briefest glance. "I might. How *valuable* do you think it is?"

Dominick held up a sixpence but snatched it back when

Hugh tried to take it. "Tell me what it is first."

Hugh sighed. "Spoilsport. That's about the least interesting thing you could've brought me."

Hugh reached into his shirt and pulled a necklace off over his head. It was little more than a length of string, but hanging from the middle of it was a similar token, the hole punched through the middle, making it a perfect pendant for a necklace.

"It's a token for a box club. You see those notches? Each member has one that's a little different. They keep a record with a tracing of all of them with the box, and if a body turns up with one, they can see who it matches up to even if they're… no longer at their best."

Dominick nodded. That was clever. And it confirmed something else he'd suspected. "And you're a member of the same club? I thought I saw you at a funeral today."

Hugh pouted. "And you didn't come over to say hello? Funny, I didn't see you. Mind, I had my coat pulled up all the way to my hat, so I probably wouldn't have noticed if the dead man himself got up and walked out of the coffin. Nasty, wasn't it? That's the one drawback to these damn clubs, you can't just have everyone come to your funeral, you're obliged to go to theirs as well, no matter the weather!"

Dominick had never before been so grateful for bad weather. He'd been keeping watch on everyone there and would recognise a member of Maeve's family by their hair from a mile off, hat or no hat. But he was glad Hugh hadn't gotten a good enough look at the well-dressed man with the umbrella to recognise him as the same one sat across from him now.

"Have any other bodies with these club tokens turned up?"

Hugh brightened. "Now that actually is interesting. So, ten, maybe twelve months back, we find a body in an alley —throat slit, no one around, nothing special. When we go through his things, we find one of these. I wouldn't have remembered it, except I thought it was a guinea at first, so I was disappointed.

"A couple months later, same thing. This one showed up with the tide. Had to fend off a bloke from the South Bank for it. Told him to stick to his own bloody side of the river!"

"This body also had its throat slit?"

"She did," nodded Hugh. "Same token too, only she had it all rolled up in her skirt at the waist. Nice little tin whistle in there too. I was going to give it to the kids, but Maeve would've had my skin."

"For giving her children something you found on a rotting corpse? I'd imagine so."

"No, no, for giving 'em something that made noise. Anyway, we found the third body about oh, three months ago now? And that was when I started to get suspicious. Also, my man at the university was starting to ask questions about why all the cut throats, so instead of taking it to him, I stashed it away for a bit while I asked around.

"To tell it short, I find this George Brine fellow, runs a pub with a burial club, and it turned out the body was one of theirs! I didn't think he'd take it well if I told him about the other two, so I kept my mouth shut. He was going to give me a reward for finding this one, but when he checked the records, turns out the dead man hadn't been paid up, so no funeral for him!

"Unfortunately, Brine said that it wouldn't be fair to the rest of the club for him to take out of the box to pay me for a member that had defaulted, but he offered to let me join the club instead and even waived the starters fee and the first month! I was very impressed by the way he ran things, and you know life is uncertain, so I took him up on it. I even got to keep the body and found a way to turn a profit on him too, so all in all, a very lucrative adventure."

Dominick needed a moment to process Hugh's barrage of words. "Let me get this straight: You found three people with their throats slit, all of who belonged to the same club, and the first thing you did was join it?"

Hugh waved a hand. "That's nothing. I once dug u— found a man with twelve fingers, then the next week, a man with twelve toes! Another time a man dropped dead of an apoplexy right into my arms. Queer things happen. Why are you asking about the club anyway? Do you want to join?"

"No. I found a man with that token whose throat had been slit."

Hugh sat bolt upright. "Why didn't you start with that? Where is he? Is he fresh?"

"He's not for sale," said Dominick. "It was the man they buried today, Larry Brennan."

"Bugger." Hugh collapsed back into his chair. After a moment he said. "I thought the fellow was a suicide. Funny he cut his own throat. Tricky, that."

Dominick shrugged noncommittally. He wasn't going to take Hugh into his confidence anytime soon; the man couldn't keep a damn thing to himself. He had no idea how Hugh hadn't talked his way onto a gallows by now with the way he ran his mouth. He'd been useful though, in amongst all the nonsense.

Three members of the same club had all turned up murdered the same way. Four, if he counted Larry. If he hadn't been certain Larry was murdered before, he was now. Of course, even if he found out who killed them he couldn't exactly put Hugh before a magistrate and say, "Go on, Hugh, tell the man about the bodies you sold. I'm sure he'll believe you didn't have a hand in killing them." But at least he knew.

He hadn't liked George Brine and hadn't liked his thug Murdoch any more. The whole time Alfie had been talking to them, Dominick had been standing behind the kitchen door, rolling pin in hand, ready to come flying out at the first sign of trouble, but fortunately that hadn't been necessary. They hadn't been stupid enough to start something in front of a constable at least, although he was sure Mrs. Hirkins would've been proud of his choice of weapon.

But even if the murdered men and women were all members of the same club, what did it mean? From the sound of it, Hugh had found the other bodies in places you'd expect if they'd been killed for the contents of their purses. There might just be someone waiting for drunk patrons to stumble out of the pub on club nights looking for an easy target. It might just all be a sad coincidence.

But Larry had been killed the same way, only in Mrs. Hirkins home, miles away and in the middle of the day. Something very strange was happening here and the club seemed to be at the heart of it.

That wasn't enough to take back to Agnes though. Mrs. Hirkins would probably appreciate it, thank Dominick for the little information he had, but it wasn't enough. He remembered the crestfallen look on Alfie's face when he emerged from each magistrate's with nothing, his shoulders slumped a little more each time. And when Mrs. Hirkins had told Alfie he'd done his best, he'd been so close to tears. He might have hidden it from them, but he couldn't hide from Dominick. Disappointing Mrs. Hirkins was hurting him, and Dominick couldn't stand it when Alfie was hurt. If only there was more he could do…

Hugh pushed back from the table. "I'm going to see if that's baked apples I smell. If there's nothing else you need?" He coughed and held out his hand. "It's really been *worth* it to see you again, Nick."

Dominick groaned and tossed him the sixpence he'd promised earlier. Then he pulled out another.

"Actually, I have one more favour to ask."

CHAPTER 8

Dominick had told him not to wait up, so naturally Alfie ignored him. He was starting to wish he hadn't though. If he'd had supper and gone to bed at a reasonable hour, he'd have no idea it was nearly two in the morning and Dominick still wasn't back.

He paced another lap of their suite and stopped to look out the window again. It was black as pitch out and the rain still hadn't let up, so all he saw was a reflection of his own worried face. Still, it was better than stationing himself in the lobby, his head snapping up every time the front door disgorged another round of drunken carousers returning from their late-night merriments instead of the one person he wanted to see.

He spun around when the door to the suite opened. Dominick shuffled in, wet hair plastered to his scalp, shoes in one hand and a pile of clothes folded over the other. He took a few careful, silent steps before he saw Alfie.

"Oh, you're still awake."

"Of course, I am." Alfie didn't mean to snap, but it was possible he'd been more worried than he let himself admit.

"I told you not to."

"Do you want to argue about that now? Or do you want to take advantage of the many towels I ordered when you walked off without your umbrella, you idiotic fool?"

Dominick dropped his soggy shoes and clothes to the floor. "Christ, I love you."

He started unbuttoning his shirt and even though Alfie had watched him do the exact same thing hundreds of times, it still sent a thrill through him. As a result, it took him several buttons to realise what was wrong.

"Hold on, why aren't you wearing your jacket? Or waistcoat for that matter? And where's your cravat?"

"Pawnbroker was mad I woke him up so late. Drove up the prices." Dominick peeled off his near-transparent shirt. The ring he always wore around his neck flashed against his bare chest, a gleam of tarnished silver against golden chest hair.

Alfie was distracted once again, then shook himself. "What pawnbroker?"

Dominick reached for the buttons on his trousers. Alfie turned his back on him and went to fetch the towels, so he had a hope in hell of finishing this conversation before he did something to scupper it completely—like dropping to his knees in the middle of their sitting room.

"Had to get a change of clothes," Dominick called out from behind him. "I pawned these, but when I tried to come back to the hotel the first time, they wouldn't let me in dressed like that. They wouldn't even take a note up to you. 'We will not be bothering His Lordship at this hour without good reason.' Good reason, my arse. They meant, 'We will not be bothering His Lordship for the likes of you at any hour.' So, I had to go all the way back to get my good clothes, but I thought the other ones might be useful to keep and the pawnbroker raised the prices so much I wouldn't have been able to buy it all back anyway."

Very little of what he was saying made any sense. Why had Dominick been pawning his clothes in the first place? And in exchange for something lesser to wear? He was about to ask, but when he returned with the towels, Dominick was sitting on the settee in the middle of the suite, his arms spread across the back, completely naked and grinning up at him.

Alfie threw the towels in his face. "Get your wet arse off that and dry yourself. And stop trying to distract me!"

"You're the distraction." Dominick laughed. "Have I ever told you how fine you look in a high dudgeon?"

Alfie made a rude gesture at that, but fortunately Dominick did as he was told. By the time he was dry and cocooned in a banyan with his bare feet so close to the fire he'd burn himself if he wasn't careful, Alfie had calmed down enough to focus on his story.

"...So that's four bodies, all tied to the same box club run out of a pub in Spitalfields called The Rose of Normandy. Only no one knows about any of the other murders because Hugh O'Donnell can't speak *and* think at the same time, and he does too much of the first to ever do the second."

A pit in the bottom of Alfie's stomach had only grown deeper with every word Dominick said. One unsolved murder was worrying enough, but *four*?

"I don't like it."

"Neither do I," admitted Dominick. "One murder? Fine, we've dealt with that before, but there might even be more than four. These are just the ones Hugh found."

Alfie shook his head. "And no one's noticed?"

Dominick didn't answer right away. Finally, barely loud enough for Alfie to hear, he said, "It's Spitalfields."

"Yes, I know that. I know how bad it is. If you'll recall, I grew up there too. Perhaps you remember me?"

Dominick shook his head. "You don't understand. You were only ever in the workhouse, not the rest of the neighbourhood. The workhouse was... bad. Outside it was worse."

Alfie found that hard to believe, but Dominick clearly wasn't joking. Alfie reached over and squeezed his hand. He'd thanked Dominick for getting him out of that hellhole a thousand times, but maybe he still didn't truly understand how much that had cost his lover.

"I have a question," he said softly. "I still don't understand these box clubs. You pay every week until you die, whether that's in a week or fifty years, correct? That doesn't seem very fair. At that point wouldn't it just be better to save your money?"

"You forget," said Dominick slowly. "The types of people who join a burial club don't expect to live another fifty years. Almost none of them will. Whether it's the cold or disease... As for saving, when your belly's empty, it's tempting to spend that penny you have saved on bread, or put it towards clothing for your children, or a glass of something to take your mind off your troubles for just a little while. You always think you'll replace it another day. But when you're hungry the next day and the day after that?"

"I see." Alfie knew that Dominick had been one of those people he'd been talking about. How close had he come to joining such a club? If things had been different, would he have been found slumped in an alley, his throat slit and a token in his pocket? Alfie couldn't bear to think about it.

He shivered. It took him a moment to realise Dominick was looking at him expectantly. He gave Dominick's hand another squeeze. "Forgive me, I was elsewhere. Did you say something?"

Dominick let out a deep breath. "I said, I have a plan to get more information, but you're not going to like it."

Alfie went still. That should be good news, but if Dominick was acting this way about it, Alfie wasn't just going to not like this idea, he was going to *hate* it.

"Go on," he said.

"I'm going to join the box club."

"The box club," said Alfie slowly. "Whose members all keep showing up dead."

"Yes, I know. It sounded ridiculous when Hugh said it too. But listen, these deaths clearly relate to the club somehow. But if we ride into Spitalfields, flashing money about and asking questions, everyone will shut up tighter than a nun's knees and we'll probably wind up with our own throats cut just to make it easier to rob us.

"But none of that happens if I go in myself, or rather, if Nick Tripner goes in."

There was something in the way he said that last part that Alfie especially didn't like. Nick Tripner, Dominick Trent, they were just different names for the same orphaned boy who'd been left at the workhouse without a name of his own and built himself into the man he was today, Alfie's Dominick. His Nick.

"I was going to go by The Rose of Normandy and see about joining the club tonight," Dominick continued. "But I wanted to get back to you so we could plan this out first. You keep working this from the rich angle, see if you can't find a magistrate willing to put his neck out a bit for an earl, and I'll work the streets."

That wasn't what he meant. Alfie *knew* that wasn't what he meant. But Dominick had been forced to "work the streets" for too many years already and this plan was taking him right back to that terrible place. Alfie wasn't going to let him.

"Absolutely not. This is the worst plan I've ever heard. You say if we go there, we'll get our throats cut. Well, what's to stop that from happening to you anyway? It's a lot easier to get the drop on one man than on two."

"I'll be fine."

"Oh, well, obviously. How silly of me. If you say you'll be fine, you'll be fine!" Alfie got up and started pacing again, unable to sit still when he was so agitated.

"Calm down," said Dominick, which had the opposite of the intended effect. Now Alfie was agitated *and* wanted to punch him in the face.

"Look, if you're so worried, I'll come back to the hotel every few days and let you know how it's going."

"And how is that going to work? They wouldn't let you in tonight. You think if the same man keeps showing up at fucking Grillion's saying he knows the Earl of Crawford, people aren't going to talk? My God, have you thought this through at all? And what am I supposed to do when you don't show up again? Just sit here staring out the window like a bloody sea captain's wife? Go see if I can buy your body off your friend Hugh? How does that work anyway? Is it a set rate or by the pound?"

"Christ, Alfie!" Dominick was shouting now. If they were anywhere else, Alfie would be worried about someone overhearing, but like everything else at Grillion's, the rooms had been designed for both the comfort and privacy of the guests. "I learned more in a fucking hour than you learned in two days of pleading with the authorities. You want to keep doing things the official way? Fine. But I'm doing this."

"Fine," said Alfie through gritted teeth. "Then I'm doing it with you."

"Like hell you are." Dominick stalked over and got right in his face. For all the way he carried himself like a giant, Dominick was really only an inch or so taller than him. The difference wasn't noticeable unless they were this close, but Alfie refused to tilt his head back to give him the satisfaction. He glared up at him through his eyelashes instead.

Dominick was all but bristling. "Alfie, it's too dangerous for you. You'll stay here where it's safe."

Alfie's voice came out as sharp and brittle as glass. "Don't you dare fucking mollycoddle me, Nick."

"You're the most stubborn man in the goddamn world."

"And you don't get to make my decisions for me. I'm not a fucking child for you to boss around anymore! Now you can either drop this idiotic plan or you can get used to the idea of me going back to Spitalfields with you."

God, Alfie hoped Dominick would just drop it. He wasn't just angry, he was scared. Scared of Dominick going back into the heart of the rookery alone. Scared of going back with him.

Dominick closed his eyes and breathed out heavily through his nose. After a moment, he leaned in further, resting his forehead against Alfie's.

"Remember what I used to call you when we were kids?"

Alfie couldn't help but close his eyes. "You called me a lot of things. Pest, imp, damned nuisance…"

"And Lord Alfie of the Mud," Dominick said softly. "Even back then I knew you were too good for that place. I don't want you going back."

"I don't want you going back either, Nick. You're too good as well. You know that, right?"

When Dominick only hummed noncommittally in response, Alfie tried another tack. "You know what I remember about the workhouse? That we were always better when we were together. A team. Nothing's changed since then. I go where you go, whether that's back to the workhouse or Spitalfields or right to the devil's door itself."

Dominick sighed. "I don't want to fight with you."

Alfie put his hands on Dominick's waist, feeling his sides expand and contract with his breaths. "I don't want to fight with you either, Nick. But I won't let you put yourself in danger. Especially not alone."

"Can we wait and talk about it in the morning?"

Alfie wasn't going to feel any differently in the morning about letting Dominick wander back into hell unprotected, but he was willing to admit that now, when they were both tired and frustrated, was not the best time to discuss it. And who knew? Maybe after a good night's rest Dominick would be willing to listen to reason. There was a first time for everything.

Alfie bit back that observation and went with something more tactful. "I think waiting until morning is a wise idea. I'm sure everything will make more sense after some tea and toast."

Dominick hummed. "You're probably right. I'm not at my best right now."

"I don't know about that." Alfie said, pleased at the chance to drop the subject. He didn't want to think about murder, or burials, or fucking Spitalfields anymore tonight. He slid his hands down until they were resting on the tie that held Dominick's banyan closed. "You're nearly naked, that's almost your best."

"And what would be my best?" He could hear the laughter in Dominick's voice.

"Completely naked."

Alfie pulled one dangling end of the tie. In the quiet of the room, the silk hissed as the knot unravelled. As the two sides of the banyan parted, Alfie couldn't help but look down. Like this, with only a few lamps lit and Dominick's back to the fire, he was almost completely in shadow, so Alfie slid his hands inside the soft fabric and let them explore what his eyes could not.

Dominick's hips met his fingers first, the hardness of muscle over bone tempting, but not what he was looking for. He let his hands roam further back until they rested on the plush swell of Dominick's arse. He squeezed gently, then harder when Dominick groaned and dropped his head to Alfie's shoulder. Pleased with this response, Alfie did it again, first squeezing both cheeks in tandem, then one at a time, roughly then soft, experimenting to see what would get him the same reaction again.

Dominick groaned once more, then nipped Alfie's neck. "For Christ's sake, is that all you're going to do?"

Alfie didn't answer his question with words, but

moved his hands, slowly sweeping up the broad planes of Dominick's back. It felt amazing. Dominick's skin, nicked and scarred in places from a life hard-lived, contrasted beautifully with the silk of the banyan against the back of Alfie's hands. He stepped closer so he could reach even more, curling his hands behind and around Dominick's shoulders.

He hadn't realised he'd stopped moving, until Dominick's arms wrapped around his waist and his mouth pressed against his neck again. A kiss this time rather than a bite.

"Everything all right, love?"

Alfie realised he'd just been standing there holding him, but he didn't want to move.

"Fine."

"Only fine? I thought you wanted me at my best?" Dominick teased. "I'm still not naked."

Despite his words, he made no move to dislodge Alfie and even gripped him tighter, not for Alfie's comfort, but his own.

Finally, Alfie sighed. "All right, let's get you at your best."

Dominick laughed and stepped backwards out of his grip. He did so deliberately slowly so Alfie's hands stayed on him for as long as possible. Then he shrugged out of the banyan, insouciant and glorious in his nudity, and padded his way to Alfie's bedroom.

Alfie couldn't help but stare after him.

"Well?" Dominick called out over his shoulder. The look on his face was wicked. "Are you coming?"

By the time Alfie unstuck his tongue from the roof of

his mouth, Dominick had disappeared into his bedroom. He was helpless to do anything but follow, tugging off his cravat and blasted jacket as he went. He cursed as he struggled with the damn things. Why had he bothered staying properly dressed while he waited? It wasn't as if Dominick cared, the shameless hedonist, and it was only delaying things now.

He tossed the jacket into the bedroom in triumph when he finally wrestled it free, but never saw it land. His eyes were fixed instead on the sight on his bed. Dominick had kicked the blankets to the floor and now reclined as languid as a sultan awaiting his due.

He looked up at Alfie from under heavy-lidded eyes, never stopping the motions of his hands, one of which slid lazily up and down his cock, bringing himself to hardness while Alfie watched. His other hand traced along the skin of his inner thigh, his legs spread wide.

"See anything you like?"

All Alfie could do was grunt in response. It'd been a year, but he still hadn't gotten used to how gorgeous Dominick was, nor how capable he was of using that beauty to reduce Alfie to an insensate mess. Every time he thought he'd built up the slightest defences, all Dominick had to do was smile at him like *that* and they all came crumbling down, along with Alfie's ability to reason, or think.

His only chance was to go on the offensive and seduce Dominick before he could be seduced. He toyed with the top button of his waistcoat. "I see plenty I like, but it looks like you have things well in hand. Are you sure you need me?"

If he hadn't been looking for it, he would've missed Dominick's eyes narrowing just the barest fraction. Perfect. The game was on. He unbuttoned not just the one button, but three. Let Dominick think he had the upper hand.

"I'm sure I could think of a use for you," Dominick growled. His voice had darkened, deepened. Alfie didn't fake the shiver that went through him. Still, he wasn't ready to cede the battle.

"Aren't you cold?" he asked. He finished unbuttoning his waistcoat and let it drop to the floor. "I swear there's a positive chill in the air." Feeling like an utter slattern, he ran his hands over his chest in a mock gesture of seeking warmth, gasping as the fine linen of his shirt rubbed against his nipples.

Dominick's jaw dropped open, but he recovered quickly, raising an eyebrow and looking down at his admittedly impressive cockstand.

"Does it look like I'm cold?" Dominick asked, not nearly as composed now as he had been when their game began. He moved his hand up again, and they both hissed when he rubbed his thumb over the head. "Why don't you finish undressing, and we'll see if it doesn't warm you up."

Alfie bit back a groan, arse clenching at the memory of Dominick inside him. Swaying, he was on the verge of surrender, but the grin on Dominick's face at his impending victory gave him the strength to rally. He shrugged. "Might be faster to just build up the fire."

"Don't you dare." Dominick's voice was all need now.

Alfie rewarded him by unbuttoning his shirt and pulling it off. Perhaps it would've been better if he'd teased it out, but his own need was making itself known and the sooner he was out of his trousers, the better.

It was then that Dominick—filthy, rotten cheater that he was—played his trump card. He pulled his knees up, and the hand that had been tracing his thigh moved inwards, circling his entrance as Alfie watched, transfixed, before pressing one dry fingertip inside.

Alfie's breath caught and he twitched in place, unsure of whether to go to Dominick, keep undressing, or just spend inside his trousers. If he didn't decide soon, the matter would be out of his hands.

"Alfie?" Dominick said his name like a prayer. "Fetch the oil from the drawer."

Alfie would walk into the sea if Dominick asked him to in that voice, so fetching the oil was the least he could do. He brought the bottle and stood beside the bed, unsure of where to look, overwhelmed by choice. Dominick's finger in his arse? His hand on his cock? The way his chest rose and fell with each parting breath? The spot where his lip went white as he bit it?

Suddenly, the hand that had been wrapped around Dominick's cock shot out, grabbing Alfie's wrist and pulling him in. He dropped the bottle with a cry and ended up in an ungainly sprawl halfway across the bed. He had one last volley on his lips when Dominick hummed contentedly and sucked two of Alfie's fingers into his mouth.

Alfie's breath left him in a soundless cry and he rutted his hips mindlessly against the mattress.

Oh God, Oh God, Oh God.

Alfie surrendered completely but Dominick showed him no mercy, snaking his tongue between his fingers in an obscene but unmistakable display, then pulling back to nibble on the pads of his fingertips. Alfie was certain he was going to spend from this alone, his vision already going hazy at the edges, when Dominick pulled his fingers from his mouth, saliva dripping onto his chin.

"Alfie," he said again. "You have ten fucking seconds to get your trousers off or I'll do it myself."

Alfie blinked, too lost in the fog of sensation. What the hell were trousers?

Dominick growled. The sound rolled through him, an unstoppable wave washing the fog away. "One... Two..."

Alfie scrambled upright, cursing the very existence of clothing. He would've made it in time had his shoes not gotten tangled in his stockings. Still, he couldn't complain as the delay meant Dominick grabbing him around the waist and ripping his drawers down. He tossed them over his shoulder. Alfie heard something rattle on the dresser as they landed, but he honestly couldn't give a fuck if they broke the damn thing in half. He had Dominick leaning over him, eyes black and cock hard, and they were both *finally* naked.

He pulled Dominick down into a kiss as hot and desperate as he felt, coming back again and again as he wrapped his legs around Dominick's hips. His thoughts swam, needing nothing but the man above him, until suddenly the need for air was even more pressing and he tore himself away.

"Christ, you're a fucking tease," Dominick panted, but he was kissing his way across Alfie's collar, so he couldn't be too angry.

"Me!" said Alfie, not yet so overcome that he couldn't be

affronted. "You were the one all spread out in that... that display!"

He felt teeth against his shoulder as Dominick grinned. "Liked that, did you? Want to fuck me?"

Alfie spluttered. "After all that teasing, that's how you ask?" His voice sounded shrill to his own ears, but he couldn't stop his hips from bucking up at Dominick's suggestion.

Dominick kissed him again. "That's a yes, then?"

"Jesus, yes! Of course, it's a yes! Where's the fucking oil?"

Ignoring Dominick's chuckles, Alfie rolled over, stretching towards the top of the bed where he'd last seen the damn bottle. Something glittered from one of the pillows and he let out a cry of victory that turned into a broken moan as Dominick took advantage of his new position and *sunk his teeth into Alfie's arse.* He collapsed down into the bed, the bottle rolling out of numb fingers as Dominick turned him over, scraping his teeth over Alfie's hipbone as it passed, then biting him again in the sensitive hollow between hip and groin, worrying the skin with his teeth until Alfie could feel the mark rising to the surface.

"We-we could do it this way instead," he said shakily as Dominick sat back to survey his handiwork.

"Just wanted to give you something to remember me by." Dominick winked.

Alfie couldn't help but pull him down for another kiss. While it began fiercely, it slowly became something different from what had come before, something soft and tender. Alfie found himself at risk of becoming adrift all over again. His body was so attuned to Dominick's that he found himself responding without having to think about it, meeting Dominick's love with love. He wound his fingers through Dominick's hair, not pulling but caressing.

He would've been happy to enjoy the slow kisses and gentle touches forever, but he really was desperate to come. Fortunately, Dominick must have felt the same. He pulled back just far enough to whisper in Alfie's ear.

"What do you want, love? I'm yours however you'll have me."

"God, Nick. I still—I still want to fuck you." The words sounded crude after such a sweet kiss, but Alfie was just proud he was still coherent enough to ask. It wasn't the way they usually did things—by both their preferences—but he wasn't going to turn down the chance now.

"Then I'd better let you get to it." Dominick rolled off him and resumed his previous position on his back, knees pulled up and head rolling against the pillows.

Alfie had to take a moment to give himself a firm squeeze. If Dominick kept this up, it would end in disappointment for them both.

He glowered as he tried to count slowly backwards from ten but unsurprisingly, Dominick only looked more pleased with himself.

"Want me to suck your fingers again?"

"You bloody well will not," Alfie gritted out once the immediate danger had passed. Once again, he had to hunt for the oil. Finding it, he viciously poured more than he needed into his palm, determined to make things as comfortable for Dominick as possible. He moved into position, kneeling between Dominick's spread legs. While he waited for the oil to warm, he let himself look his fill at the man spread so trustingly beneath him. Dominick seemed content to be admired, watching Alfie in return and running his finger back and forth along the chain around his neck, pulling it taut and causing the ring hanging from it to thump against his chest with each pass.

The wait had the added benefit of calming Alfie down, so that when he slid one well-oiled finger in, he could focus only on Dominick's pleasure and not his own. It was just as well they so rarely did it this way; Alfie could easily get addicted to the way Dominick's eyelashes fluttered when Alfie breached him, and the way his body opened so easily under Alfie's fingers, welcoming him into that satiny heat.

He gave Dominick plenty of time to adjust before adding a second finger, groaning as the muscle clamped tight around him, already imagining how it would feel around his cock.

"I've got you, Nick. It's just me," he murmured.

With his free hand, also now slicked with oil, he captured Dominick's cock and pulled slowly, his grip neither light enough to tease nor firm enough to bring him to climax. He'd had a year to learn Dominick's body, just as Dominick had a year to learn his. The effect was exactly what he'd expected. Dominick relaxed, allowing Alfie to move both fingers of his other hand in and out, spreading them, and when Dominick was ready, pushing in and crooking upwards.

Dominick jolted, throwing a hand over his mouth to cover his cry as Alfie found that perfect spot inside him, touching it again and again, until he was able to add a third finger without Dominick even noticing.

"Oh, you bastard," Dominick sighed when Alfie gave

him a moment to catch his breath. "You utter, complete, fucking bastard."

Alfie couldn't help but grin. Usually, *he* was the one falling to pieces. It was nice to be in control for once, even if his need to be touched was starting to grow painful.

"Do you want to keep calling me names, or do you want my cock?"

Dominick threw his head back. "I want your cock," he mumbled. "You fucking bastard."

Alfie would've laughed if he wasn't so aroused. Instead, he poured out more oil, slicking his cock, then readying himself at Dominick's entrance. This was the part he loved most. He pressed in slowly, watching Dominick's eyes close as he adjusted to the sensation. His mouth fell open in wet gasps punctuated by the occasional curse and his arms came up, hands scrabbling at the solid headboard for purchase but finding none, then falling back and twisting in the sheets.

Alfie couldn't help but think about how it felt from the other side as well, that first overwhelming minute when he had to remind himself that he existed at all beyond the sensation of Dominick inside him, filling him, pushing out any room for doubt or fear or anything other than unimaginable pleasure.

He pulled himself back to the task at hand with difficulty. He was hardly going to give Dominick the buggering he deserved if he was too wrapped up in thoughts of Dominick buggering him.

Dominick's breaths steadied. Tentatively, he lifted his legs even further, not quite wrapping them around Alfie, but with his ankles pressing tight against his thighs.

"Ready?" Alfie asked breathlessly.

At Dominick's nod, Alfie pulled back and took a moment to calculate the perfect angle, shuffling forward on his knees and manoeuvring Dominick by the hips as best he could. Then he thrust in.

Dominick's response was ferocious. With a howl only barely muffled by his hand, his back bowed off the bed, and a beautiful pink flush began to spread down his neck. Alfie thrust again and again, changing his approach just a little bit every time until he found the exact angle that made Dominick cry out and moan. The sight was astounding—his confident and stalwart Nick turned feral with lust. And the feel of him, so hot and tight around Alfie that he didn't know whether to scream or cry.

He was too wound up to last long, so he wrapped his hand around Dominick's cock, determined to feel Dominick fall apart around him before he spent. He was nearly knocked off the bed as Dominick thrust up into his grip, but held on. He only had time to give him three or four strokes before Dominick's entire body seized up, as rigid as if he'd been struck by lightning. Then he was coming, long white pulses shooting up his belly and chest, another one with every thrust. If Alfie had thought him beautiful before, it was nothing compared to the way he looked now.

Alfie dropped his head, unable to watch, but with Dominick now clamped tight around him, the sight of his cock disappearing into Dominick's body was too much to bear. He came with Dominick's name on his lips, his vision greying out around the edges and sparking white as wave after wave of pleasure rolled over him.

When he was finally able to breathe again, he slowly

pulled out, apologising as Dominick hissed. He sat upright while he gathered his bearings, rubbing his thumbs over Dominick's ankles, unable to bear losing contact completely. Then his leg, so easy to ignore when he had Dominick writhing beneath him, finally began to make its protests known. He lowered himself to the bed on shaking arms.

"Christ," said Dominick after a few minutes. "How do you bear that all the time? I feel like my head's not going to be on right for a week."

Alfie chuckled. "Maybe I'm just better at it than you are."

Dominick swatted at him. Either by planning or luck, his blow landed right on the bitemark he'd left on Alfie's buttock.

Alfie blushed and buried his face in the pillows. He wasn't going to be ready for another round any time soon, but if Dominick did that again, he might change his mind.

To remove himself from temptation, he got up with a groan and limped over to the wash basin to fetch a fresh cloth. They cleaned themselves and Alfie felt himself being pulled down into slumber. As Dominick prepared to head back to his own bedchamber, Alfie caught his arm.

"Stay with me tonight?" he mumbled.

Dominick's arm tensed under his hand. "I really should go."

Alfie gave him a tug. "Please? Just for now. I'll make sure to wake you early enough to get back to your own bed."

The silence while Dominick hesitated was longer than Alfie expected before he gave in.

"You can't always have things your way, you know."

Dominick said as he gathered up the blankets and pulled them over them both. He draped a heavy arm over Alfie's waist.

As Alfie tucked himself up against Dominick's shoulder, warm and content, he thought, *Perhaps not, but as long as I'm with you, I'll have enough.*

❋ ❋ ❋

When he woke the next morning, Alfie reached out blindly across the sheets, not ready yet to face the day when he was so warm and content. His fingers found nothing but cool linen. He smiled without opening his eyes. Good. Dominick actually had gotten out of bed of his own accord without Alfie having to kick him out. Not that they were likely to be disturbed by the staff, having given strict instructions to the contrary, but if they were, the consequences would be far worse than at Balcarres. There, they'd only have to deal with Jarrett leering, but here...

And that unpleasant thought was enough to spoil his good mood. He got out of bed with a groan and limped his way over to his washstand. His leg was always stiff in the morning, exercises or not. After he got himself ready, he collected his clothing from where it'd been strewn across the room the night before. While it wasn't really proof of anything if he left it scattered about, it was a touch suggestive. Besides, no reason to make more work for the staff than he needed to.

As he tried to determine which side of his shirt was the inside, he remembered Dominick saying he'd pawned his clothes to get the secondhand bundle he'd dropped in the sitting room the night before.

Oh wonderful, they'd put off their argument until this morning, hadn't they? Well, no use hiding from it in his bedroom. He walked out into the suite, seeing that the door to Dominick's room was open.

"Do you want to quarrel before or after breakfast?" he called out. "Either way I'll need tea first, but since we so rarely have the opportunity for decent eggs, I'd hate for them to go cold."

When he got no response, he checked Dominick's bedroom. Finding both it and their private bathroom empty, he came back out into the sitting room, befuddled. Something was off, more off than just Dominick stepping out to order breakfast without telling him. Then he realised what it was and his blood ran cold.

Not only had Dominick disappeared, but the bundle of clothes he'd bought to wear in Spitalfields was gone.

CHAPTER 9

"Christ, what's wrong with you? I've seen cheerier folk climbing the gallows," Hugh said, with his usual lack of tact.

Dominick didn't bother scowling at him. As much as pushing Hugh in front of a cart might have cheered him up, Dominick's foul mood wasn't his fault. That was all of his own making.

He could've stayed in bed with Alfie, woken up in his lover's arms, then had a fine breakfast brought right to their table before letting Alfie talk him out of such a foolhardy idea. Instead, he'd snuck out like a thief before dawn and was now tired, hungry, and itchy in his ill-fitting clothes. Not to mention stuck with fucking Hugh O'Donnell. And he had no one to blame but himself.

Dominick shook his head. He'd done the right thing, no matter how angry Alfie would be when he got back. The box club was the only lead they had in solving Larry's murder. He hated the thought of being back in the world of the rookery even more than Alfie did, but for Mrs. Hirkins, he would. He liked the old cook and knew how much she meant to Alfie, so if finding Larry's killer brought her and her family any measure of peace, then he'd do whatever he could to help. Even if it meant returning to Spitalfields.

He knew that if he'd stayed in bed, Alfie really would've

talked him out of it. He'd have offered several sensible reasons why this was the stupidest thing Dominick had ever done in a long line of stupid things and he would've been right. But Dominick would've relented not because of that, but because Alfie was worried about his safety and despite all evidence to the contrary, he hated making Alfie worry.

It wasn't lost on him though, that he only felt able to do this because he knew Alfie was safe and sound back at the hotel and Dominick didn't have to worry about *him*.

He shoved his hands in his pockets, clenching the small handful of coins tightly so they didn't jingle and attract the attention of the sharp-eyed men and light-fingered children watching them as they passed.

"How much further is it to this blasted pub?"

Hugh showed no such desire to go unnoticed, nodding to a few of the men and all of the women they passed, responding to the jibes of the braver children with good humoured but equally coarse replies.

"Hmm? Oh, just a few blocks, although actually we might want to go the longer way along Grey Eagle Street rather than pass through Corbet's Place."

"What's wrong with Corbet's?" Dominick frowned. "Nothing there but whores. As long as you don't catch anything, it's probably the safest street in Spitalfields."

Hugh let out a truly aggrieved sigh. "And at least the perfume covers the stench of the refuse, I know. But I happened to hear a certain woman has set up shop there who I'd rather not run into."

Dominick didn't want to know the rest, but that had never stopped Hugh.

"You see," Hugh continued, leaning towards Dominick in a way that was either conspiratorial or just an attempt to step around the remains of a rotting... something. "A few years back, she found herself having done away with a particularly forceful client—it was his life or hers, of course—but with no way to dispose of him. My talents were called for and I disposed of her disposal, so to speak. What a shock then, when she tracks me down, looking for her share of my profit! She threatened to expose my crime, I threatened to expose hers, and so things have stood ever since."

Dominick frowned. "What crime did you commit? Body snatching isn't illegal."

"True, and while I appreciate you understanding the basics of the law, you fail to grasp the subtle complexities. Like the fact that not only did I help conceal a murder, but I stole the contents of his pockets, his clothes, and a truly lovely pair of boots. All hanging offences, but absolutely worth it. Don't you agree?"

Hugh stuck out a leg to display a remarkably well-shaped boot.

"You know," said Dominick, "if you don't find yourself another line of work, you're going to end up with your neck in a noose."

"I'm not interested in earning a living by letting men punch my face or fuck my arse, so you'll forgive me if I don't take your bloody career advice," Hugh replied airily.

Dominick stumbled and almost ended up face down in a pile of horse shite. How Nick Tripner earned a roof over his head had never been a secret, but for a full year the only person around him who'd known was Alfie, and he only mentioned it in the vaguest terms when absolutely necessary. It was a shock to hear the words spoken so bluntly by an acquaintance, and a not particularly liked one at that.

He was about ready to let Hugh sample a punch to the face to see how he liked it when a building with a hanging sign came into view.

"There it is, The Rose of Normandy!"

Dominick looked more closely at the sign. He didn't know much about Normandy, but the uneven, vaguely obscene blob carved into the sign didn't look like any rose he'd ever seen. The building's windows were made of small diamonds of glass, but impressively, he could only count two broken ones. Either this Mr. Brine was doing well enough that he could afford to have them replaced frequently or his patrons were too cowed to break them in the first place.

He reluctantly followed Hugh inside. The interior of the pub was much the same as any other in Spitalfields, so much so that Dominick wasn't sure if he'd been here before or not. He'd boxed in so many soot-stained pubs with sticky floors and dirty tankards that they all blurred together after a while.

"What can I get you gentlemen?" The barman gave the two of them a quick glance as they entered. He had the look of an old hand about him, so he likely got more from a quick glance than most men would get from an hour's conversation. Dominick tried not to let that rattle him. The man was neither particularly tall nor short, neither dark nor fair. He could've worked in a hundred pubs Dominick had been to before and never been noticed. On guard now,

Dominick took in every detail to relay to Alfie later.

Recognising Dominick's scrutiny in answer to his own, the man gave him a quick nod of approval. "You look familiar. Have you been in before?"

"No, hello for me, Toller?" said Hugh, ever aware when attention had drifted from him for even a moment.

The barman, Toller, pursed his lips briefly, then switched to a smile no doubt crafted from years of service behind the bar. "Can't seem to get rid of you long enough for hellos or goodbyes, O'Donnell. A pint for you and your friend?"

"If you would," Hugh pulled up a stool as Toller poured their drinks, the barman keeping his eyes on Dominick all the while. At a distance, Toller looked past his prime, but as he slid two tankards across the bar his rolled-up sleeves revealed sinewy bands of narrow muscle running down his forearms. Dominick had seen similar arms on men who'd spent their lives at sea climbing rigging and hauling in sail. That sort of wiry strength likely served Toller well, not so obvious that a drunken lout wanted to fight him to prove himself, but still useful for throwing the sot out on his arse at the end of the night.

Dominick laid coin enough to cover both drinks on the counter.

"I'd be careful paying for that one's drinks if I were you," said Toller amiably. "I've never seen O'Donnell buy a second round, myself."

Dominick laughed. "I appreciate the warning. It's a bit late though, he's been testing my generosity for years now."

"That's a shameful lie, Nick. You've never had the money to pay for anyone else's drink before. And I should know, I always ask."

Toller snorted and held out a hand for Dominick to shake. "Simon Toller. Pleasure to meet you."

His grip was steady, just as firm as a barman's should be but no stronger. Before Dominick could introduce himself, Hugh cut in.

"Oh, of course, Toller, this is Nick Tripner. You probably remember him as Nick 'The Terror' Tripner though. That was the name you went by, wasn't it? Or was that the nickname of that murderer they hanged last week? I swear I can never remember—"

"That's where I've seen you," Toller said, raising his voice to be heard over Hugh. "You had a couple matches here a few years back. Quick with a left hook. Not many men your size are that fast, especially on their weaker side. Been a while since I've seen you fight though. Injury?"

"Private employment," said Nick quickly. Christ knew what Hugh would interject given the chance. "Less likely to get punched in the face."

Toller rapped his knuckles against the bar. "Cheers to that. You change your mind though, let me know. Mr. Brine never turns down a chance to bring in a bit of entertainment."

Dominick never found two men beating each other into the ground to be particularly entertaining, especially if he happened to be losing, but he didn't say anything. Not that Hugh gave him the chance.

"Speaking of Mr. Brine, is he around? Nick is interested in joining the box club." Hugh had somehow finished his pint in the few seconds he'd had since last speaking. He must have made the choice between drinking and breathing.

Toller raised an eyebrow. "He'll be in his office upstairs. I'll let him know you're here."

Dominick took the few minutes the man was gone to steady his nerves. If the barman recognised him from his fights—*matches* made them sound far more civilised than the ruleless contests of blood they actually were—then no doubt Brine would too. He was doubly glad he'd stayed hidden at Mrs. Hirkins' house. The fewer people who'd seen both Nick Tripner and Dominick Trent, the better.

When Toller returned, Dominick cursed under his breath. Brine followed him, arms wide with welcome and already calling out a greeting, but behind him was the same hulking shadow he'd had before, the thug Jack Murdoch.

Dominick had watched the entire confrontation over Larry's body through a gap in the kitchen door, ready to step in at Alfie's word. Now that he had a better look at Murdoch though, he was glad he hadn't been needed. Dominick wasn't used to feeling like a small man, but next to a living wall like Murdoch, it was hard not to.

"Hugh O'Donnell, good to see you!" Brine boomed. "And I hear you've brought someone to join our little society. Welcome, welcome, Mr. Tripner! Such a shame Toller says you're out of the business. Are you sure I can't lure you back for a bout or two? I'd offer a thruppence for every round you go and be willing to negotiate a fair cut of drink sales as well."

Dominick's head swam, a year ago the offer would've been too good to refuse, now it was impossible to believe he'd been willing to sell his life so cheaply.

You've sold more than just your life for less money than that, he reminded himself sternly. If it wasn't for Alfie, he wouldn't just be visiting his old haunts like a tourist with a taste for the lurid, he'd be living in Spitalfields still, neither knowing there was better nor hoping for it. He had to remember that this was where he really belonged.

And this is who you really are, Nick Tripner.

The thought didn't sit well with him, but he didn't have time to examine it. Hugh was giving a recounting of how he came to extoll the virtues of the box club to Dominick—leaving out any mention of corpses, for both their sakes—and he was nearly finished.

"—So, Nick asked if I'd be willing to bring him down and see about his joining up too, and here we are!"

"And we're very happy to have you," Brine chuckled. No wonder Hugh enjoyed the club; if Brine was hiding any real annoyance at Hugh's… everything, he was doing an excellent job of it.

"I still have a few questions though," said Dominick. "Make sure this club is as good as Hugh makes it sound."

Brine chuckled again and joined Toller behind the bar. He poured Hugh and Dominick each another pint, as well as one for himself, waving off their murmurs of payment. From behind Brine's shoulder, Toller didn't look pleased at this, but since Brine owned the pub, there was little the barman could do about it. Dominick took the drink with thanks, but his focus was on Murdoch instead.

The hulk had shifted himself towards the front of the pub. Seated at the bar with his back to the door, Dominick could do little to track his movements other than listen for the floorboards creaking under him as he moved. He didn't like having Murdoch behind him, but he liked the idea of raising suspicion by confronting him about it even less.

"Can you tell me a bit more about your club?" Dominick asked. "Now that I've got a steady income, I've been thinking more about the future, but I wasn't sure where to start."

"Well, to be clear, I don't know what O'Donnell here told you, but we're not a bank or anything of that sort. Never seen a use for banks myself, if you've got the money today, enjoy it, I say. Who knows what tomorrow will bring?" Brine took a sip of his ale and let out a satisfied sigh. "Take this ale, for instance. A good, strong brew. I never dilute it. You'll be hard pressed to find its like anywhere this side of the city. Now, you may say it doesn't make sense to sell such a thing when there's cheaper to be had, but think about it, who drinks more at a pub than the publican himself? If I die tomorrow, at least I can guarantee my last drink will have been a good one!"

Dominick took another sip of ale to be polite. It was fine, no better than whatever Jimmy served up, and both were a far cry from the rich wines on Alfie's table every night, or the many bottles of spirits, elegantly decanted into fine crystal, that went down so smoothly that they were like drinking liquid gold.

He couldn't think about such things now. This burial club was their only link to Larry's murder. He needed to know everything he could about it.

He said, "You must think a bit about the future, to be running a burial club."

"Of course, that's something else entirely," Brine nodded sagely. "None of us can say when we'll die, but we all know it's going to happen. Now there's some that don't care what happens to their bodies after their souls have departed, but that's a horrific and blasphemous way to look at things, if you ask me."

Dominick couldn't help a sidelong look at Hugh. To his surprise, the man was nodding in agreement.

"Not to mention lonely," Hugh said. "Forgotten somewhere and left to rot."

"Precisely. Which is why I started the box club. Now any man or woman can know that when their time inevitably comes, they'll get a proper Christian burial attended by those who cared for them."

Brine's words didn't exactly match Dominick's memory of the indifferent vicar and restless mourners at Larry's funeral, but he only said, "That does sound good. Comforting."

"*Comforting*," Brine beamed. "Exactly that, Mr. Tripner. Exactly that. And we try to make it more so, more of a gathering of friends. We collect dues here every Wednesday and many of our members stay to socialise after the meeting."

And I'll wager you turn a handsome profit on that. No wonder you're trying to recruit more members, especially with so many turning up dead.

Dominick listened patiently while Brine laid out the basics of the club, the tokens, and the services provided. It was all roughly the same information Hugh had given him. Whether it was at all useful was the question. But they had no other leads and four club members with slit throats were certainly suggestive.

There was more than that though, something about the

pub put Dominick's teeth on edge. Whether it was Toller's too-knowing stares, Brine's too-wide smile, or Murdoch's entire fucking presence he wasn't certain. But he was sure there was more to The Rose of Normandy and its box club than he was seeing.

"That all sounds good," Dominick said when Brine finished his explanation. "How much does it cost?"

"Six pence to start, then three pence every Wednesday after that. That's guaranteed not to change whether you drop dead tomorrow or live to be ninety. Attendance at all other members' funerals is required. There's a fee for missing them, of course, so you know yours will be just as well attended as my own!"

Hugh interrupted. "Don't forget to come to the meetings either! You don't want to lose out like that poor bugger I found."

"Thank you for the reminder," said Brine. "Mr. O'Donnell stumbled across one of our former members some time back and was kind enough to let us know, but unfortunately the man had skipped several weekly payments and not paid the interest, so we were unable to provide him any burial services. It may sound cold, but it's only fair to our paying members. Never fear though, if you do fall behind for whatever reason, you'll be eligible again the moment you've paid up."

"That sounds fair," said Dominick. He felt for the remaining coins in his pocket. There hadn't been many in the hotel room. Most of the things they required were paid for by writing to their bank, and the few notes they had would've been enough to buy The Rose of Normandy itself, not just membership in the club. Finding small enough coins to go unnoticed in Spitalfields had been a challenge. Especially doing so without waking Alfie.

He didn't let himself feel guilty about that while he counted out six pennies. It left him a single one for the rest of the day, but seeing as he planned to head straight back to the hotel, he shouldn't need it.

"Wonderful!" Brine exclaimed when Dominick handed him the coins. "Toller, go and fetch the book, and find a token for Mr. Tripner as well!"

Brine poured Dominick yet another ale while Toller did the administrative work of adding Dominick's name to a line in a large green ledger. Dominick watched him print out "Nick Tripner" in a neat, even hand, then take a token similar to the one he'd found on Larry's body and trace its outline beside Dominick's name.

Dominick tried to focus on the other names in the book, memorising them for later, but Brine was right, the ale was a strong brew. The words printed on the thin green lines that ran across each page blurred and ran into each other. He squinted, but it was almost impossible to focus with Hugh and Brine both chattering excitedly in his ear. Then the hairs on the back of his neck rose, and he fought the chill that rushed down his spine as he sensed something large looming behind him. He readied himself for a fight.

"Don't forget to make your mark." Murdoch's voice was deep, with an undercurrent that threatened, despite the mundanity of his words. That Murdoch's voice was coming from somewhere both behind Dominick and well over his head made every muscle in his back tense.

He duly signed where indicated, pleased when all the letters stayed on the appropriate line, despite having to take a minute to remember if he put one "p" in "Tripner" or two.

Toller dropped the token in his palm. It felt heavier than it should, the rough nicks that identified it as his threatening to cut his palm when he closed his fist around it.

"I'm so glad you're joining us," Brine said effusively as Dominick rose to leave. Hugh looked happy to stay and finish Dominick's untouched third ale for him. "Now don't forget, the meeting is here on Wednesday, eight o'clock. And if you are ever looking for work, remember me first. The return of Nick 'The Terror' Tripner would be too good a draw to pass up!"

Murdoch didn't step back to allow Dominick room to pass, but it was easier to slide past him than to raise the issue. It wasn't until he stepped out of the pub into the street that he could take a full breath. The air outside wasn't any fresher than that indoors, but he'd take the honest smell of shite and refuse over whatever secrets were festering in The Rose.

All Dominick wanted now was to leave the entire stinking mess and get back to Alfie.

❊ ❊ ❊

The day had stretched into evening by the time, exhausted and footsore, he finally made his way up the steps of Grillion's.

Only to have the way blocked by two footmen.

Shite. He hadn't brought any of his wealthy clothes to change into. All he'd been thinking about was getting out without waking Alfie. Even after what had happened yesterday, he hadn't thought at all about getting back in. Alfie'd warned him about this. Served Dominick right for not listening.

He sighed heavily. Alfie had warned him not to do this either, but it was worth a try. "I don't suppose you'd tell Lord Crawford he has a visitor?"

Neither of the footmen deigned to respond. Dominick sighed again and retreated down the steps. Looking back up at the gleaming marble of the hotel, he pondered his options. Alfie said he wouldn't be waiting by the window for his return, but that didn't stop Dominick from craning his neck back. Maybe if he knew which windows belonged to their suite he could throw some pebbles against the glass... And immediately get himself arrested for attempted property damage and probably whatever other charges they could make stick.

He could try going around to the stables to find either the driver or footman from the other day—*What were their names again?*—and see if they would let him in. Of course, that would mean explaining why the earl's cousin they'd met was now dressed in little more than rags. And even if they let him in, how long would it take for the story to spread, first among the servants, then the rest of London society? It might not matter to him, but he wasn't sure what trouble it would cause Alfie.

He felt his pockets, but knew he only had his token and a single penny. That wouldn't buy him a night in anywhere but the worst doss houses. It could buy him something to eat at least, a trotter or a bowl of eels. If it came to it, Jimmy had always let him sleep on the floor of The Barge when things were bad and surely Maeve would show him some pity for putting up with her brother all day. Maybe they'd even let him use that closet of a room above the pub if no one had rented it for the night.

He took one look back up at Grillion's. Warm light was spilling out of the windows into the twilight. Somewhere behind them was a hot bath, a hearty supper, a soft bed, and most importantly, Alfie.

He sighed and began the long walk back to Spitalfields. Hopefully Alfie wouldn't worry *too* much.

CHAPTER 10

Alfie paced the length of the sitting room again, his entire frame tense with worry. He'd barely been able to sleep the night before, settling into a light drowse before jerking awake at the slightest sound, hoping it was Dominick returning from God knew where. But each time it'd only been some muffled noise from the street drifting up to him. He was already so used to country living that he hadn't realised how loud the city he'd spent his whole life in actually was.

Now, even within the pampered walls of Grillion's, every night watchman's cry or horse's hoofbeat rang louder than church bells in his ears, jangling his already fraught nerves. Finally, he'd wrapped himself in his banyan and sat in the dark of the sitting room, watching the embers glow and waiting for the dawn.

The noise hadn't bothered him on any of the other nights. He'd been able to sleep peacefully with Dominick beside him. And that was the problem, wasn't it?

He paced another lap of the room.

He'd let the footman bring in a breakfast tray, but hadn't been able to sit since. The eggs and coffee had long since gone cold and Dominick still wasn't back. He'd been gone a full day now, if not longer. What could that mean? Dominick, the damned pigheaded sod, had snuck out of their bed like a guilty lover and hadn't come back.

Alfie's steps picked up pace until a warning twinge in his leg forced him to slow down and collect himself.

Dominick hadn't just acted like a guilty lover, he *was* one. Hopefully, he was choking on his guilt. He knew Alfie hated the thought of him going back to Spitalfields, back to some strange semblance of his old life, even for a day. Not to mention trying to track a killer through Spitalfields alone! So, what had he done? He'd fucked Alfie's brains out then slunk out the door before they could discuss matters the next morning. Of all the caddish, stubborn, overbearing, stupid things he'd ever done! Alfie would never forgive him for it.

If he even got the chance to.

And that was what had him wearing a path through the oriental rugs. Alfie hadn't wanted Dominick to do something dangerous. Dominick had done it anyway. And now Alfie had no idea where he was. Yes, the years that Alfie had spent learning the proper arrangement of seating at a dinner party and the correct dress for every occasion, Dominick had spent scraping a living out of the worst corners of the darkest rookeries in the city, but that didn't mean he was safe there now. Even without a murderer on the loose, every day in Spitalfields was a gamble and yesterday might have been the day Dominick lost.

Alfie shook his head. He couldn't think that way. If he had to think about what he'd do if Dominick was gone, if something had happened to him and Alfie never even had the chance to say goodbye, he'd go mad. No, it was better to wait, and worry, and think about the righteous fury he'd unleash upon Dominick when he returned from his little adventure. He absently scratched his chin. He hadn't bothered to shave since Larry's funeral and the stubble rasped against his fingertips. He might as well go take care of that, although if Dominick returned while Alfie had a blade in his hand, he wouldn't be responsible for what happened next.

There was a knock at the door. Alfie flew to it, sprinting across the suite and nearly knocking an inconvenient table over in his haste, uncaring as the vase atop it teetered precariously.

"How dare you!" The admonishment was already out of his lips as he threw the door open, revealing a startled footman.

"Beg your pardon, my lord," the man stammered. "I can return at a more convenient time."

Alfie didn't bother trying to compose himself. His legs were suddenly weak, although from the exertion or the disappointment he didn't know. He clutched the door frame to support himself.

"What do you want?" he asked dully. The footman wasn't Dominick, so it hardly mattered.

"A letter for you, sir. Just delivered. It's marked urgent."

Alfie took the letter and shut the door before the footman even had a chance to bow.

The paper was rough, but he'd recognise Dominick's blocky, deliberate handwriting anywhere. Heart pounding in his chest, he tore the letter open.

Right Honrable Earl Alfie,

If youre not to mad, please bring some clothes to missus hirkins by supper time. Nice ones.

- Nick

Alfie read the letter again and again. It didn't take long. His hand shook as he dropped it to the floor, barely making it to a chair before collapsing himself.

Dominick was alive. Thank God, Dominick was alive. Relief washed through Alfie, but in its wake came an even stronger emotion. The blasted man had been gone for over a day and all he had to say was "bring clothes"!

❋ ❋ ❋

Alfie let his mingled waves of relief and annoyance buoy him through dressing and packing a bag, then propel him into a carriage and all the way to Mrs. Hirkins' door. It wasn't until he was standing on her stoop he realised that even by the most generous of margins it was still several hours before what could reasonably be considered "supper time".

Still, he wasn't going to sit on her front steps and wait. Out of spite, he'd intentionally packed some of Dominick's best and most uncomfortable evening wear, with appropriately matching shoes and cufflinks, but was dressed much more inconspicuously himself. Well, as inconspicuously as an earl's wardrobe would allow. He was already catching stares from a squinty-eyed woman across the street. Better to be early than have to deal with the entire neighbourhood coming out to gawk at the goings on at the Hirkins house. Again.

He'd barely given a single rap with his cane before the door was flung open.

"You're early," Mrs. Hirkins said. "Thank Christ, I thought I'd be stuck with him for hours."

She led Alfie in, but rather than staying in the sitting room, they turned into the small kitchen. It was warmer in there, Alfie noticed, the scent of something rich and savoury bubbling up out of a lidded pot. A small table with four chairs sat to the side of the room holding a pot of tea and a plate of what looked like currant buns.

But none of that even registered, because sat at the table was Dominick. He looked tired and dirty, and his clothes were fit to be burned, but at least he was here. He was *here*. Not crumpled in an alley or wrapped up on the back of a resurrectionist's cart. Here.

He smiled as he got to his feet, that same blinding grin that made Alfie lose his train of thought every time. As he walked closer, whatever words Alfie had meant to say spluttered out and died on his lips.

"Hello, Alfie. I see you got my note."

Alfie slapped him.

At least, he tried. Just before his hand could connect, a tight grip wrapped around his wrist.

Curse Dominick's boxing reflexes. Alfie tried to pull away, knowing it was useless. Swearing, he was about ready to drop his cane to try again with the other hand when he looked into Dominick's eyes. He wasn't sure how to take what he saw there—surprise, guilt, love, apology— he even saw some of his own worry reflected back at him. Before he could parse through them all, Dominick gently pulled Alfie's hand to his face, resting his cheek against Alfie's open palm.

"We'll talk about it later. We *will* talk about it later." Alfie could barely get the words past the lump in his throat. He waited for Dominick's slight nod, then his fingers closed of their own accord, stroking Dominick's temple.

When he'd tried to slap Dominick, Alfie had dropped the bag he'd been carrying. He nudged it now with his foot. "I brought your bloody clothes. Go get changed."

Dominick nodded again, squeezing Alfie's wrist just once before bending to pick up the bag.

"Bedrooms are upstairs," huffed Mrs. Hirkins. "Don't think you can just strip off in the sitting room like an animal. You've got two grieving women here—it'd likely kill at least one of us."

A bubble of laughter came from the kitchen table. Alfie hadn't noticed Agnes sitting there before, he'd been too focused on Dominick. She held a handkerchief to her lips too late to stifle the laugh. But though her eyes were still red from sorrow, she didn't look like she'd mind all that much if Dominick decided to get changed right there in the kitchen.

Fortunately, he had more of a sense of decorum than Alfie would've given him credit for, as he disappeared up the stairs with little more than a wink in Mrs. Hirkins' direction.

"And don't be going in my bedroom either! Choose one of the others!" Mrs. Hirkins called after him. Then she turned back to Alfie. "Walk into the sitting room and come back."

Alfie did as he was told. She shook her head. "Men! Agnes, what's wrong with him?"

Alfie was ready to happily list Dominick's many flaws, when he realised Mrs. Hirkins meant *him*. Agnes hesitated, likely unwilling to point out an earl's flaws no matter her grandmother's manner.

"He's limping," she said timidly. "More than before."

"Good girl," Mrs. Hirkins nodded approvingly. "Those buns you made came out a treat too. Come over here and I'll show you how to make something useful now. Master Alfie, you sit and try those buns. Tell me they aren't just as good as any I could make."

"Impossible," replied Alfie, but he did as he was told.

It was nice to just sit, knowing everyone he cared for was safe, even if only for the moment. The shifting creaks of Dominick's movements overhead punctuated the two women's conversation as Mrs. Hirkins guided her granddaughter through the grinding and mixing of whatever potion they were brewing.

Eventually Dominick came back down, still haggard, but brighter somehow in his evening wear. His outfit should've appeared out of place at the worn table, Alfie noted as he poured himself a cup of tea and topped up Dominick's own. But Dominick's cravat hung untied around his neck and somehow that was just enough to make everything feel right.

Something rapped against Alfie's shoulder.

"Here you are then. Why I don't just make it up by the bucketload, I don't know."

Alfie took the offered tin from Mrs. Hirkins. The familiar arnica scent of her healing balm rose from it.

"Thank you," he said as she and Agnes settled themselves back at the table. "And the buns are very, *very* nearly as good as yours."

He hesitated. Neither of them had said anything about Dominick's state of dress either before or now, so he must have told them something. Had he told them where he'd been since he disappeared? Jealousy rose in him at the thought that they knew before he did. "Did Dominick explain…"

Agnes cut in breathlessly. "He told us he needed to borrow some money to send a letter and the clothes were part of your investigation. Does that mean you have something?"

Alfie and Dominick shared a look.

"It's still early days," Dominick said. "I don't want to get your hopes up."

"Not much chance of that," sighed Mrs. Hirkins. "Not enough hope to go around these days."

That worn-out look had returned to her. The peace of the little house felt different now, too quiet, too solemn.

"Still," said Dominick. "I'd rather keep you both out of it as much as possible."

Agnes gave a sad nod, but it was no surprise to Alfie when Mrs. Hirkins proved troublesome. "Well, at least leave those rags you came in here with. Lord knows where you found them. They need a wash and good mending. I imagine whatever you're up to, it won't do to have you be seen with Master Alfie even carrying those dreadful things about. You can pick them up here whenever you need them."

It was a good idea, even if the, "That way I can press you for details later." part was obvious in her tone.

"Thank you," Alfie said. "I hate to ask again, but have you thought of anyone else who might know why Larry was killed? Any friends, or people he worked with?"

"Larry didn't talk about himself much." Agnes twisted her handkerchief. "He was such a good listener. I could prattle on to him all day and he'd remember every word. I think that's why it took me so long to notice he never said much himself. He was a member of a social club. I don't know the name, but he might have had friends there."

That must be the burial club. Alfie was about to ask more, but Dominick caught his eye and gave a quick shake of the head.

"Where did Larry work?" asked Dominick, changing the subject. "I don't think you said."

Agnes hesitated and glanced over at her grandmother. Apparently Alfie and Dominick weren't the only two capable of silently communicating about something that shouldn't be mentioned.

Mrs. Hirkins took her granddaughter's hand. "You can blame me if you want, Master Alfie, but remember that he was going to be the father of my great-grandchild. It was the innocent babe I was looking out for, not him."

Alfie didn't like where this was going. Mrs. Hirkins continued anyway. "When a man won't say what he does for a living and comes courting one too many times with bruised knuckles and blood on his shoes, there's only a few reasons why, none of them good. So, when Agnes announced she was in a family way, I put my foot down. I said, 'Larry Brennan, you'll have a real job or never darken our door again.' I don't care what the church may say about needing to be married. Agnes wouldn't be the first woman on the street with a 'husband at sea'."

"Nan's making it sound worse than it was," Agnes interjected on the dead man's behalf. "Larry wanted to take care of us! He leapt at the chance when she found him a position!"

Mrs. Hirkins raised her chin. "Word got round Lord Sempill was looking for a new footman. I told Larry to say he'd been in service with you, Master Alfie. I could vouch for him if anyone asked, seeing as you were out of reach at the arse end of the Earth."

"Scotland," said Alfie, rubbing his eyes.

Mrs. Hirkins' sniff made it clear that, in her opinion, there wasn't a difference.

"What's the problem?" asked Dominick, clearly at a loss.

"Mrs. Hirkins used my name to get an untested, untrained, and unknown man into the home of a member of the peerage. That's... a highly sackable offence at the very least."

"Good thing she doesn't work for you anymore." Dominick pointed out. Considering how annoyed Alfie already was with him, it was not the wisest thing he'd ever said, even if he was right.

"It puts my reputation on the line as much as Mr. Brennan's if he acted improperly. And seeing how things ended up..."

"I needed to make sure the child would be provided for," said Mrs. Hirkins. Alfie had met admirals with less steel in their voices.

"Well, it's something I can look into at least." Alfie relented. A sudden thought struck him and he turned to Agnes. "Will you be all right now? How will you get on without him?"

She looked down at the table and wiped her eyes with her handkerchief. "I'll manage somehow."

"*We'll* manage," said Mrs. Hirkins, giving her hand a

squeeze. "There's plenty of room here now, and I can take care of the little one once she finds work. I'm teaching her all I know in the kitchen, so I'm sure it won't take long. It'll be nice to hear children's laughter again, now that mine are all grown and gone."

That was the nature of the silence Alfie had noticed. It wasn't just in the home—it was in the air around Mrs. Hirkins. With her husband dead and her children and grandchildren out and living their own lives, it was an echo of the stillness around her, a silence not created by the recent tragedies, but made worse by them.

It reminded him of the silence in the house on Bedford Square in the time between when his parents had died and Dominick had come back into his life. It'd been only Mrs. Hirkins and him then, all the other servants pensioned off or departed for better opportunities. The stillness of a house not only marked by death, but filled with a loneliness born of lack of purpose. Neither of them had known what to do with themselves at the time. Looking back now, the threats on his life and chaos that ensued had almost been a relief.

But now Mrs. Hirkins was surrounded by silence once again. At least Agnes was here for her. And the baby, when it came, would give her someone to take care of the way she'd taken care of Alfie when he was a scared and lonely child. That was something at least, but with all his heart, Alfie wished there was more he could do.

"We'll keep working," he said roughly.

"Thank you, sir," Agnes whispered.

"You'd best get going then," said Mrs. Hirkins, rising from the table. She gave Alfie a pat on the arm. "You've got that tin I made up for you? Won't do you any good on my kitchen table."

Alfie recognised it as close to thanks as he was likely to get. And his nod, she turned and gave Dominick a long look. "And I won't have this one dirtying up my home any longer. Off you go."

Alfie was headed to the front door, when he heard Agnes gasp. "We forgot to show them!"

A swirl of skirts brushed by him as Agnes rushed up the stairs, returning a few minutes later with something cradled in the palms of her hands. She hesitated before handing it over to Alfie.

"We don't know if it's important. We found it in the fireplace. Neither of us has any idea how it got there."

Alfie took the item carefully. It was a scrap of paper, burned at the edges, but with a little writing still visible. Alfie squinted at the fragments of words remaining on the neatly lined paper, but he couldn't make much of the jumble of letters and numbers.

"What is it?" he asked, handing the paper over to Dominick, who frowned at it.

"That's what we were hoping you might know," said Mrs. Hirkins. "A grocer's bill for a large house was our best guess, they ordered fifteen pounds of something."

"Is it helpful?" Agnes asked, her eyes pleading for him to say 'yes'."

Alfie looked to Dominick for an answer he couldn't give her.

"It might be," said Dominick kindly. "If it was in the fireplace it very well might be. If nothing else, you found something I overlooked, which I don't think many can say."

True, thought Alfie, *but you were looking for a murder weapon, not a shopping list.* Aloud he said, "May we keep this?"

At Agnes' nod, he took the paper back from Dominick and made a show of tucking it into an inner pocket where it would be safe. He had no idea if it actually was useful at all or just a bit of burned trash, but until they knew for certain it was best to err on the side of caution. Then he bid both women farewell and let himself out.

As he paused in the doorway to adjust his jacket, out of the corner of his eye he saw Mrs. Hirkins pull Dominick firmly aside. He had to strain to catch her whispered words, clearly not meant for his ears.

"You take care of that one. He's been away far too long."

"It hasn't even been a year," was Dominick's whispered reply. There was a small smile at the corner of his mouth that vanished at her next words.

"You know what I mean. The sorts of places you need clothes like those rags for. He's been away from *there* for too long. He's forgot what it's like. You keep him away from that, for his own good."

Dominick only nodded in reply. Alfie looked away, pretending he'd seen and heard nothing.

CHAPTER 11

The walk back to the hotel was one of the more uncomfortable ones of Dominick's life. It was just as well Alfie had dismissed the carriage when he'd arrived at Mrs. Hirkins' home. Judging by the look on his face, he probably would've used the privacy to strangle Dominick and tipped the driver extra to throw him in the river.

He took several jogging steps to catch up with Alfie's furious pace, his cane clapping like thunder every time it struck the ground. Suddenly, Alfie wheeled on him, eyes blazing in the falling twilight.

"I don't need looking after," he gritted out between clenched teeth. "Not by you, or Mrs. Hirkins, or anyone else."

The street they were on was quiet, caught in the strange lull between people going home to their suppers and going back out for entertainment.

"This is about me leaving before we'd talked about it." Dominick said.

"My God, is it really?" Alfie threw his hands up, knocking Dominick in the side with his cane. He wasn't completely sure it was an accident.

"I don't regret what I did," said Dominick. And he didn't, not really. "Although I'll admit I didn't go the right way about it. I'm sorry."

"You'd better be," Alfie hissed. He turned and continued walking, although this time when Dominick caught up, he didn't try to speed away.

"I was worried sick, Nick," Alfie said, voice barely a whisper.

"I'm sorry. I didn't mean to be gone for so long. They wouldn't let me back into the hotel. I should've listened to you about that. We could've come up with a plan."

"Going to Mrs. Hirkins was a good idea. I don't think there's much you could do to surprise *her*, at any rate."

"Still, it was stupid of me to go about it like that."

Dominick meant every word. He'd had a long cold night in Jimmy's attic room to think about the difference between what he'd done and what he should've done. If he'd stayed to discuss things, at first Alfie would've tried to talk him out of going back to Spitalfields or insisted on joining him, but eventually they'd have sorted something out. Even when they were children, they'd always done better when they worked together than when they were at each other's throats. And they both had the scars to prove it.

"I meant what I said before. I don't want to fight you, Alfie. But I will if it means keeping you safe."

Whatever plan they might have come up with could've been one that put Alfie in danger and it was Dominick's job to make sure that didn't happen, just as it'd always been.

Alfie sighed. "That's exactly what I mean, Nick. Despite appearances, I'm not some naive little lordling who enjoys sticking his nose in dark alleys. And I'm not a damn child who needs you to look out for him anymore. At least credit me with brains enough to decide for myself if something is worth the risk."

"You stuck your nose in a dark alley after my last boxing match. Chased me down it, if I recall correctly."

"Yes, well," Alfie glanced around to ensure the street was empty. "We've previously established that I'm rather stupid when it comes to you. I won't do it again if it matters that much."

He didn't think Alfie did things like that because he was stupid, but because he was one of the bravest men Dominick had ever met.

"All right. And in return I promise to warn you every time I think about running off to Spitalfields without any money or a plan to get back, or anything else equally foolish."

"If you do that, I'll never have any peace." The barest smile teased Alfie's face and the furrow in his brow relaxed. Dominick knew this wasn't the end of the conversation, but at least Alfie wasn't quite as mad at him anymore. The rest could be worked out later. They were still some distance from the hotel, but Dominick needed to be back as soon as possible so he could kiss him.

"I don't suppose you have any money, do you?" he said. "We could hire a hack."

Alfie grinned. "Unlike you, I plan ahead *and* have money. Flag one down and you can tell me what you found out on the ride back. Look for one with open windows. Mrs. Hirkins was right, I don't know how you got so filthy in a single night, but I'm not letting you out of the bath until I've inspected you for nits."

Dominick grinned, sure that was likely to turn into a *very* thorough inspection.

❋ ❋ ❋

Dominick scrubbed a towel through his hair. Alfie had been damnably literal about his inspection, only allowing Dominick the barest few kisses and meagrest fondling before declaring him pest-free, then leaving to go to check with the concierge for any correspondence and secure them both a belated supper while Dominick finished bathing. That was all right though. At the mention of a decent meal, Dominick's desires had shifted. After all, he'd do a better job of expressing his apologies to Alfie with a well-deserved ravaging if he wasn't distracted by his stomach rumbling the entire time.

He pulled on a pair of trousers just as there was a knock at the door. Odd for Alfie to knock. Maybe he'd been delayed and had a tray sent up instead.

Dominick wrapped a banyan around himself for decency's sake, which was just as well, for when he opened the door it was to see a small, elderly woman in the black dress and white apron worn by all of Grillion's maids. Dominick stepped aside as she slowly shuffled into the room, pushing a cart carrying several covered dishes from which enticing aromas rose.

She couldn't have been much older than Mrs. Hirkins, but if this woman had ever had an ounce of that woman's vitality, it'd long since been worn away. Her short stature was made even smaller by a pronounced stoop and her hands shook as she lifted the dishes onto the table.

Dominick rushed to help her. Christ, if this was the same maid who was responsible for cleaning his rooms, he felt like an utter cad for complaining. She should be tucked up in a comfortable chair somewhere, not bending down to check under beds for lost stockings.

"Let me get that for you," he said, taking the largest tray off the cart before she could even touch it. It sloshed with some sort of soup inside. "I'll handle the rest of these, why don't you sit a moment, I'm sure you're run off your feet in a big place like this."

"Pardon. Non, non thanks. I thank you. I… non." The woman didn't take a seat, but her murmured series of broken thanks sounded off to Dominick's ear.

"Here now, please rest a bit? Or have you eaten? I'm sure there's more than enough here. His Lordship and I wouldn't mind sharing with such a fine lady."

Dominick bent over as he spoke so he wasn't towering over her. Her uncomprehending eyes met his briefly, but as they flicked away, she jerked and her eyes locked firmly on his chest. She let out a cry.

"Mon Dieu!"

Dominick slapped a hand to his chest, blushing when he felt only his necklace over bare skin. Even worse, he must have made quite a sight, still flushed warm from the bath with tiny droplets of water clinging to his chest hair. Bending over in that way must have caused the banyan to gape and given the poor woman a view she hadn't been expecting. He pulled the fabric fully closed, pinning it at his neck with one hand as if he'd been the one inopportuned.

"Christ, I'm so sorry!" He stammered. "I didn't mean anything by that, ma'am. It was an accident, I swear!"

The woman let out another cry and began babbling at

him fiercely.

"What's going on here?"

Alfie's voice cut through the maid's nonsensical speech like a dropping blade. She gasped as she spotted him silhouetted in the doorway, a bundle of papers in his hand. It dawned on Dominick how ridiculous they must look with him clutching his clothing like an endangered maiden in a melodrama, recoiling from a tiny old thing like her.

"I wasn't as dressed as I should've been," he said when it seemed the maid wasn't going to offer anything. "I tried to apologise but she just started talking and I don't know what she said."

"In French. She was talking in French. That's why you couldn't understand her."

"Oh," Dominick turned back to the maid. "I... I am sorry. I do not speak French."

He said each word slowly, feeling a little ridiculous. She looked between the two men, then cocked her head sideways, appraising Alfie before turning back to Dominick. There was something knowing in her gaze, like a confidant acknowledging a shared secret that other people in the room—in this case Alfie—weren't meant to be privy too. Whether she and Dominick actually had something in common or the poor woman just thought they did, he had no idea.

"Ah, oui." To Dominick's surprise, she winked at him. "Apologies, monsieur. I had the mistake."

"Not at all," he said. "The fault was mine. Do you need help with the cart?"

To his surprise, she nodded. But when he stepped closer

to help, she gripped his arm, her spidery hand like a vise around it.

She hissed in his ear. "They is in a bath."

Then she wrenched the cart from his grip and pushed it out the door, not deigning to look at Alfie even as he stepped hurriedly aside to keep from being run down.

"What was all that?" Alfie asked.

"Not sure," said Dominick, rubbing his arm. "She was fine at first, but my robe came open a bit and that seemed to unmoor her? Then she said a lot of nonsense in French and told me I'd left someone or something in the bath."

"Did you?"

Dominick shrugged. "Perhaps one of my many other lovers. I'll check, but even if I did, there's no way she'd have known. All she did was bring in the cart. Do you think she might be a bit barmy?"

"I suppose. It's certainly not unheard of for women her age to be a bit doddering. Although I think in establishments like this, they'd call it 'unwell'. Although since she's French it may be just 'eccentric'."

"Should we say anything? I don't suppose she'll be given a fine pension and a house like Mrs. Hirkins has."

Alfie shook his head. "More likely she'll be turned out on the spot. Probably without even her last month's wages. And if she really is foreign, she's unlikely to have family nearby who can take care of her."

Dominick knew what would happen then. What little money the old woman had managed to save over the years would be gone soon enough. She might be able to survive the summer on charity, although many purses would be closed to a wretched creature seemingly muttering nonsense. It wouldn't matter either way. The first freeze of winter would kill her. Dominick had seen Hugh and others like him going through the slums after the first frost, bodies stacked in carts like firewood.

"She didn't do any harm," he said, shaking away the images of blue lips and frost-tipped fingers. "I don't think it's anyone's business. If she wants to issue warnings about the bath water, she'd hardly be the first. Seems there's always someone saying how too cold water can kill you or too hot leads to immorality. Though I'm not sure I've ever had a bath that was too hot!"

"Just as well," said Alfie, setting his letters on the table and lifting the lid of one of the covered trays. "You're immoral enough already. I imagine you're only one warm dunking from utter depravity."

"You've had a good decade of warm baths more than I have. What's that make you then?"

Alfie plucked a morsel off the tray, popping into his mouth before licking his fingers slowly and far more thoroughly than necessary.

"I believe most would consider me an unrepentant deviant."

"An unrepentant bloody nuisance is what you are. Make up your mind, food or bed. I'm not going to drive that poor old woman even further round the bend by losing peas in the bedsheets."

Alfie laughed. "In that case, food first. Have you had anything to eat between when I saw you last and Mrs. Hirkins' house? I'm still grossly annoyed at you, but that doesn't mean I wanted you to starve."

"My friend Jimmy and his wife took care of me. She's a

fine cook, though I'd be the last man to ask the origins of some of her ingredients. You don't see so many feral dogs around The Barge as you used to, but her stew is worth it."

Alfie's nose wrinkled in distaste. "She's the sister of the body snatcher, correct?"

"Resurrectionist, yes."

"Then I suppose dog is the more preferable of her meat options."

Dominick laughed. "Don't think she hasn't heard that one before. She threatened to turn me into Sunday roast if I made another crack about it."

Alfie didn't seem very hungry after that, picking at his plate while Dominick had second servings of everything, taking advantage of the privacy to run his bread around his soup bowl in a very ungentlemanly manner.

"Did you know Louis XVIII stayed here at Grillion's when he came through five or so years ago? He was on his way to Paris to reclaim the French throne." Alfie said. He'd deigned to eat a few bites of syllabub, but Dominick knew from experience it'd take more than a little morbid conversation to keep him away from such a treat.

"Oh? And how did that go for him?"

"Well enough so far, although why he wants that wasps' nest back when he could have simply remained in extravagant exile, I'll never understand. I was merely wondering if that's where our continental maid came from. Several of his servants were smart enough to stay behind. Why, the Clarendon Hotel just down the road is famous for the Jacquiers in their kitchens. They were the king's personal chefs before deciding that an elite hotel in London might be better suited to their skills than whatever awaited them in France. Perhaps our maid made a similarly wise decision."

"So, I got pinched by a hand that might've pinched royalty?" Dominick mused. "Not every man can say that. You think that'll help her any? I mean, even if we don't say anything, it's only a matter of time before she's let go if she's acting like that."

Alfie let out a heavy sigh. "I don't know. Possibly. I could make discreet enquiries into servants' homes. But there are so few of them and so many women like her and I can't find places for them all. Of course, I'll try, but it's ridiculous that after years of service it's up to the whims of someone like me as to whether she lives out her final years in comfort or squalor."

"I know," said Dominick, "Believe me, I know. But you did right by Mrs. Hirkins."

"Nick," Alfie laughed, but his tone was bitter. "If another noble knew what I spent on her pension, they'd say I did *obscenely* by Mrs. Hirkins. A home with more than one room and money enough to maintain it? I've heard of nobles whose children outgrew their nursery maids while the family was abroad, so they just left them behind in foreign cities. It's repulsive."

Dominick said softly, "Or ones who buy children from a workhouse just because they don't have one of their own."

The silence hung heavily over them both.

"I do remember, you know." Alfie said so softly that Dominick could barely make out his words. "I know you think I don't, but I do. Bits and pieces. I'm not... I'm not just *this.*"

Dominick didn't think Alfie was *just* anything. It hurt

his heart to hear Alfie refer to himself that way, but he knew what he meant.

"I know, love. I'm not just this either. Not just Dominick Trent, I mean. Going back, it made me see I'm still Nick Tripner too. They're different people. The money you gave me, the clothes, the knowledge that I never have to worry again about where my next meal's coming from or what I'll have to do to earn it? It made me different.

"I didn't realise it until we came back, not fully. I think it was harder to see in Scotland, but here, where all this grandness is just a walk away from the rookeries? It's not harder exactly, but it's bloody uncomfortable."

Alfie gave him a look like Dominick was a stone he was turning in the light to see little flecks of something in it that he hadn't noticed before. Then he got up from his chair and dropped himself onto Dominick's lap without a word. Dominick's arms wrapped around him instinctively so he wouldn't fall. He hadn't realised until he had the warmth of Alfie's body under his hands, his weight pressing down on Dominick's legs, just how much he'd missed him. They'd only been apart a day or so, but just as Alfie had lived too long in comfort to really remember what their childhood squalor was like, no matter what he said, Dominick had grown so used to having Alfie with him that their time apart had been a shocking reminder of how bad things were when they weren't together.

But it was more than just not being together. There were plenty of days at Balcarres where they both were so busy they hardly saw each other at all. It was when they fought that was so unbearable. The being apart in spirit even worse than being apart in body.

I'll try harder, he thought. But whether it was Dominick Trent promising or Nick Tripner, he wasn't sure.

"I can see gears turning behind those stupidly blue eyes of yours," Alfie said. He poked Dominick in the middle of his forehead. "Whatever you may think, you're not any different now than you were when I fell in love with you or when I used to hide your socks under the mattress because they stank too much to sleep top-to-toe. You're still as overbearing, stubborn, and *kind* as ever. Nick Tripner and Dominick Trent are exactly the same man. One just wears better trousers."

Dominick wasn't quite convinced. "And who am I without the trousers?"

"Oh, that's the best of all," Alfie's grin went from caring to wolfish in a heartbeat. "Because that's when you're *mine*. And now if you've dined sufficiently, I think it's time you take me to bed so I can remind you of that."

CHAPTER 12

Alfie adjusted his sleeve minutely while he waited for the butler to take his card to Lord Sempill. One advantage of being an earl was being allowed to wait inside rather than standing on the stoop. A walloping spring rain poured outside the windows of the cosy salon to which he'd been ushered after the whisking away of his drenched coat and hat. For now, he was content to gently steam by the fire while he waited.

The fall of his jacket sleeve was perfectly correct, but he couldn't help tugging on it again, sure that some mark of Dominick's would be visible from the night before. Their reunion had been...

Dominick's teeth at his throat, his hands worshipping Alfie's body as he nipped murmured apologies into his skin. The contrast of Dominick's hard body forcing him down into the soft mattress, the pillows muffling Alfie's cries of pleasure. The scent of sweat and sex rising as their pace increased, their movements becoming frantic, wild, until finally—

Alfie shook himself. This was hardly the time or place for such thoughts. It wouldn't do to greet Lord Sempill with a raging cockstand, although if the man left him here to languish much longer the social awkwardness would be the least he deserved. He'd intentionally arrived later in the day to be sure the man was awake to receive visitors but apparently Lord Sempill kept even later hours than he'd anticipated.

He ran a hand over his face, grimacing at the prickle of stubble. He'd forgotten to shave yet again. It was completely unacceptable to make calls while so dishevelled, but it was also unacceptable to keep an earl— even an unannounced one—waiting nearly half an hour. Alfie couldn't help but laugh. He really was a spoiled little lordling if he was railing against being left to wait in comfort after having arrived unannounced at the home of a man he barely knew. Perhaps he should take a moment to count his blessings.

At least the weather had waited until today to turn foul. He shuddered at the thought of Dominick being caught in it with nowhere to go and only those damn rags to keep him warm. The thought that Dominick had survived the same and worse before unsettled him, but he was comforted by the memory of where he'd left him this morning. When he'd last seen his love, Dominick had been devouring a late breakfast with single-minded intent. He'd been wrapped up warmly in a banyan, hair still tousled from their activities the night before. He'd declared it his turn to lounge about the hotel while Alfie did some of the investigating work for once. Only the fact Alfie knew he was deliberately being baited gave him the strength to walk out the door rather than drag Dominick back to bed for another round. Had he known how long he was going to be left to cool his heels, he might have anyway.

Footsteps approaching the salon announced the belated arrival of Lord Sempill. For a brief moment, Alfie hoped the man was somehow involved in Larry's death.

Not only would it mean Dominick had no reason to go back to chasing leads across Spitalfields, but perhaps cooling his heels while awaiting his trial would give the man some appreciation for promptness.

If Lord Sempill was a murderer however, it wouldn't explain the other bodies found with the burial club token. Unless he was some sort of repeat killer preying on the most lost souls in London. Who knew how many victims the man might have that had gone unnoticed. Stranger things had happened before. Did he have a fiendish assistant in his nefarious deeds? The butler perhaps? Had Larry stumbled across something incriminating during the course of his employment—a grisly souvenir or a blade still wet with human blood—and needed to be eliminated?

If Dominick was here, he'd tell Alfie he'd been reading too many gothic novels again. Nevertheless, he should stay on his guard. His cousin had moved in the same circles as this man, which was suspicious enough. That alone was reason enough to avoid Lord Sempill, but Alfie also had a vague recollection of the man resembling some sort of dog in human form. Whether that was a flattering description or not, he couldn't recall. If only he could remember which breed.

Then the door opened and Alfie didn't have to wonder any longer. Lord Sempill was a young man within a year or two of Alfie's age, but his fair hair was so blonde it was nearly white. Despite the ample time his valet had to dress him before he came down, wisps of Sempill's hair stuck out in all directions. No doubt the intended effect was meant to be Byronic, but combined with his fashionably pale skin and overly intricate cravat in snow white linen, he much more closely resembled one of those fluffed up white dogs that shivered from fashionable ladies' laps.

A Pomeranian. That's what he reminds me of, poor man.

The effect was only enhanced by Sempill's dark eyes that were spaced just a little too far apart in his face and the wide mouth that opened into an even wider smile when he spotted his guest. The resemblance was so uncanny Alfie wondered if the man would expect a treat for sitting or staying. Despite his dog-like appearance, he clearly kept cat's hours. It was well past the usual time for luncheon, never mind visiting, and Sempill was still blinking sleep from his eyes.

"Lord Crawford, so good to see you again," said Lord Sempill with the distracted air of a man who'd just awoken and had yet to fully realise the fact. "It must be… some time since we last met? Forgive me if we had an appointment, I just can't keep the blasted things in my head from one day to the next. Never had a head for dates."

Alfie rather thought the numerous glass decanters along the sideboard might have something to do with that as well, especially as the man was already pouring himself a drink.

"Well over a year," Alfie said. "Perhaps two? I believe it was at a party at my cousin's home, Mr. Reginald St. John."

"Ah, yes." Sempill toasted the air with his glass as he handed Alfie one of his own. "Terrible business. I did send a condolence card, didn't I? Yes, I must have, Johnson would have told me if I hadn't. Very capable man. I know it's the done thing to pretend we're all for the raising of the lower orders, but some men are just made to be butlers, you see? It would be as unfair to Johnson to make him be a banker as it would be for me to polish my own silver!"

Sempill laughed heartily at his own wit—it was difficult to think of the sound as a laugh rather than a bark. Alfie was reminded once again why he'd never associated with his cousin's friends of his own will. For the sake of his mission however, he ignored the multiple offensive things Sempill just said and took the opening he'd been granted. He tried to match Sempill's airy tone.

"You're quite fortunate to have found competent help. I've had a devil of a time myself. I don't suppose I could poach any of yours, or perhaps you've any recent cast offs to recommend? If your Mr. Johnson is as capable as you say, I'm sure even an unsatisfactory servant trained under him would be much more suitable than most I've looked at. No doubt due to your expert leadership. A man's only as good as his master after all."

Sempill visibly swelled with pride at Alfie's words. He leaned in as if imparting great wisdom. "That's true, that's true. The secret is not to concern yourself with the smaller matters. Give your man the run of that and it leaves you free to focus on the larger issues. For example, I've no idea if we've gained or lost anyone lately. As long as there are no angry letters from my solicitor, meals are on the table at the appointed hour, and the sherry decanter is never empty, I leave it up to Johnson to keep everything running while I handle the more important things."

Sempill tapped his nose knowingly before pulling the cord to ring for a servant. If the man didn't concern himself with his calendar, bills, social obligations, staffing, or even his spirits, Alfie wondered what other matters he was possibly handling.

He knew the many horror stories of employers exploiting their staff as a matter of common practice, but he wondered how often it went the other way. It sounded like Sempill had almost no involvement in the happenings in his own home. If that indifferent ignorance extended to his accounts as well, then who knew what sort of things could be done without his notice. Alfie hoped whole-heartedly that Johnson was taking advantage of his position to rob Sempill blind.

He barely had time to conceal his smile in his glass before the butler himself was at the door in answer to Sempill's summons. In contrast to his employer, Johnson had the look of a man accustomed to rising early and accomplishing a good many things every day. His black suit was neat, neither too well-made nor too plain to attract notice. Somewhere in his late thirties or early forties, he had the perfect posture of a man who'd known military service, an assumption that Alfie felt comfortable making when he noticed the mirror shine to the man's shoes and his brutally regimented hair and side whiskers.

"Yes, my Lord?" the butler asked with perfect deference.

"Has anyone been let go lately, Johnson? Lord Crawford here is in need of staff. I don't remember writing any references."

"You didn't, sir. May I inquire as to which positions Lord Crawford is looking to fill?"

Alfie could almost hear Dominick snickering at the question. Just as well he'd left him behind.

He floundered a moment; he didn't plan on being in London long enough to need a staff and hoped Johnson wouldn't get any out-of-work servant's hopes up by mentioning he asked. "I don't recall off the top of my head, a maid or two, perhaps a footman?"

Johnson hesitated before replying. "I'm afraid I'm not aware of anyone that would suit, my lord. We haven't had any maids leave us recently."

His omission was so obvious that even Sempill noticed. "Did we lose a footman then? I don't remember you saying anything."

Johnson lips pressed flat for just a moment before he returned to the image of the perfect butler. "I believed I mentioned it once or twice, sir, but perhaps I was mistaken. An under-footman had to be let go after proving himself unfit for service. However, I believe Lord Crawford is already acquainted with the man, as it was on his recommendation that he was hired."

Damn. Alfie should've thought of that. Mrs. Hirkins had gotten Larry the job on Alfie's alleged word. Ridiculous to have expected a drunken carouser like Sempill to do any of the hiring. Of course, Johnson had been the one dealing with it all and of course, a man like him would remember that it was Lord Crawford who'd sent Larry his way. Too late to do anything about that now, however. Perhaps if Johnson was used to dealing with Sempill, he'd expect all nobles to be equally useless.

"Was it really?" said Alfie with feigned surprise. "I'm sure I just signed whatever recommendation my secretary put in front of me. You say you let the man go already? Was there a problem?"

Johnson's lips tightened again. "I'm afraid so, sir."

When no more was forthcoming, Alfie cursed internally. Dominick was right. No one wanted to confide in an earl. So be it. He hadn't meant to turn this into an interrogation, but Johnson could hardly refuse to answer a direct question in front of Sempill.

"Did he have issues with other members of the staff?"

"No, sir. He was quite well liked in the short time he was here."

That was something at least. Johnson's answer didn't sound like the sort of rote response Alfie would expect if he was lying. There was a ring of truth to it and Alfie had no doubt that if anyone under Sempill's roof had problems with Larry, Johnson would've been the one to know. Interesting that Larry had been let go. Alfie had expected Johnson to just say he'd stopped showing up. Say, roughly around the the time he'd been murdered.

"Why did we get rid of him then?" asked Sempill before Alfie had the chance.

"I'm afraid he just wasn't a good match."

For God's sake, Johnson wasn't meant to be a butler. He was meant to be a diplomat.

Fortunately, Lord Sempill wasn't. "That's not much of an answer." He scoffed. "Come on, man, out with it."

Johnson took a moment to find appropriately bland phrasing. "While I hope the footman in question, Mr. Brennan, served well during his time originally in Lord Crawford's employ, he unfortunately proved unreliable here."

"How so?" asked Alfie.

"I'm afraid he was absent on multiple occasions that did not coincide with his half-day off. And while I tried to be forgiving on the occasion of the first funeral out of respect for the man's grief, by the *third*..."

Sempill laughed. "Three funerals? Surely the man could come up with a different excuse."

"Indeed, sir," said Johnson. "Which is why he was relieved of his employment several weeks ago. Unfortunately, when his valise was searched upon his departure, several small items of value were discovered among his things."

"My God, Freddie!" Sempill laughed again. "Did you send a jewel thief into our midst?"

Alfie gritted his teeth at the hated nickname his cousin and his friends had always used.

"I had no idea," he replied distractedly as his mind raced with the new information. So, Larry hadn't been able to balance his employment with his responsibilities to the burial club. Odd that he'd tried to attend all the funerals though. They couldn't actually expect all members to attend every single one. Dominick had mentioned there being some sort of penalty for skipping out, but surely it couldn't be so high that a man would risk his employment. But perhaps that explained the purloined items in his bags.

Larry's thievery was surprising. Alfie wouldn't have expected Agnes to tell him if her fiancé was light-fingered, but it would've been the first thing out of Mrs. Hirkins' mouth. And being let go weeks ago meant Larry was an unemployed thief at that. Had the Hirkins women even known? Mr. Hirkins' illness and death might have been some distraction, but Larry would've needed to find a way to fill his time to avoid arousing suspicion. And some way to fill his pockets if he was let go without pay.

"In Lord Crawford's defence, sir," said Johnson. "It is possible he was an unknowing victim as well. None of the items Mr. Brennan attempted to steal were of great significance, so it is likely their loss would have gone unnoticed for some time in a different household."

In a household not run by me, his words clearly said. Alfie was offended on Mrs. Hirkins' behalf, even though all of this was partially her fault to begin with.

"It certainly doesn't sound like you want this fellow back!" exclaimed Sempill.

"No," said Alfie. Not that he could. "I'm sorry if he inconvenienced you."

While he ostensibly made the remark to Sempill, he didn't miss Johnson's slight bow in acknowledgement.

"Nonsense, nonsense," said Sempill cheerily, tossing back the contents of his glass. "But I'll let you make it up to me regardless. There's a club I've been meaning to try. They offer this new card game that's all the rage. American, I think, or French. Some blighted place at any rate."

Alfie couldn't help glancing at the clock. It was admittedly late in the day for a social call, but still many hours until darkness—the customary time to visit the sort of club that advertised such distractions.

"Club" indeed, Alfie was sure the more appropriate term was "hell".

"It's rather early for that sort of thing, isn't it?"

"Ah ha! So, you're interested!" Sempill crowed. "If you had other engagements you'd have said so! Come on then. Johnson, grab Freddie's coat and we'll be off."

❊ ❊ ❊

Without knowing quite how it happened, Alfie found

himself swept off to not one, but three gaming hells, gathering friends of Sempill's at each. It was all far too reminiscent of the way his cousin used to drag him around as little more than a billfold with legs. At least none of Sempill's friends asked him for money. They didn't seem inclined to accept his polite excuses either though, so he did his best to ignore the bite of cheap gin as they ordered round after round and the shouts of victory and defeat from the betting men around him. It was all rather like the night he'd been dragged to Spitalfields to see a fight and found Dominick in the ring.

The thought made him smile around his glass of truly awful gin. If Dominick was here now, it would be much more bearable. It might even be fun. Alfie only occasionally indulged in gambling, but from what he could follow, this new game could be quite exciting if played in the right company. While similar to one of the ones Gil had taught him to play at Balcarres, Alfie doubted he'd be able to remember all the rules to this version on his own. Maybe if Dominick was here, they could muddle it out between them. Had Dominick ever come to places like this when he wasn't fighting? He wouldn't have had the money to waste, but he might've enjoyed the sport of it all.

One of Sempill's friends pulled a laughing woman into his lap and Alfie's smile slipped off his face. Dominick might not have come to places like this to fight, but he might have in search of other employment for the evening. He watched the woman lean across Sempill's friend in a way that displayed her bosom with unmistakable intent.

He looked away before he saw more than he needed to, his eyes falling on a man at the table across from theirs. His back was to them so Alfie couldn't see his face, but misery was writ in every line of his body.

"Well, Freddie!" Sempill slurred. "Are you going to wager or just sit there?"

As Alfie watched, the man at the other table slumped down, head buried in his hands. He was stripped to his shirtsleeves, the back of his waistcoat catching the eye with bright swirls of blue and green in some lavish pattern that stood out even amidst the riot of movement in the hell. His jacket lay on the table, and one of the grinning players took it and added it to his own pile of winnings.

So much to be lost in a place like this, Alfie thought. *A small wager becomes a larger one, but you can't keep it up indefinitely. And what happens if you can't afford to lose?*

The room swayed as he got to his feet but that didn't stop him from leaving without a word, ignoring the shouts of Sempill and his friends behind him. He didn't care what they thought of his leaving so abruptly. He wasn't going to learn anything useful about Larry's death here and he'd had enough misery for one day.

CHAPTER 13

"I still don't like this."

Dominick sighed as he examined a mended patch in his shirt. Mrs. Hirkins really did excellent work. However, it still didn't make the material any less coarse, especially after removing a silk banyan to put it on. He turned to Alfie, still smugly wrapped in a banyan of his own, his feet kicked up on the settee beside him as he watched Dominick dress.

"I know you don't," said Dominick. "But the club seems to be our only real lead. It'd be foolish to give up on it now."

"Why does the burial club have so many members, anyway?" Alfie asked from his perch. "Not to be unkind, but Larry's funeral was... shabby, at best. Paying every week of your life just for that?"

Dominick took a moment before responding. Sometimes it felt like he and Alfie had never been separated, but other times he would say something that made the gulf of their thirteen years apart almost impossible to navigate. Looking at him sitting in a warm and lavish room dressed in silk with a tray of the finest delicacies at his elbow, to be eaten not because he was hungry, just if he desired something sweet, was one of those times.

"It might seem shabby to some, but for those who

expect little more than to wind up in the back of a resurrectionist's cart, it's nearly the same as a royal funeral. A burial on consecrated ground with a real priest, a real casket, people to mourn you, and even your own headstone? Those are fineries most in Spitalfields could never even dream of for themselves. Not to mention how much more all that means for religious folks."

"I suppose," said Alfie slowly. "But is it worth it? It seems like such a commitment, especially for the young."

"Larry was young," Dominick pointed out.

Alfie conceded the point with a nod. "I suppose so. And you're sure this burial club holds our answer? You don't think Larry's death might be related to his stealing from Lord Sempill instead?"

Dominick raised an eyebrow. "Do you?"

Alfie scrunched up his nose the way Dominick loved but could never tell him was adorable.

"No, as much as I don't want my aching head from spending all night in that hell to have been for naught, I don't. If Larry had been the only one to show up dead, perhaps. But that several other members of the club turned up with their throats slit and he just *happened* to be killed the same way by someone else entirely?" Alfie shook his head. "I'm willing to believe in coincidence, but that seems a little much."

"I agree," said Dominick. He'd enjoyed Alfie being the disreputable one for once, stumbling into their suite in the late hours, stinking of smoke and gin. He'd spent the next day with a cup of tea clutched between his hands, eyes squinted shut despite the blizzard of headache powder he'd consumed. He hadn't done much the next few days at all, but honestly there was little for them to do. They'd had this conversation again and again, but with no other leads, all they could do was wait until Wednesday rolled around again.

Fortunately, Alfie's anger at him for running off had lessened somewhat, although Dominick suspected it was more a matter of the embers being banked to reignite later. Perhaps it would've been better if he'd had spent the days in Spitalfields instead, readjusting to being Nick Tripner, but he couldn't bring himself to spend more time there than he had to—even if Alfie would've let him.

But now it was Wednesday. The package from Mrs. Hirkins had arrived around suppertime, but that gave them precious little time before Dominick had to dress to go to the burial club meeting. He could've prolonged the misery by waiting to change until he arrived at Mrs. Hirkins' home to drop off suitable clothes to change back into, but a greatcoat hid any number of sins and he was a little worried that he wouldn't have the resolve to go through with it again without Alfie's support.

Alfie selected one of the confections from the tray beside him and nibbled it contemplatively. "I suppose that rules out Mrs. Hirkins and Agnes as well."

"Rules them out from what? Surely you don't think they're killers?" Dominick asked in surprise.

"Not now that we know about the other deaths," replied Alfie. "But when it was just Larry..."

Dominick gave the idea serious thought. "I could understand why Mrs. Hirkins might have. She certainly didn't hide her dislike of the man and I don't doubt she's capable. She wouldn't have done it in her own home though. Too much mess."

Alfie wrinkled his nose. "That and she likely would've just told us. Or at least strongly hinted that we needn't waste our time elsewhere. It's not like we have enough evidence to send her to the gallows."

Dominick laughed. "You wouldn't dare even if we did! Not if you didn't want to wake up to her ghost swinging a frying pan at your head."

Mrs. Hirkins could probably admit to overthrowing the monarchy and Alfie would do little more than look aggrieved. He'd be even less likely to turn her in than he would Dominick because at least Mrs. Hirkins didn't steal all the covers.

Dominick shook his head fondly. "Why not Agnes? She was in a family way from an out-of-work thief. She couldn't have been happy about that. Maybe she thought she'd be better off without him."

Now it was Alfie's turn to look thoughtful. "That would still leave the problem of the other murders. And I don't think the timeline makes sense, she was at Mr. Hirkins funeral right beside her grandmother the whole time. Besides, we have no proof she knew anything about Larry stealing from Lord Sempill."

"Not to mention, she deserves to be on the stage if she's faking those tears. I'd wager a thousand pounds she really loved him."

Alfie hummed in agreement but the look on his face was forlorn. "I suppose that leaves us back at The Rose where we started."

"I'm still glad you looked into Sempill," said Dominick, pulling on his waistcoat. The fabric was greasy under his fingers. "In case you're moping about that being a waste of time.

"Earls don't mope," replied Alfie, despite doing exactly that. "And I don't think my time was wasted looking into it, even if I'd preferred the butler had admitted to murdering Larry and presented his wrists for handcuffs. That would be much simpler and not put you in any more danger. It is interesting that Larry was stealing from the household. Agnes never mentioned anything about him being a thief."

"Perhaps she didn't know."

"Perhaps." Alfie's face brightened and he swung his feet down from the settee. "You could ask her when you drop your clothes off."

Dominick couldn't help but laugh. "I thought you wanted to keep me out of danger! If I did that, I'd be the next body found with a slit throat!"

Alfie's expression darkened. "Don't say that. Not even in jest."

"All right, I'm sorry. I'll do my best to keep my throat intact."

"And the rest of you as well."

"And the rest of me as well."

Alfie was quiet as Dominick finished dressing. Finally, he said in the softest voice, "Are you sure you have to do this?"

Dominick bit back a sigh.

"I know, I know," said Alfie before he could respond. "I just hate the idea of sending you into the serpents' lair. I don't suppose there's anyone else it could be? What about Hugh?"

"What about him?" Dominick frowned

Alfie shrugged, but clearly it was something he'd been thinking about for a while. "He sells corpses for a living. Is it that hard to believe he's decided to make his own? Especially when he's been the one to find all the bodies so far?"

"All the bodies we know of," Dominick pointed out. "There could be more."

"That's not as reassuring as you think it is."

Dominick considered it. "I don't think he did it. If you met him, you'd know why. Hugh could find every dead rat in East London if he thought he'd turn a profit, but he just doesn't seem the type to murder."

"All the more reason to be suspicious. Isn't the murderer always the last person you'd suspect?"

Dominick snorted. "I don't think the Prince Regent did it either. Does that mean he's our killer?"

"I wouldn't put it past him," grumbled Alfie.

"I'll keep an eye on Hugh, just to be safe." Dominick pulled the greatcoat over his shoulders. "How do I look?"

He fought the urge to preen as Alfie eyed him up and down.

"Thoroughly disreputable," Alfie announced at last. "Best make sure that coat is fastened up tight or you'll frighten the maids on your way out."

"Mm, we'd hate for them to think the Right Honorable Lord Crawford was dragging good, honest prostitutes out of the slums for his own deviant purposes."

"Well, if he'd known that prostitute was going to be silly enough to try to go back to the slums, and root out a murderer in the bargain, Lord Crawford might have left him bleeding out in the alley where he found him and bestowed his deviant purposes on someone more appreciative."

Alfie rose as he spoke and was now running his hands down Dominick's lapels. Dominick caught them both up and pressed a kiss to his knuckles.

Alfie sighed. "You will be careful, won't you?"

Dominick kissed his hands again. "I promise."

"I still don't like this."

Kiss. "You've said."

"At least you're not sneaking off this time. Will you be back tonight?"

Dominick hesitated. "I don't know. It depends on how long the meeting goes and how raucous it gets. I'll stay at Jimmy's if it goes too late, don't worry."

"Of course, I'm going to worry," said Alfie. "But considering where I spent most of the other night, I can hardly scold you now, as much as I want to. Which reminds me, I keep forgetting to give you these…"

He broke away, returning a few moments later with a handful of coins. Dominick looked them over. Mostly pennies, with nothing larger than a sixpence.

"I thought you might need some smaller coins. I won them at the tables. It was quite the challenge to win only the small pots."

"Thank you," said Dominick as he dropped the coins into an inner pocket where they'd be safe from all but the most brazen of pickpockets. "I think that's everything. Oh no, you've forgotten something important."

Alfie brow furrowed. "What?"

Dominick grinned. "A kiss for good luck."

Alfie rolled his eyes. "And you say I'm the one with the

deviant purposes. You're incorrigible."

Despite his words, Alfie went easily when Dominick reeled him in with an arm around his waist. Before he could kiss Alfie though, he was stopped by a finger to the lips.

"Just the one kiss," said Alfie. "We don't want you to be late for your meeting."

*　*　*

Dominick breathed in the smoky air of The Rose of Normandy as he pushed his way through to a less crowded corner. Despite his best intentions, he wasn't actually late, but he was clearly one of the last club members to arrive.

He pressed himself more tightly into the corner. The years of grime worked their way into his clothes, but it hardly mattered. He wasn't in one of the delicate outfits that required careful brushing and washing and pressing that he'd become so used to wearing. This wasn't the first packed pub these togs had seen.

He knew the club had a lot of members, but he hadn't been expecting a crush like this. The pub was packed, nearly from wall to wall, every chair and table filled with men and women of all ages, all tired and thirsty from a hard day's work—or from the looks of some—a hard day's searching for it. There were linkboys and cutpurses, stevedores and washerwomen all talking and joking and shouting over one another to order a pint. Behind the bar, Toller the barman was being run off his feet, pouring drinks and pocketing pennies, while the owner George Brine was spending more of his time socialising than making sure his pub stayed in business.

Not that he needs to worry. Dominick thought as he took another look at the mob. He had a growing suspicion that Brine operated the burial club less to ensure the proper rest of his fellow men and more for the additional money they spent on drink at the weekly meetings.

He looked around the rapidly filling room in vain. He'd arrived with Hugh and while normally he'd be thrilled with the man's disappearance, he wasn't sure he wanted to be alone either. He'd been out of Spitalfields both too long and not long enough. There were few faces left he wanted to see, so he was surprised when he saw one he did.

"Helen!" he shouted.

"Nick!"

A woman of indeterminate age made her way towards him. She had the stretched look of someone who had either lived many years well or few years poorly. He suspected it was a mix of both. Her brightly coloured skirts marked her for the doxy she was, although not as obviously as her bodice which creaked under an acre of bosom and dipped so low the faintest hint of pink nipple was visible. The bright green ribbon she had tied high around her throat only accentuated the amount of skin on show. Despite her obvious display of wares, she wore less make up than most of the female prostitutes Dominick knew. She'd been considered a great beauty in her prime, even making her way into *Harris's Lists of Covent Garden Ladies*, although those hadn't been published since before he was born.

She threw herself against him in a fierce embrace. "I didn't know you were a member of the club!"

"I only just joined. I saw Hugh O'Donnell at a funeral a

week or so ago and he made introductions."

"Ugh, that ghoul." Helen shuddered. "Explains why I hadn't seen you yet. Had to skip that one. Was sleeping off one of *those* nights of work. You know the kind I mean?"

Dominick let out a shudder himself. "One of *those* nights" could mean many things, none of them good. He'd had more than a few of *those* nights himself when he was working her job.

"I know exactly the sort. Let me buy you a drink after all this is done?"

"Well, I won't say no to that." She batted her eyelashes at him. "You look well."

Dominick laughed. "I don't—"

Before he could finish, he was interrupted by a great cheer that rose up from the crowd. They turned to see Brine standing on top of the bar, hands raised in the air.

"Welcome everyone to The Rose Burial Club!"

Another cheer went up.

"Thinks he's on stage at the Theatre-Royal, he does." Helen sniffed.

"One or two pieces of business tonight before we get started. We've a few new members that I won't trouble by naming, but make them feel welcome if you see them. Now I've gotten this question more than once, so I'll say again…"

Dominick tried to focus on Brine's words so he could recount them to Alfie later, but the man was far too fond of the sound of his own voice. He might've been interesting enough if he hadn't been talking about club by-laws and technicalities, but as it was, Dominick felt the same way he did whenever Gil tried to explain investments to him.

Namely, like he was a cat in a sack and could hear a rushing river; he wanted out *desperately*.

He distracted himself from the urge to claw his way to freedom by watching Toller instead. He'd stopped pouring drinks when Brine began speaking and had disappeared into the back only to return with the large book Dominick had signed his name in. He set the book on the bar with a thud that didn't even cause a ripple in Brine's flow of words, then disappeared again. When he returned this time, he was carrying a wooden chest. He appeared to be struggling under its weight and Dominick instinctively stepped forward to help, despite there being dozens of people and an entire room between them. When Toller hefted the chest onto the table, another cheer rose up, finally drowning out Brine.

"That's the money chest," said Helen. "God, can you imagine how much is in there? All the money that goes in every week? Would take someone braver than me to try to crack it though."

"Has anyone tried?" Dominick couldn't help but think of Larry and his pocketed silver. Had he tried to steal from the club and ended up with swifter justice than he'd expected? Had the other victims made the same mistake? Four thieves sounded like a lot, but Dominick bet there were at least twice that many in the room with him now. And that was only if he was counting the dedicated professionals. Likely there were dozens more who'd done a bit of light-fingering or housebreaking here and there, himself included.

But Helen was shaking her head. "There's few things that only the worst man would steal: a babe's milk, a parson's candles, and another man's grave. If the curse of doing such a thing wasn't enough to frighten you off, it only gets brought out for these meetings and I'd like to see the man brave enough to try to make off with it while in a room full of people whose money is inside! He'd be lucky if the only thing they did was kill him!"

"It's locked up the rest of the time?"

Helen eyed him suspiciously. "Why? You're not thinking of trying, are you? I'll remind you my money's in there too."

Dominick shook his head. "I just want to make sure my money will be safe."

Helen hummed. "See that that's all it is. But yes, locked up tight and guarded by that brute Murdoch half the time. That's him there."

Dominick looked where she pointed. He hadn't seen Jack Murdoch when he'd arrived, but there he was sure enough, barely visible in the shadows save for the outline of his rectangular bulk. Dominick wondered how he'd found a spot dark enough to hide his hideously bright neckcloth and striped waistcoat.

"...and I think that's all the important news," Brine finally concluded. "If Toller's brought out the box, it's time to get things well under way. Thank you, Simon. You've brought the book as well?"

Toller grunted and began flipping through its pages. He started calling out names, and one by one, people made their way to the front to pay their dues.

"Helen Moore." He called out then added, "Penalty."

Brine chuckled good naturedly. "Oh Helen, what've you done to make our Toller sound like that?"

"Lack of attendance at a funeral," said Toller solemnly. "One florin penalty, with an additional pence added in interest for every week it's late."

Dominick had to keep from gasping. It was an outrageous sum for such a minor offence. No wonder so many of the club had been willing to stand out in the rain for Larry's funeral. He kept from touching the pocket which held his coins. He had far more than that on him, but it would take Helen all week to earn such a sum. Still, she seemed unmoved.

"I've only enough for my dues tonight, but I'll get the rest soon," she shouted back. "Unless you want payment in kind?" Grinning, she pulled up her skirts to a chorus of hoots and cheers.

Brine only laughed. "We only accept payment stamped by the face of the king, not the regent!"

The uproarious laughter that followed drowned out any retort Helen made but she was smiling as she made her way to the front and cheekily dug around in her cleavage for a few coins and dropped them in the box.

"There you go, Toller," she laughed. "I'll have the extra for you later."

"See that you do, Ms. Moore," he said flatly. "As you know, all persons in arrears are ineligible for payouts in the event of death."

Helen made an obscene remark about her own "arrear" that set the crowd off again.

One by one, all the others were called forward to make their payments, including Hugh, who waved at Dominick when he caught his eye, but fortunately returned to a boisterous table of friends instead of making his way over.

When his name was finally called, Dominick made his way to the bar. When he glanced down at the ledger, he froze with his hand in his pocket. As Toller tapped his finger under his name in the ledger, Dominick realised he'd seen a page like that before. Those faint green lines that ran across the page were the same as those on the piece of paper Agnes had found in the back of the fireplace—singed, but unmistakably the same.

He cursed himself silently. Hadn't he already signed his name into this very same ledger before she'd found the paper? If he hadn't been half drunk on Brine's ale when he'd signed up, he'd have noticed it was the same paper the first time he saw the scrap. He tried to remember the writing on the page she'd found as he stared down at the book before him, but he couldn't tell if the handwriting was the same or not. There had to be thousands of similar ledgers all across the city, but the coincidence was too great. For a brief moment, he wished Alfie was with him. Surely he'd be able to tell if they were the same.

It did raise an interesting question though; what was a page from the burial club's ledger doing in Mrs. Hirkins' fireplace?

He watched Toller place a check beside his name in the book and at his nod, added three pennies to the box. As the latest member, his was the last name called, and he'd barely let go of the coins before Brine began booming once again.

"Another meeting nearly completed! To conclude, if you have a glass already, raise it for our members who've gone before us and in memory of the comfort they have in resting properly and peacefully."

He raised a tankard, as did most of the room.

"Now let us eat, drink, and be merry, my friends! And if you didn't have a glass to toast, come up the front and let's see if we can't fix that!"

The crowd cheered a final time. Dominick had a moment's peace before being crushed against the bar, shouted orders filling his ears. Toller ignored them all, making a final few notes in the ledger before closing it with a snap, no doubt smearing the still wet ink. He stacked the book on top of the chest, then disappeared into the back with both. Murdoch peeled off from his place in the shadows to follow him, no doubt to ensure the box returned to its usual hiding space safely.

This left Brine alone in the pub he allegedly ran. It looked like the actual work of a publican didn't suit him, for he only grudgingly started pouring drinks for anyone other than himself when after several minutes Toller hadn't reappeared. Even then, he could only work at half Toller's pace and those who ordered beers received mugs that were half head.

"Two gins," Dominick said, when he finally caught the man's attention.

"You're doing well for yourself." Brine said as he grabbed an unmarked bottle and two glasses. "You paid your dues. I can't tell you how many people forget to save up their first week."

Dominick shrugged. "I've enough for dues and a few drinks. Nothing more."

"Well, if you're looking for more, I might have some work for you."

Dominick nodded and slid his payment across the bar.

As he carried the glasses back to Helen, he wondered if he should give her enough coin to cover her penalty. It would only be fair after all her kindness to him over the years, but it might raise questions as to how he'd come into such funds. And this was the last place he wanted to be flashing his money around.

Still, the least he could do was buy a round for an old friend. Who knew what useful information she might "remember" for the price of a free drink. After all, it was for the sake of the investigation. And he couldn't question only her. While he was here, he should try the same with other members of the club. Subtly, of course. It wouldn't do to let the murderer know he was interested.

That stopped him in place. If the killings were related to the club, it was likely the killer was here too. Drinking, laughing, searching for his next victim.

He staggered back into motion, but when he reached Helen, he handed her both glasses. He had to remain on his guard. She knocked back the first in a single go, the ribbon around her throat bobbing. Then she looked at him questioningly over the second one.

"Not thirsty anymore," he said. "Anyone here I should meet who'd want it?"

By the time Helen had finished leading him around, his feet were sore, his clothes itched, and he was silently cursing every person he'd bought a drink for without getting one for himself. None of them had any useful information. It'd been a waste of both money and time. Now it was late and he was too tired to make his way halfway across London to Mrs. Hirkins' house for his clothes, then across the other half to get back to the hotel and Alfie.

* * *

Jimmy barely glanced at Dominick as he stumbled into The Barge, too busy with his own last few patrons of the night who had no interest in leaving a nice warm pub.

"You're in luck. Room's free tonight," Jimmy said, jerking his thumb in the direction of the stairs. "You know where it is."

Dominick slowly plodded his way up to the tiny attic room. As he undressed for bed, he counted out his remaining coins with a chuckle. He should've gone ahead and given Helen the money. He'd spent almost that much on drinks and didn't have anything to show for it, not even a single pint for himself.

He debated going back downstairs and getting a drink from Jimmy, but his head hit the pillow in exhaustion before he could make up his mind.

* * *

A thunderous series of knocks sounding at his door startled Dominick awake. Outside the small window, the sky was still grey with dawn. It couldn't have been more than a few hours since he'd left The Rose.

He got to his feet with a groan and flung open the door.

"Christ, Jimmy, what the hell do you want?"

But instead of Jimmy's bearded face, preferably with a mug full of coffee held out in front of it, Dominick found himself eye level with a garish handkerchief.

The handkerchief was above an equally ugly waistcoat and tied around a neck as thick as Dominick's arm.

Jack Murdoch grinned down at him, but there was no mirth in it, only violence.

"You'll come with me," he said, darker than a storm cloud. "If you know what's good for you."

CHAPTER 14

When Dominick hadn't returned by the time he went to bed, Alfie wasn't overly concerned. Unhappy, yes, but Dominick had at least warned him this time before staying out all night. When he hadn't returned by breakfast the next day, the first few drops of unease began to trickle in. By the time the sun rose on the second full day of Dominick's absence, he was definitely worried. By the third morning, he was decidedly panicked.

Unwilling and unfit to rub shoulders with the rest of the gentry beginning their day with a meal downstairs, he had breakfast brought up to the suite and was busy glaring at the tablecloth while two servants set out the dishes.

A cough to his right drew his attention. Turning to the source of the sound, it took him a moment to recognise the maid standing beside him as the same one who'd had the strange encounter with Dominick only a week ago. Had it really only been a week? It felt like he'd been trapped in this bloody hotel with nothing to do but worry for fucking years. His scowl deepened before he realised the old woman was staring at him, the look on her face no more pleasant than his own.

"Can I help you?" he snapped. He'd usually never speak to a servant that way, never mind a woman, but he was at the end of his rope.

With a distinctly Gallic disregard for his higher station, she asked, "Où est le... Ah! Where is the... other man?"

"I'd like to know that myself," Alfie muttered. "What business is it of yours?"

Even without his limited French he'd have known her response was uncomplimentary from the way the other servant, a footman, blanched.

"Forgive her, sir!" The footman said, all but bending himself in half bowing. "The French, they're ruled by their passions. Please, truly she meant no offence! I'm sure it's only the disappointment of not seeing the earl himself. There's not many of those in France, you know."

"With good reason. I believe they went out of style some decades ago, along with their heads."

If possible, the footman went even paler.

"Besides," said Alfie, "*I'm* the Earl of Crawford. And she doesn't appear particularly excited to see me."

"No, my lord. I mean—yes, my lord! That is... we have a letter for you, sir."

The moment the footman set the letter on the table, Alfie snatched it up.

"Leave me," he said, not even waiting to see if they followed his instructions before tearing the letter open.

Dominick's handwriting was clear although yet again his message was frustratingly short.

Staying in Spitellfields, don't know how long. Might be followed. Rose of Normmandy definately involved, but not sure how. Am safe. Stay where you are. Will return when can. DO NOT DO ANYTHING STUPID.

With a roar of frustration, Alfie sent the contents of the breakfast table clattering to the floor.

* * *

By the time a further two days had passed without any word, Alfie was ready to tear down the walls with his fingernails. He hated himself for doing nothing, but at the same time, what could he do? He'd barely left hotel, hoping word would come, his terror growing with every moment none arrived. It wasn't just that Dominick was alone in one of the worst parts of the city. As much as Alfie hated it, he'd brought himself to accept that Dominick had spent all but the last year of his life in Spitalfields and had emerged—relatively—unscathed. But the fact he was alone in one of the worst parts of the city *while tracking down a murderer* added an all new edge of terror. And what had he meant by, "Might be followed?"

No, he thought, throwing his knife down on top of an untouched slice of toast. *If Nick can't return on his own, then I'm going down to that rotten warren of rat holes and dragging him back by his collar.*

He'd done it before, he could do it again. Granted, the last time he'd gone into Spitalfields in search of Dominick, he'd found him more by luck than skill and had ended up killing a man in the process.

The thought of that drove Alfie to his feet. What a fool he'd been. Clearly Dominick couldn't be trusted on his own with murderers about, look at the trouble he'd gotten in last time.

He marched into his bedroom. If he was going to retrieve his wayward lover, he was going to need clean stockings, and a shave, and an outfit that effectively conveyed "Do not even think of robbing me". The sword cane would go a long way to convey that last part, but he could hardly focus on retrieving Dominick if he was fending off thugs and pickpockets left and right.

He grabbed a jacket in deep maroon and held it up to the dresser mirror to see if it would suit. But the image he saw reflected back wasn't the wrathful man on a mission he'd been hoping for. After days of freedom from its pomade, his hair ran riot, curls floating around his face like an auburn halo, only serving to make him look that much younger and his skin that much paler.

Spoiled little lordling.

His own words echoed back at himself. He didn't have to imagine the jeers if he went storming into Spitalfields on his own with a gold handled cane and unmarked skin. He'd heard them all before.

Pretty, spoiled, *useless* little lordling.

He set the jacket down with a sigh. It was true. So far, he hadn't been any use at all. Maybe Dominick was right; the best thing Alfie could do was stay put and let him figure things out on his own. Dominick was certainly smart enough to do so, not to mention tough enough to handle anything that came his way. And Alfie wasn't. Not with his leg that still got in his way, or his refined looks— so carefully cultivated to fit in amongst other nobles—that now only marked him as a target.

He no longer belonged in the place he'd been born.

The thought filled him with a queasy sensation he didn't fully understand. It was true, he was made of Spitalfields mud just as much as Dominick was, but he'd spent half his life in one world, half in the other. He didn't want to go back. He *desperately* didn't want to go back. After he retrieved Dominick he'd be happy to never see Spitalfields again. But the idea that he no longer belonged in the place he'd spent his childhood left him feeling oddly, like he was reaching out in the dark for a lantern always kept in the same place, but his hand passed through nothingness instead.

He let out a deep sigh and rubbed his face. The unfamiliar prickle beard growth scratched against his palms.

He snorted. Pretty, spoiled, useless, *unkempt,* little lordling.

He couldn't remember the last time he'd shaved. Looking into the mirror again now that he wasn't focused on the disgustingly artful tousle of his curls, he could see the hair growth on his chin and cheeks. Not enough to be called a proper beard yet, but noticeable nonetheless. The hair on his face was redder than that on his head, but darker too. It might not actually look that bad if he allowed it time to grow in. Perhaps making him less pretty and more what? Distinguished?

It certainly wasn't distinguished as it was now though. Dishevelled, certainly. A bit rough even. It actually changed his appearance quite a bit.

Disreputable, that was the word he was looking for. It was a good thing he'd been taking his meals in his rooms. He'd never be allowed in the Grillion's dining room looking like this.

His heart thudded in his chest. He didn't look like he belonged in polite society at all...

Heart still pounding, he stared at himself as a plan

came together in his mind. It was a terrible plan, risky, foolhardy even, and if he was caught the consequences would be horrific.

He remembered the last line of Dominick's letter. *DO NOT DO ANYTHING STUPID.*

Oh, my love. It's like you don't know me at all.

He couldn't help but smile. In the mirror, a pretty little lordling smiled back.

Well, he thought, *I can fix that.*

CHAPTER 15

Dominick clenched his fists as he followed Murdoch out of The Barge. This early in the morning, the streets of Spitalfields were quiet. If Murdoch meant him harm he couldn't rely on help. Not that he expected any. He rolled his shoulders. He wasn't looking forward to a fight with Murdoch, but if that's what it came down to, he'd beaten bigger men than him before.

Well, maybe not quite, but he'd beaten some pretty big ones.

And been beaten yourself.

He tried to focus on their surroundings. To his surprise, the route they were taking was familiar. Very familiar, in fact. He'd just come this way a few hours ago.

"We're going back to The Rose?" he asked.

Murdoch grunted and Dominick relaxed just a hair.

"Any reason you couldn't have just asked? Or spoken to me last night for that matter?"

"Mr. Brine has an offer for you. Too busy to ask last night." Murdoch grinned. "And now we know where to find you. Been trying to figure that one out since you showed up. Started thinking you were a ghost."

Fuck, fuck, fuck. If Brine had been looking for him, then it was only luck that kept them from tracking him to Mrs. Hirkins. Or Alfie. He couldn't risk that happening. He'd have to stay in Spitalfields until this was all over.

It meant having to find a way to get messages to them so they wouldn't worry, but he'd deal with that later. Mrs. Hirkins he wasn't so concerned about, but Alfie? Christ, he'd have to spell it out to keep him from doing something stupid.

The interior of the pub looked worse for wear from the previous night's revelry, but Toller was already there, half-heartedly pushing a mop over the floorboards. Did Brine ever let any of them sleep?

The publican himself was seated in a chair by the fire, feet propped up on the table in front of him.

"Ah, Mr. Tripner!" He beamed as Dominick followed Murdoch over to him, but didn't offer either of them a seat.

"Murdoch here said you wanted me?"

"Oh, knowing Jack, I'm sure what he said was actually much more threatening, but I appreciate that you could see through that to the true meaning of his words! In that spirit, I'll speak bluntly. I'd like to offer you a job, Mr. Tripner."

"You've mentioned that. I appreciate the offer, but I don't think I'm interested."

Dominick knew he should probably at least hear the man out, in case it related to Larry's death, but all his instincts were screaming at him to get out. Murdoch lurking over his shoulder wasn't helping his unease either.

"Now, Mr. Tripner, I don't see how that can be the case. I believe you told Toller you were in 'private employment' but I'm quite the centre of the local community these days and I've asked a few questions here and there. It seems you fell off the map about a year ago, no one knows where you went. And now you've returned but no with no legitimate employment I can discover, no boxing matches and even the..." Brine coughed. "Even the members of the other *profession* in which you've sometimes indulged haven't seen you about. Until last night, I wasn't even sure if you had lodgings at all or just sprang up from the ground like a mushroom."

Dominick's cheeks reddened at the mention of his other profession, but he kept his face blank.

"Now," Brine continued, "there's many reasons a man might suddenly reappear with money in his pocket after a long absence, most of them unsavoury. I could, if I had reason enough, look into it. I assure you I'm *very* thorough when I have reason to be. But I don't think either of us wants me to spend my time doing that, do we?"

Christ, no. Whatever Brine thought Dominick's secret was, he couldn't risk him getting too curious and discovering the truth.

"What's the job then?"

Brine's smile turned oily. Dominick would have to keep an eye out, to make sure he hadn't piqued Brine's curiosity anyway.

"I'm so glad you're interested! It's nothing distasteful, I assure you. You'll merely be assisting Jack here with collections."

"Collections?" said Dominick slowly.

"Yes." Brine's head bobbed up and down comically as he nodded. "It's a funny business running a pub, all sorts of unsavoury characters trying to take advantage of you by overcharging for goods or asking for a loan but never repaying it. Then, of course, there are the known troublemakers that won't seem to take a hint when their presence is unwanted."

Is that what happened to Larry? Dominick knew asking that would be suicide, but he couldn't help but think it. He knew what sort of a job Brine was talking about. An attack dog. He wanted to aim Dominick, set him loose, and expect him to return with flesh between his teeth.

Brine continued. "As you can imagine, Jack is very accomplished at this sort of work, but I've found teams of two are preferable. They keep each other honest and people are less likely to be difficult when there are *two* strapping gentlemen carrying about my business."

"What happened to the other man then?" Dominick asked before he could think better of it.

"Don't ask questions," rumbled a deep voice slightly behind and above him. Dominick fought the urge to shoot an elbow back into Murdoch's gut.

Brine only laughed. Dominick cut a look sideways. Toller had stopped mopping to watch, but when he saw Dominick looking he dropped his head and went back to it. No help from that quarter.

Dominick sighed. There wasn't going to be an easy way out of this. It was clear Brine wasn't going to let him leave without agreeing. On the upside, it sounded like the "job" involved more threatening than actual violence. And if Brine ordered them to slit someone's throat, Dominick could kill both him and Murdoch and be done with it. *How* he was going to do that he wasn't exactly sure, but as long as he said the right things now, he'd have time to work out the rest.

"When do I begin?"

* * *

By the end of the week, Dominick felt dirty down to his soul. To his immense relief, so far he hadn't had to hurt anyone or even issue any threats himself, just stand menacingly inside of doorways while Murdoch held whispered conversations with nervous shopkeeps. A few times he'd seen money exchange hands, so whatever scheme Brine was running was clearly profitable, but was it worth enough to kill over? Had Larry owed the man more than he'd been able to afford and paid for it with his life? Or was his death completely unrelated to this other business? He'd hoped to find out more once Brine decided he could be trusted, but he and Murdoch stayed maddeningly close-lipped. He hadn't even gotten a chance to look at the ledger again to confirm it matched his memory of the scrap of paper. But there was more to be discovered here. He knew it.

He mulled that over with a heavy heart as he followed Murdoch back to The Rose of Normandy. As soon as they were inside, Murdoch and Brine disappeared into the back, as they had every day so far, making it clear with a glance Dominick wasn't invited.

He debated whether or not to leave. All he wanted to do was get back to Jimmy's and go to sleep. Or even better, go back to Grillion's, but he knew he couldn't, not while doing so might put Alfie at risk. He sighed and pulled a stool up to the bar.

He was vaguely surprised not to see Toller behind the counter. For the first time, there was someone else there instead. The man had his back to Dominick, but he was much taller than Toller was, perhaps even of a height with Dominick himself. He was younger than Toller as well, if his straight back and shoulders were any indication. His close-cropped hair was so short Dominick at first thought he was bald, but a few nicks and cuts on his scalp suggested he either did the trim himself or had a barber with a drinking problem.

"I'll have a pint," Dominick said, rooting in his pocket for payment.

When the man turned around and set the mug in front of him, Dominick's coins fell from his nerveless fingers.

The man had the beginnings of a ruddy beard covering most of his face, but those eyes! Although he was used to seeing them sparking brightly with happiness, not bruised and sunken from lack of sleep, Dominick would know those eyes anywhere.

"Alfie?"

For a moment, Dominick thought he had to be mistaken. That all the days of worry and fear had corroded his mind, giving him a vision of the person he most longed to see where he couldn't possibly be—serving ale in a Spitalfields pub in a striped shirt and faded trousers. Then the vision spoke.

"Nick Tripner, you damned buck finch! Here, have a caulker and bring your arse to anchor!"

Dominick started. That wasn't Alfie's voice. It sounded like him, but the words and accent were all wrong.

He suddenly remembered being ten years old, dragging a fuming Alfie behind him as he let out an unbroken chain of obscenities in his sweet child's voice, his accent thicker than the workhouse mud. Alfie had mentioned Mrs. Hirkins teaching him to speak proper, but it appeared he'd never forgotten his native tongue.

"Alfie?" Dominick said again, still in shock.

Alfie tipped his head and gave Dominick such a look of, *Of course it's me, you idiot.* that all Dominick's doubts vanished. It wasn't a vision. Alfie really was here.

Christ, Alfie really was here.

Before the panic could truly set in, Alfie raised a finger in warning. "Right good of you to point me this way, knowing I was in need of work. I told Missers Brine and Toller how we was old friends, long lost until I ran into you again. They were happy to offer me a job on your good word."

Don't say anything now, Alfie's look said. *I'll explain later.*

Dominick took a moment to catch on. "What? Oh, right, of course." *You'd damn well better.*

"Is everything all right?" Toller came slinking out of the shadows from somewhere. "This cove said he knew you."

"Who, old Alfie? Sure. It was kind of Mr. Brine to hire him on. I'm sure you don't mind an extra hand."

Toller's thoughts on the matter were cut off by the reappearance of Murdoch and Brine.

"Ah, I see the new barman has made his introductions. But of course, you two have already met, haven't you?" Brine was wearing his usual publican's smile, but Dominick couldn't help the feeling of ice cracking under his feet.

"We knew each other back in the day. I just told Toller it was good of you to give him a chance."

"Hardly out of the goodness of my heart," Brine

beamed. "He came in asking for no pay, just a chance to work for tips. I'd be a fool to turn that down, despite his lack of experience."

Christ, Alfie. No wonder they were leery. He'd be lucky to earn a tuppence a night on that arrangement. The people around here barely had coin enough to buy their drinks, they didn't have any generosity to spare for the man who poured them. For Alfie to have made an offer like that sounded suspicious. Or desperate.

"Well," Dominick said. "It's still good of you. Once you've worked a certain profession, it's hard to find anywhere else to take you on. Especially us men. No one minds if their maid is already used to having her arse grabbed!"

"Oh, I see!" Brine laughed. He looked much more pleased with himself than he should at finding himself the employer of not one but two former whores. It was a good reason why Alfie would take a job for little to no pay though. That was what mattered. "Well, you can tell your friend he doesn't have to worry about that here."

Brine turned to Alfie. "Now, if you're still, ah, seeing clients, I can't have that here either, but there's a boarding house down the way that would be happy to rent you a room for—"

"None of that. He's staying with me 'til he gets on his feet." Dominick said, in response to Alfie's widening eyes. Like he was going to trust Alfie out of his sight for a minute. "In fact, I'd best show him the route back from here, if you don't need anything else."

Brine laughed again. Dominick was really starting to hate that sound. "I'm done with you for today, but the dinner rush will be starting any minute. I'm afraid your friend's work is just beginning."

Alfie didn't look nearly as alarmed at that as he should, following Toller at a snapped word to go help him bring out another barrel. Dominick picked up his pint and found himself a comfortable seat by the fire. If he was going to be stuck in this thieves' den all night, he was at least going to be warm.

He gave Murdoch a nod as the man headed out the door, although whether on his own business or more errands for Brine, Dominick didn't have the energy left to care.

Murdoch halted. "Your *friend*," he sneered, clearly making assumptions. Just because his assumption was correct didn't make Dominick want to punch him in his fucking face any less. "He doesn't even have the money to join the burial club, does he?"

Dominick was uneasy with both the question and the man asking it. "I doubt it."

Murdoch nodded. "If he steps out of line, I hear Hugh O'Donnell's been making good money lately. It'd be easy enough to send more work his way. Understood?"

I'll snap every bone in your body if you even think of touching Alfie.

Dominick smiled tightly. "I'll keep an eye on him."

Murdoch grunted, but thankfully left. Dominick tried to settle back into his chair, but it didn't feel nearly as comfortable as it had before. He sipped his drink, careful to make it last. He had to be ready in case he needed to drag The Right Honourable Earl of Crawford out of a gin-soaked hellhole.

Christ, Alfie. He thought with a groan. *What have we*

gotten into now?

CHAPTER 16

By the time the last few stragglers stumbled out of The Rose of Normandy and Toller gave him a pinched, "That's enough for today." Alfie was dead on his feet. He glanced around for Brine, but the publican and that brute Murdoch had their heads bent together at the other end of the bar. When Alfie set his apron on the counter, Brine raised a hand in his general direction, so he assumed that was permission enough. He followed an unspeaking Dominick out of the pub and into the near total blackness of the Spitalfields streets.

Normally, his mind would be racing. *Why wasn't Dominick saying anything? What did it mean that he'd stayed, sipping that single pint for hours while Alfie worked harder than he ever had in his adult life? Was there anything to be discovered at The Rose at all or was he wasting his time?*

But tonight it took all his mental effort to keep from toppling over into a pile of refuse. The walking stick he'd acquired along with his change of attire was better than nothing, but he still wavered on the pockmarked streets. Keeping up with Dominick in such a state would usually be impossible, but it didn't escape his notice that Dominick shortened his strides to stay close. He took Alfie's elbow to guide him through a particularly lightless alley and didn't let go until he pushed open the door of an empty pub not so different from the one they'd just left and headed up a flight of stairs.

Alfie hobbled up behind him as quickly as he was able. When Dominick unlocked a door, all Alfie needed to see was a bed before he was pushing past him and collapsing onto it with a groan. He lay there waiting for his muscles to stop screaming at him, dimly aware of Dominick moving around the room and lighting a candle.

"Go on then," Alfie said struggling for a moment to sit back up, then abandoning the cause as lost. "Let's hear it."

"I've nothing to say."

"Of course, you do, Nick. I could see you glowering at me all night. Go ahead, I can guess the gist of it, but I'd hate to deprive you of expressing the fullness of your ire."

The bed dipped with a squeak of the mattress ropes. "I don't want to yell at you, Alfie."

"No?"

Dominick sighed. "No more than usual."

"You're not angry that I didn't stay wasting away with worry at the hotel?"

"Of course, I'm angry. Angry you didn't stay where it was safe, angry you threw yourself into the middle of something you don't understand, angry that you put yourself in the path of dangerous men. Dangerous men you've already met while dressed as an earl! Jesus Christ, Alfie! I'm not angry, I'm furious!"

Dominick was shouting by the time he finished speaking. He made a strangled noise as if there was too much he wanted to say at once, then fell into stormy silence. Alfie turned his head to see him better. Dominick was sitting at the foot of the bed, his profile lit by the single candle. It threw the angles of his face into sharp relief, turning his handsome features into something darker, almost violent. But if his face was that of a god of war, the slump of his shoulders was that of a general who'd lost the battle.

"I don't know how many times I have to say it to get it through to you," Dominick continued, but he was looking at the floor and not Alfie. "You shouldn't be here. You don't belong here."

His words cut Alfie more deeply than he'd expected. "I used to."

Dominick just shook his head. After a long minute he gave a sigh. When he spoke, his tone was blank. "And I gave up everything to make sure you never had to come back."

The words struck Alfie like a blow. He hadn't considered that. He'd thought about how terrible it must be for Dominick himself to come back, but not what it must be like for him to see Alfie here. Not after all he'd sacrificed when they were children, protecting Alfie at every turn, and when the chance came, giving up his own escape for Alfie.

"I should've come back for you," Alfie whispered. "I'm so sorry, Nick."

Dominick shook his head again. "We were children. I never blamed you. Besides, it all worked out in the end, didn't it? Until this mess."

"Until this mess," Alfie agreed. "Nick, I was going out of my mind with worry. If things were reversed, you'd have done exactly the same. Don't pretend otherwise."

"Of course, I would. And you would be just as mad at me as I am with you for doing something so recklessly stupid.

But…" Dominick let out a huge rush of breath. "I figured most of this out in the second hour of waiting while you played barkeep. Make no mistake, I wanted to wring your scruffy throat for the first hour. But I spent the second one thinking about why you'd do such a cork-brained thing and while I'm still angry, I understand."

Alfie couldn't help but ask. "How did the rest of the hours go?"

"Oh, I went back to wanting to wring your neck quite a bit. Christ, Alfie. Do you realise what a risk you took? How did you know they wouldn't recognise you?"

Alfie raised a hand and ran it over his head. He'd done the best he could with the mirror and scissors, but had been too afraid to try a razor or risk a loose lipped barber spreading word about The Mad Earl of Crawford, so he knew the results were a mess. Some spots were bare all the way to the scalp, often ringed with small cuts, but he could feel other patches where the hair was a little longer. The short hair brushed gently against his palm, so much softer than the itchy stubble on his face.

"You barely recognised me," he pointed out. "They'd met a dandified earl throwing his weight about like a particularly finicky Persian cat. They were hardly going to connect that to the mangy creature who dragged himself in begging for a job."

When he'd first stepped foot in the pub, he'd hardly been as certain as he sounded, but he was never going to let Dominick know that. He also wasn't going to let him know that he'd wandered through Spitalfields for over an hour trying to find the place, no doubt putting himself in the way of even further harm.

"I don't need you mother henning me, Nick. I know coming here was a risk, but it was a risk for you too. I wasn't going to leave you here again."

Dominick said nothing in return, just sat staring at the floor.

"Besides," Alfie said. "I'm not exactly helpless, you know."

That earned him a snort. Dominick turned just enough to look at him sprawled limp on the bed and raised an eyebrow.

"As I was saying," Alfie continued. "I'm trained in fencing and while I lack a sword at present, a solid walking stick is nearly as good. And I can provide a second pair of eyes, talk to people who might not talk to you, and most importantly, I can watch your damned back, the same way you always watch mine. Not to mention, of the two of us, *I'm* the one who's killed two men and usurped an earldom. So. Hardly helpless at all."

A small smile twitched at the corner of Dominick's lips and Alfie nearly wept with relief.

"I suppose not," Dominick said. "Does that mean you don't need me to rub your leg?"

"Oh God, would you?" Alfie breathed. "I think it hurt less getting shot in the first place."

Dominick rolled his eyes. "There's something I need to do first."

Before Alfie had a chance to ask what was more important than his agony, Dominick leaned over and kissed him long, hard, and deep.

Alfie's head was spinning by the time he finally pulled away.

"I've needed to do that for days," Dominick said, his lips brushing Alfie's. "You're a damned nuisance. And a distraction. And you'd better not get us both killed but…"

He wrapped his arms tightly around Alfie, nearly pulling him off the bed with the force of his hug. In his surprise, Alfie could do little more than hug back, gently at first, then desperately as the full scope of their situation hit him. They were committed now. No way out without finding answers and no one to come to the rescue if they needed it. Alfred Pennington, Earl of Crawford and the wealthy Mr. Dominick Trent didn't exist inside Spitalfields. Only Alfie and Nick did, all alone except for each other.

"I'm glad you're here," Dominick whispered into his neck. Alfie felt tears prick the corners of his eyes.

Eventually Dominick pulled back and eased Alfie gently back down onto the bed.

"Your leg, then?" he asked, his voice rough.

"Please," said Alfie. "And when you're done with that, my other leg? And my feet? And perhaps my back? Lord, I think I walked twenty miles back and forth behind the bar tonight. My shoulders too. How does Toller do it every night?"

Dominick shook his head. "Be thankful you never had to work the docks. That nearly broke me. You'll get used to it. You didn't remember to bring any of Mrs. Hirkins' salve did you?"

"Coat pocket."

Alfie lay still while Dominick rummaged around, only to let out an affronted noise when Dominick tapped the tin against his nose.

"Are you too tired to undress yourself or are you just

pretending you are?"

Alfie considered the question. "Bit of both?"

Dominick laughed but a moment later he was pulling off Alfie's shoes. Then his hands were at Alfie's waist working on the buttons of his trousers. Alfie did his best to struggle out of his upper layers and between them they finally got him naked. He blushed as he felt Dominick's eyes on him, but couldn't help but shiver from more than just desire.

"Here," Dominick said, then he was tugging the blanket out from under Alfie and draping it over all of him save his injured leg. The first press of his fingers made the wound sting as it hadn't in months.

Alfie gritted his teeth. Slowly, the tension eased, but not enough and not nearly quickly enough.

"What have you found out?" He asked, desperate for distraction.

As Dominick worked, he laid out everything he could remember from the time they were apart, from the box club meeting to being pressed into service as Brine's thug. By the time Alfie's leg began to relax, the rest of him was tense with worry.

"I should've come sooner," he muttered.

Dominick huffed out a laugh. "You're making it very hard to be cross with you, love."

"Good. Because now I'm cross with you. For God's sake, Nick, you have to see how dangerous this is for *you* and I know you don't want to be doing Brine's dirty work anymore than I want to be cleaning spilt ale and vomit in his damned pub."

He struggled to sit upright, then took both of

Dominick's hands in his. The blanket pooled around his waist, but it wasn't as if Dominick hadn't seen him in far more compromising states.

"Mrs. Hirkins will understand. And Agnes… Well, she might not take it so well, but she won't have our blood on her hands and frankly that's all I really care about. We tried. *You* tried. My God, you say you never wanted me to come back here? When you walked into the pub today, I nearly dragged us both out on the spot. I should've known how badly coming back was going to wear on you."

"I didn't know myself," said Dominick. He gave Alfie's hands a squeeze but didn't say anymore. Alfie gave him time to think. Finally, Dominick dropped his head and let out a heavy sigh.

"You're right. It's clear that Brine and his whole lot are crooked as politicians, but there's not a magistrate in London that would do anything about it. If they went after every man with underhanded dealings, East London would be empty. We've no proof Murdoch killed anyone or that Brine ordered him to. And I'm no closer to finding out who killed Larry than I was the day we found his body."

Alfie ignored his protesting muscles long enough to press a kiss to Dominick's temple.

"I don't like giving up either," he said. "And the idea of letting down Mrs. Hirkins is honestly terrifying, but I hate seeing you like this even more. It's your decision though. If you want to see it through, we'll see it through. But *together* this time. I'm with you, vermin and stink and itchy clothing and all."

Dominick hesitated and for a terrible moment Alfie wasn't sure which choice he wanted him to make.

"You're right," said Dominick slowly. "We tried. We more than tried. But it's not worth the risk staying any longer just in the hope of finding something. We'll leave in the morning. Christ, I want a bath and a hot meal where I can safely guess what animal the meat came from."

"I'll have both drawn up the moment we get back to Grillion's... Wait, in the morning?"

Dominick raised an eyebrow at him. "You think you're in any fit state to make it back down those stairs? Never mind how far we'd have to walk before finding a hack driver brave enough to pick up the likes of us?"

"In the morning it is." Alfie agreed.

"A shame we couldn't decide that before you cut off all your gorgeous curls." Dominick liberated one of his hands and ran it over Alfie's head.

The sensation of his palm against Alfie's scalp was indescribable. The direct heat against his skin, the way the rough calluses that hadn't gone away even after a year of easy living caught against the stubble of his hair. It didn't feel quite as good as when Dominick twisted his fingers into Alfie's hair and *tugged*, but the novelty of the feeling made something heavy flutter in Alfie's stomach. He leaned into the touch, like a cat wanting to be petted.

"I-I'll..." he swallowed. "I'll have to invest more in hats."

The words were completely inane, but it was hard to think of anything when Dominick stopped stroking his head and began scratching, his hand moving down from Alfie's scalp to along his jaw.

"Rather like this, though," Dominick murmured. "You'll look damned good with a beard once it grows in."

Alfie couldn't keep from groaning. "Don't get used to it.

Damn thing itches like the devil."

"Perhaps I'd better distract you then," said Dominick wickedly. "Nowhere to go until morning, a tin of salve, and an already naked man in my bed? I think I might be able to come up with something."

"Oh, might you, indeed?" Alfie shifted, intending to pull himself onto Dominick's still clothed lap in a manner both beguiling and blatant, but halfway through his leg gave out and he found himself heading rapidly towards the floor face-first.

Only a pair of strong arms around his waist hauling him back saved him certain ignominy and possibly a broken nose.

"The spirit is willing, but the flesh feels like it's been dragged behind a mill cart or possibly underneath it."

For the sake of his pride, Alfie ignored Dominick's chuckles as he helped him lay back down. Then he nearly shot off the bed again as Dominick's hand wrapped around his cock.

"Nick…" he groaned.

"You're still wound tighter than a watch spring," Dominick said. "Nothing fancy, just something to help you sleep. Besides, I've missed you, missed *this*."

Alfie used the last of his strength to loop his arms around Dominick's neck and pull him in for a kiss. God, he'd missed this too. The feeling of Dominick over him, touching him. It'd barely been a week, but he hadn't realised he was starving until the feast was before him.

Dominick kissed him back, again and again, each kiss only making Alfie hungrier. Dominick shifted, doing something Alfie couldn't see and then Alfie felt Dominick's cock slide against his own, the drag of it long and hot and welcome. His head dropped back against the pillow when Dominick's hand closed around them both, the remnants of the salve just enough to smooth the motion to a glide as he worked them together from root to tip. Hips twitching, Alfie was helpless to do any more than lie there and enjoy as Dominick took away all the misery of the last few days —last few weeks—stroke by stroke. He watched Dominick's face, drinking in the sight of him. He never got tired of looking at his lover, whether it was slouched in his chair in their study asleep by the fire or on horseback, bathed in midday sun as he galloped across the estate. He never looked more beautiful than he did in bed though, his skin flushed with exertion and handsome features twisted in pleasure.

Dominick's breath hitched and he gasped out Alfie's name as he climaxed. His knuckles smeared his spend across Alfie's bare stomach as he continued to stroke. When Alfie's own climax overtook him just moments later, it did so in gentle, rolling waves, his worries sinking as he floated away, knowing that Dominick was with him, safe in the protected harbour of this squalid little room.

His eyelids were growing increasingly heavy, but he could still see that pleased little smile on Dominick's lips that he loved so much. When he awoke, they'd leave Spitalfields behind for good. What a perfect thought to drift off to.

Then a frantic pounding noise filled his ears. He jerked up, muscles screaming at the sudden movement. Dominick was already off the bed, cursing as he tucked himself back into his trousers. Alfie cast around frantically for his own clothes, barely taking a second to wipe himself off before throwing them on as Dominick cursed louder.

"For Christ's sake, do you know what time it is?" he bellowed.

There was a muffled response from the other side of the door and Alfie's mind finally surfaced through the shock to place the sound just as whoever it was began another frantic barrage on the door. The doorknob began to rattle but Dominick caught it before the door could open.

Alfie stared at him wide-eyed. Even dressed, there was no way to mistake what they had been doing. They were both dishevelled and the room reeked of sex. It dawned on him suddenly that if they were caught together like this, no one would believe he was an earl. By the time things got sorted out, they might already be on their way to the gallows. He saw his own terror reflected in Dominick's face.

"Who is it?" Dominick boomed, body braced against the door.

Alfie couldn't make out the reply, but whatever it was must have assured Dominick enough because he relaxed his stance and before Alfie could protest, he stepped back from the door and let it swing open.

A man with bright red hair and an unfortunate moustache stood in the doorway. Alfie had never seen him before, but based on Dominick's description, it had to be Hugh O'Donnell, brother-in-law of the man who owned the pub below, and fellow box club member.

And body snatcher.

Dominick all but growled. "Hugh, what the fuck are you doing?"

"Hello, Nick. Hello, Nick's... friend." Hugh bobbed a

quick nod at them both, but seemed neither surprised nor disgusted to find an only partially dressed man in Dominick's bedroom.

"I think you need to see this right away. I found another one, only this one I recognised. Definitely from the burial club."

Hugh held out his hand. Dangling from it was a length of ribbon that Alfie first thought had been dyed in several colours before he realised the truth. The ribbon was stained in places with a reddish brown so dark it nearly turned the bright green of the fabric to black.

Dominick let out a choked gasp.

"It's Helen."

CHAPTER 17

Dominick followed Hugh down the stairs on numb feet. He was dimly aware that he was leading them towards one of the backrooms, but still wasn't prepared for the sight of Helen's body lying still on a table.

She looked nearly identical to the last time he'd seen her, her cheeks red with rouge and the same bright dress worn far too low. But now her pale skin was drained a ghastly white and where she'd once worn her green ribbon, a yawning gash cut across her throat.

"Maeve'll skin me if she knows I brought my trade here," said Hugh. "But I knew you'd want to see her, after all the questions you were asking. I don't frighten easy but I'll be the first to say I don't like this. It's unnatural and I don't need to tell you she was a member of the box club as well. I'm starting to think it might be best to quit the club myself, but then that's money down the drain. What a waste."

"Where did you find her?" Dominick asked.

"Whitechapel. There's a mews behind Thrawl Street where the whores—"

"I know the place," Dominick interrupted.

"Right. Well, it's on my rounds. I've been lucky there more than once. She was there, all rolled up against the wall like she was asleep. 'Course I can spot the difference a hundred yards off. Didn't recognise her 'til I got her in the light, but when I did it made the hair rise on the back of my neck, it did."

"It was good of you to bring her here," said Alfie. Dominick had almost forgotten he was there.

Pushing that thought aside, Dominick stepped forward to see if there was anything on the body—on Helen—to give some clue as to what had happened to her, but found his hand hesitating. It wasn't his first time seeing the corpse of someone he knew, but it was hard to reconcile the raucous, lively woman he'd known with the cold body before him.

"Weren't nothing on her," Hugh said, interrupting his thoughts. Dominick couldn't help shooting him a look.

Hugh clicked his tongue. "Don't give me that. You were about to do just the same. Besides, it's not like I'm going to earn much for her in the state she's in. So, I had to make it worth my while, especially after taking the time to bring her all the way back here."

Dominick's stomach roiled at Hugh's careless words but he tried not to take them too much to heart. He looked over at Alfie to see how he was handling it. Alfie's lips were pressed tightly together and his hand kept twitching like it wanted to press a non-existent handkerchief to his mouth. Still, it didn't stop him from coming closer. He knocked his shoulder against Dominick's. A small show of comfort, but one he desperately needed.

"There was nothing on her at all?" Alfie asked, the tinge of suspicion clear in his voice.

"Knife tucked into her waistband of course, but it was clean. I might get a half shilling for that if it's any good. But

I checked all the places a woman like herself would be likely to hide something and that was it," Hugh drawled. "If you want to get your hands up her skirt, be my guest. She's past caring."

"Shut your damn mouth!" Dominick snapped.

Alfie laid a gentle hand on his arm. "What about her token? For the box club."

Hugh nodded and dug around in his pocket. "Oh, sure. But nothing that's *worth* anything."

"It's enough to get her a decent burial," said Alfie softly. "That must be worth something for your friend? And perhaps Mr. Brine would be willing to offer a reward for your trouble."

A worrying thought crossed Dominick's mind. Surely the murders hadn't been committed for a few shillings reward?

Hugh snorted.

"She's not worth anything to me or herself. Silly girl, she should've paid her dues."

Oh, Christ.

The coins in Dominick's pocket were as heavy as lead.

"Nick?" Alfie asked. "What does he mean?"

It took several tries for Dominick to speak around the lump in his throat.

"The last box club meeting. She didn't have the money to cover her dues."

And I did. I did and I didn't help her. And now she's dead.

Hugh finished for him. "If you miss a payment or a funeral, you can't claim club benefits until you've paid up. Keeps people paying and playing their part. But it also means that if you fall off the perch before you've paid back what you owe..."

The silence in the room said it all. Helen had been horrifically murdered and now wouldn't even have the comfort of the burial she'd been so desperate to buy.

"I see," said Alfie after a long moment. "Mr. O'Donnell, can you transport Miss..."

"Moore."

"Can you transport Miss Moore to Canonbury? There's a churchyard there."

"I know it," Hugh said.

Dominick wasn't going to ask why Hugh knew the churchyard. He recognised the church not as the one Larry had been buried in, but the far nicer one where Mr. Hirkins had been laid to rest.

"Good," said Alfie. "Tell the rector there will be a woman coming with funds sufficient to cover a burial and all other necessary arrangements."

Dominick raised an eyebrow. He must mean Mrs. Hirkins. It wasn't as if Alfie could walk into a bank in his current state and unless he had a sheaf of bank notes rolled up inside his walking stick, they wouldn't have access to the sort of money needed for a funeral until they were out of Spitalfields. They'd been planning to leave in the morning.

Not now though. Not with another murder.

He couldn't think about that now. Gathering his courage, he leaned over Helen's body, looking for something, *anything* that could lead him to her killer. One at a time, he picked up her cold hands and looked them over. Her nails were unbroken and there weren't any recent marks of violence on her.

She'd known her attacker then. Helen was a shrewd woman, toughened and taught by the life she led not to let her guard down. But whoever killed her had been able to get close enough to cut her throat without alarming her enough to fight back. A random client wouldn't have been able to do that. It had to have been someone she trusted enough to follow into the mews without worrying. A frequent customer? Or someone she had a reason to trust, perhaps even another woman. After the events at Balcarres, Dominick would never think of them as the weaker sex again.

Hugh's voice interrupted his thoughts. "That's all good for Helen, but what about me? Why should I go through the trouble of dragging her all that way and delivering cryptic messages to rectors about mysterious women with money when I could just take her to the anatomists instead? A man's got to earn a living."

Dominick wasn't sure whether he wanted to wring Hugh's neck or pummel him to death. Fortunately, his moment of indecision gave Alfie time to slip between them.

"And how many bodies with slit throats have you brought them now?" he asked coolly. It was strange to hear the icy tones of an aristocrat come out in Alfie's original accent, but the intensity of it was enough to make Hugh hesitate.

"Even the most unscrupulous surgeon is going to grow uneasy eventually. I wonder if they've started to talk amongst themselves yet, comparing notes? How many obviously murdered victims do you think it will take for one of them to go to a magistrate? Four? Five? How many did you say you were up to again?"

Hugh squinted. "Not like it would matter if they did. They don't care about this side of town. If they thought I'd done 'em in, they'd probably thank me for 'improving public morality' or such rot."

Dominick was far too tired to deal with any of this. "Hugh, I'll make sure it's worth your while to do what he says. I don't have enough now, but talk to Jimmy, he'll tell you I'm true to my word."

He watched as Hugh weighed his options.

"Fine." Hugh huffed. "But only because it seems like bad luck at this point to not bury a fellow club member, lapsed or not. If these killings keep up though, I might think about ending my membership myself before someone else does it for me!"

CHAPTER 18

Alfie woke the next morning feeling distinctly chilled. Dominick must have stolen all the blankets in his sleep again, curse him. He stretched, trying to reclaim the purloined bed linens, and promptly fell off the bed.

The sudden shock was enough to fully wake him—or so he thought until he got a good look at his surroundings.

"Mmfie?" Mumbled a bleary voice somewhere behind and above him.

"Nick? What's going on?"

"You fell."

"Where the hell are we?"

"Spitalfields."

Alfie leapt to his feet in a shot. The last decade and a half, had it all been a dream? A beautiful dream of luxury, money, adventure, and love? Had he made all that up? Oh God, he'd never made it out of Spitalfields. He must have eventually aged out of the workhouse but he was still here and thank God so was Dominick, but that was little consolation because...

"Whoa, whoa! Steady on! Christ, Alfie, what's wrong?"

Alfie spun in time to see Dominick drag himself from their bed, although Alfie had no idea how two grown men had fit on what was little more than a cot. As Dominick groped around for his shirt, some of the finer detail of the last few days began to filter in. At the same time, so did all the aches and pains.

"My God, why did I think coming back here was a good idea?" Alfie asked as he slumped gingerly back down onto the bed.

Dominick mumbled something Alfie didn't catch, but he could guess the general idea.

"Yes, well, we're here now. Along with the rats and fleas and—Helen! Is she still downstairs? Tell me I didn't spend my night sleeping over a corpse!"

"Just sleeping *like* one," said Dominick, but the jest was thin. "Don't worry, Hugh will have gotten her out before your head even hit the pillow last night. He's more scared of his sister than you need to be of any ghosts."

Alfie wasn't sure he agreed with that, but in fairness, he'd been too tired to do anything but fall into bed even after seeing Helen's body, so he didn't have much right to complain now.

"I'd better send word to Mrs. Hirkins about the money. Is there a safe way to do that?"

"You mean, without worrying about being spotted by Murdoch or any other spies Brine might have? Jimmy and Maeve's kids would be happy to carry a message. They're as reliable as any postman and if they know there's an old woman who likely made too many biscuits on the other end, you'll have the fastest mail service in Britain."

"And they're..." Alfie hesitated, "trustworthy?"

"They were brought up right. Won't say a word to a soul."

"Not even their uncle?"

Dominick hesitated in the act of pulling on his shoes.

"I know you've known Hugh a long time." Alfie jumped in. "But we can't be too careful."

"You still think he might be involved in the murders," Dominick said slowly.

"Yes! I mean, no. Well… give me a moment, I'm still not fully awake."

Alfie limped over to the tiny window, hoping some fresh air might sweep the cobwebs from his mind.

"I wouldn't do that," Dominick said around a yawn. "Room faces the back. The privy's probably the least of the things stinking up that alley. That's why there's rags around the frame. Keeps the worst of the smells—and vermin—out."

Alfie snatched his hands back from the window frame as if it was on fire.

Dominick laughed. "Jimmy and Maeve keep the inside as clean as they can. Sit on the floor, we'll stretch your leg and I'll let you tell me how Hugh is our murderer while you do."

"I never said he was!" Alfie said, dropping his voice to a whisper halfway through. "And I know you don't think he did it. It's just that we've been foolish enough before to not consider all the possibilities and both times that ended with me in no small amount of mortal peril. I'd like to avoid that again if possible."

He took Dominick's offered hand and lowered himself to the floor. He had to shuffle back until he was almost against the wall to have enough room to extend his leg without hitting the bed. Dominick sat in front of him to give him something to brace his foot against, which Alfie did with a hiss.

"Keep your voice down. We're not in a bloody castle anymore. Don't want to be overheard." Dominick shook his head. "You haven't been doing your exercises the last few days, have you? And fair enough about Hugh. I suppose finding several dead bodies does look a bit suspicious."

"A bit," said Alfie between repetitions. "And that's assuming we can take him at his word. From what you've said, no one would blink twice at seeing him with a dead body. It might all be a cover for the fact he's killing them himself."

"True," said Dominick. "I'd like to say he's not the sort, but he'd probably check his own mother's teeth for gold fillings if he had the chance. It *might* be a matter of if he thought he could turn a profit."

"Which may be a factor in his favour," Alfie pointed out, switching to a new, yet equally painful, position. "If the anatomists really are starting to get nervous about the increased numbers of bodies with slit throats, surely Hugh would at least strangle or smother a few."

"How comforting," Dominick said. "But I see your point. It also wouldn't explain why he was only going after club members, especially before he had joined himself. There's easier targets he could've gone for than grown men or women fit enough to earn or steal their weekly club dues."

"Unless healthy bodies are worth more?" Alfie asked dubiously. "I have no idea how the pricing for that works."

Dominick snorted. "Well, I know a man you could ask…"

"Ignorance is bliss."

"It wouldn't explain why he killed Larry though," said

Dominick contemplatively. "Not in the middle of the day like that. And not in Canonbury. It's not like Spitalfields. He might have got away with Larry's murder, but in Canonbury people would notice him carting away a dead body to sell with a knife still sticking out of it."

Alfie shuddered. "I wish we'd found that knife. I don't like knowing it's still out there. You're right though. Unless he didn't go to Canonbury meaning to kill Larry? Perhaps they were in on it together and had a disagreement. Or it was done intentionally, to throw anyone looking into the deaths off his scent."

"In which case, he's stupider than I think he is," added Dominick. "Seeing as we only found out about the murders because of Larry's death. And we know for sure that no one else was investigating.

"Do you think Hugh's lying about how long he's been in the box club? If he's been a member since the killings started that would make him look guiltier since he'd be more likely to know all the victims. I suppose I could ask at the next meeting, but I'd have to be careful about it."

The idea of Dominick putting himself in further harm's way made Alfie's stomach tighten. "Let's just keep our ears open for now, see if there's another way to find out."

Dominick snapped his fingers. "It'll be in the ledger!"

"What ledger?"

"Christ, it slipped my mind with everything else going on. There's a big book, a ledger that Brine brought out at the last meeting with the money box. I had to sign my name in it when I joined too. It's how they keep track of who owes what. If we could look at that, it might be able to tell us more about Hugh's involvement. Not only that, but I think that scrap of paper Agnes found in the fireplace is from the same book. I don't suppose you brought that with you?"

Alfie groaned. He knew exactly where the scrap of paper was. It was lying held down by a crystal paperweight on the mahogany desk in their hotel suite.

"I suppose if we could find a place where pages are missing, that might prove something." Alfie turned the thought over in his mind. Honestly, he had no idea what matching the ledger to the burned paper would prove, but at least it was *something* to go on after so much nothing. "And there would be more information on other club members. I could see when each member joined. I might be able to get a glimpse of the ledger at the pub. Did you see where they kept it?"

Dominick shook his head. "Both times, Toller fetched it from somewhere in the back. I imagine it's kept under lock and key except for meetings or signing on a new member."

"We'll keep it in mind."

Alfie reached out with both hands to let Dominick pull him to his feet. Then Dominick was gracious enough to provide Alfie with a steady shoulder to lean on while he held his balance for as long as he could on one leg, then the other.

"That does lead us nicely to our other suspects." Alfie panted as he finally dropped his right foot to the ground. "I believe we've agreed it isn't Mrs. Hirkins nor Agnes."

"Agreed."

Alfie lifted his left foot off the ground and looked for anything to distract him from the pain. "T-then shall we begin with your friend, the gorilla?"

"Jack Murdoch's hardly a friend. And I don't know that

he'd have the brains to do this on his own. I'm not saying he wouldn't kill, say if Brine ordered him to, but unless he's doing it for the pleasure of the slaughter, I don't know that he'd have any reason on his own."

"Do you think it's something Brine would order?" Alfie asked, releasing Dominick's shoulder and sitting down on the bed. Rather than sit next to him, Dominick crossed his arms and leaned back against the wall.

"Hard to say. What do you make of him?"

"Me? I've only met the man long enough for him to tell me I had the job and point me in the direction of the bar. After that I was too run off my feet to pay him much notice at all. And before, when we were arguing over Larry's body at Mrs. Hirkins' house, I had other things on my mind than his character."

Alfie took a moment to think about his brief interactions with the publican. "I don't like him. This is going to sound odd, but somehow he doesn't seem real, does he?"

"He's a character." Dominick nodded. "The Merry Publican. It slipped a bit at the last meeting when he had to cover the bar for Toller. And when threatening me into doing his dirty work. Still, it almost makes you wonder if his nose is really that red or it's just a bit of rouge."

"Like for the stage? I could see that. You mean he's a bit too graced with bonhomie?"

"I do if that means he's not acting right. Have you met Jimmy?"

"Just the once. I gave him ten pounds to keep you from getting your teeth knocked out last year. Then he threatened me."

"I still say I could've won that fight if you'd given me a few more minutes."

Alfie didn't rise to the bait. "What about Jimmy?"

"Well, you said it yourself. He's a publican too, but you don't see him acting the way Brine does, like everyone's his friend. Hell, I *am* Jimmy's friend, and he'd still be happier if I only paid for my drinks then left. He'll be downstairs, I can smell Maeve cooking breakfast. I'm sure they're both dying to meet their new lodger."

"You're not worried about him recognising me?"

"Oh, now you're worried about that?" said Dominick. Alfie couldn't help but flinch at the sting in his voice. Especially since Dominick was right.

"I'm sorry—"

Dominick held up a hand. "Let's not go through all that again. I shouldn't have said anything. But no, you won't have to worry about Jimmy. As far as he's concerned, all white men look the same. Now, his wife Maeve on the other hand..."

"But I haven't even met her before!" Alfie protested.

"No, but I have and I'm fucking terrified of her, so the least you could be is a little worried."

Alfie laughed. "I suppose it's just as well I got a job at The Rose and not here then. I'd hate to have unknowingly put myself in danger."

Dominick moved close enough to gently kick Alfie's good foot. "That's not funny. What about Toller? He seemed an all right bloke at first, but since I joined the club about all I've seen of him is his sneer. A bit temperamental, if nothing else."

"You've seen as much as me," admitted Alfie. "He had

some choice words, but if he was going to cut my throat, I think he would've done it last night in front of everyone when I dropped that bottle."

Dominick kicked him again.

"I'll be careful," said Alfie, raising his hands. "He's under Brine's thumb, too. No knowing if that means Brine threatened him the way he did to you or if Toller is happy to follow him. Or Toller might have motives of his own that we don't know about. Not to mention, he'd certainly have known all of the victims, at least by sight, since they were club members. And even if Toller didn't commit the murders, he might know something. I can see what he has to say."

"Don't bring up the killings yourself," said Dominick. "I'm sure word of Helen's death will spread soon enough. She was a popular woman."

"I'm sorry for your loss," Alfie said sincerely. He almost left it there, not sure if pressing further would bring up dark times in Dominick's past. But he couldn't help wanting to know about everything in Dominick's life he'd missed in their years apart. "Last night, you spoke as if you knew her well?"

Dominick sighed and settled on the bed beside him. When it seemed like he was just going to sit there silently with his shoulders slumped, Alfie took his hand and gave it a squeeze.

"She was a friend of mine," Dominick said finally. "When I was a... In the times I had to work as a prostitute, we'd run into each other often. Even London only has so many dark corners. She was one of the few women who didn't treat me like competition come to steal their nice, decent lechers away with my shapely arse. No, Helen said there'd never be a shortage of men looking to swive even if buggery was also on offer. And she wasn't wrong. She deserved better."

Alfie squeezed his hand again. "*When* we catch Larry's killer, we'll catch hers too. She'll have justice at least."

When he looked over, Dominick was staring at him.

"We're not leaving Spitalfields this morning, are we?"

"It's up to you," Alfie said. "Everything last night still holds true. We've gone further into this than any sane men ever would. But neither of us hopped out of bed this morning and ran to find the nearest coach, did we? You talked about breakfast with Maeve and me meeting Jimmy and I got down on the floor—risking splinters in my own shapely arse—to do my exercises like the start of any other day. Even before we found out about Helen, I think we both knew we weren't going to give up that easily."

Dominick exhaled heavily. "I wish we would."

"I know, Nick. Me too." Alfie plastered on a smile he didn't quite feel. "Now come on, I could face down Medusa herself for some eggs. I doubt your friend's wife is quite that terrifying."

"Close, but not quite," Dominick admitted. When Alfie tried to encourage him up off the bed though, he resisted, keeping Alfie's hand in his and rubbing his thumb over his knuckles.

"Thank you," Dominick said. "For what you're doing for Helen. Arranging a proper burial and all, since the club won't. Most people wouldn't bother for a whore."

Alfie bit back the first dozen things that ran through his head. *Most people wouldn't bother for someone like me,* is what Dominick meant?

The idea he thought so little of himself made Alfie's blood boil. He took a deep breath before he could say something that might come out the wrong way. It wasn't just what Dominick said that infuriated him, it was the growing unease that Alfie'd been pushing down ever since he spotted Dominick walking into The Rose the day before. The Dominick he knew would usually brush aside reminders of his past with a joke or at least a shrug. But now, Alfie could see the way he was being dragged back, dragged down by all the reminders of his old life.

One of the bodies could've been Dominick's, too. A prostitute, alone at night, having to follow a man into the dark for the promise of a few pennies. If Dominick hadn't left London with him, that could've been his fate any night over the past year.

And you brought him back here.

Alfie couldn't dwell on that now. As soon as this entire sorry affair was over, he and Dominick could leave their pasts behind for good and never return to this stinking, sprawling, cesspool of a city that had brought them both nothing but pain.

"Regardless of the station of Helen's birth or the choices she made from the few she was afforded, she was still a person," Alfie said emphatically. "She still had value."

Dominick's face softened. "Still, thank you, love. I know it's a small thing..."

"But a worthwhile one." Alfie finished for him. He pulled on Dominick's hand. "Now, I really would face down any number of horrors for some breakfast. Why don't we go introduce me to your friend and let his wife terrorise me appropriately?"

CHAPTER 19

"We got royalty visiting I don't know about? Enough sweeping and come help me with this!"

Alfie looked down at the pile he'd swept off the floor of The Rose so far. Amongst the expected dirt and dust were several large shards of broken glass and what looked suspiciously like a tooth.

Still, orders were orders, even if the sound of Toller screeching for him from across the pub made Alfie feel as if iron nails were being driven into his ears.

I can't speak for royalty, you obnoxious toad, but I can confirm the aristocracy is severely unimpressed.

It'd been over a week since Alfie had started working at The Rose of Normandy and he was afraid that if he and Dominick went much longer without finding any new hints as to who their killer might be, he'd go mad and burn the place to the ground out of spite. It wasn't so much the exhausting work, although each day the pain in his leg increased no matter how much of Mrs. Hirkins' salve they rubbed on it. By the end of every night, he felt like his hip was on fire and his shoes filled with iron spikes that drove up into his leg with every step. But he could handle the pain. He could even handle the stink of too many unwashed bodies crammed into too small a space and the results of too much alcohol with nowhere to relieve it.

After a while, even the fear that he could be in the presence of a killer at any moment dulled to a buzzing hum, like that of a wasp somewhere out of sight—impossible to ignore, but eventually becoming little more than another in the list of irritations.

No, what Alfie couldn't take was Toller's constant shifts in mood. Some days he greeted Alfie with a clap on the back, others with sneers and comments about Alfie not even being worth the nothing they were paying him. Worse still were the dismissive glances of everyone else, not just Brine and Murdoch, but even the customers who came in every evening for a pint, the way they looked right past him as if their mugs refilled themselves, only noticing when he was too slow to keep up with the pace of their drinking.

He knew it was a petty thing to be bothered by in the midst of greater concerns. Really, he should be trying to not be noticed at all. But it was because it was so petty that he allowed himself to be distracted by it. If he feared being gutted like a fish every time he followed Toller into the cellar to drag up yet another cask of too-weak ale or too-strong gin, he'd never be able to get through a day without falling to pieces, never mind hunt their murderer.

Despite how they grated on his nerves, the casual dismissals did serve some purpose. He hadn't eavesdropped on anything pertaining to the murders yet, but he'd learned far more about the current schemes, crimes, sorrows, and affairs going on in Spitalfields than was good for him, so surely it was only a matter of time. If he could hold out that long.

The one bright spot in his days was his nightly walk

home with Dominick. Each night he'd share the juiciest morsels of gossip he'd learned in an attempt to take their minds off another day with nothing but aches to show for it. They'd then go up their sparse room and collapse into bed, tangled tightly together to keep from falling off.

And *only* to keep from falling off. The endless, frustrating days in the heart of human misery were hardly conducive to putting Alfie in an amorous mood. Even if he wanted to, he doubted he'd have the energy. And he wasn't the only one who felt that way.

He wasn't blind to how Dominick was growing quieter, speaking less and less about the things he got up to when he went off with Murdoch each day. Yet every night, Dominick held him tighter, clinging to him as if he was afraid of losing Alfie all over again.

Once, Alfie had awoken to Dominick running his fingers against Alfie's new beard, the gentle caresses easing the constant itch. He hated the beard, hated the itching, hated not being able to trim it, hated not knowing if it made him look like something dredged out of the river or not. It made him not look like an earl, that was the important thing. But lying there in the quiet of the morning, weary in both body and heart, the simple pleasure of Dominick's touch was almost enough to bring him to tears.

With enough moments like that, Alfie could withstand the rest of it. After all, he'd survived all the years in the workhouse, albeit with more than a little help from Dominick, but those peaceful moments were few and far between. The night of the latest burial club meeting, Alfie had dragged Dominick back to their room, reeking of alcohol and tripping over his own feet. He'd still been snoring in bed when Alfie went off to The Rose the next day, but when he'd shown up in the pub that night, Dominick hadn't said anything about the night before. Instead only wearily asking Alfie if he'd found out anything as they'd picked their way through refuse-strewn streets back to their room. That had been a week ago, and Alfie was dreading a repeat performance at the club meeting tonight.

He was worried. What must it be like for Dominick to be back? It had been over a decade since Alfie had been plucked from the muck, but Dominick had barely been free a year. True, the circumstances were now better. They had a stash of coins in their room to pay for their essentials and didn't have to worry about where their next meals would come from. And in theory, they could leave at any time, although doing so would mean not only letting themselves down, but Mrs. Hirkins and Agnes as well.

Alfie knew he'd have to be the one to drag them out. Dominick was too stubborn for his own good and too used to fighting long after there was any hope of winning. So far, Dominick hadn't had to do any more than stand behind Murdoch when he made his threats, but Alfie swore the first time he came back with blood on his knuckles, they'd be gone, murderer or no murderer.

"Interrupting your beauty sleep, princess?" Toller's snarl cut across Alfie's thoughts.

"Sorry," said Alfie, his Spitalfields accent coming as naturally now as if he'd never left. "Just distracted is all."

"Well, undistract yourself. We're running low on firewood. Go out to the yard and get enough to last the rest of the week."

Alfie bit back his questions. He'd been trying to predict a pattern, but so far, Toller's moods remained as unpredictable as the weather.

They'd used hardly any firewood since Alfie started working and he'd know. The one night it'd been cold enough to chill even The Rose's stuffy interior, Toller had sent Alfie out in the rain for more. The small, stinking yard behind the pub had become a pig sty in the rain, the sucking mud trapping Alfie halfway up his calves. His single pair of trousers still bore the mud stains. At least, he was going to tell himself it was only mud.

But the weather the last few days had been mild, even warm for the season. A lit fire in such weather would make a crowded tavern unbearable, especially on the evening of the burial club meeting, their busiest day of the week.

He's trying to get rid of me, Alfie realised. *He's up to something he doesn't want me to see.*

"Might take me some time," said Alfie cautiously. It would, especially if he took a break to see what Toller was up to.

"So does everything else!" Toller snapped. "Get to it!"

Alfie almost hoped Toller was their murderer. At least it would justify his violent fantasies about the man. He tapped his knuckle against his forehead in a quick sailor's salute and headed towards the back door. With every step, he made sure to exaggerate his limp and clomp down heavily on his left leg. The more noise he made now, the less Toller would be listening out for him.

He went out to the yard, the piss and vomit smell stronger out there. The yard was little more than a triangular patch of earth formed by the awkward meeting of buildings. A shed belonging to the pub sat opposite an alley so narrow Alfie would have to turn sideways to get through it. The yard was open to the sky and neither of the other two buildings that formed its walls opened onto it or had any windows looking down, creating an unseen pocket of space that made Alfie feel like a cornered rat. He wouldn't have been surprised if instead of being scattered across the East End, Hugh had found all the bodies stacked up in the shed beside the firewood. It was the sort of place where all sorts of terrible things could be done with no one the wiser.

With a shudder, he gathered up an armful of wood and stomped back into the pub. He didn't acknowledge Toller, who still stood where Alfie left him, but merely stacked the firewood with just enough exaggerated slowness that by the time he returned with a second armful, he wasn't surprised to see Toller had disappeared. Working just slowly enough to annoy whoever gave you the task without making it obvious was a skill they'd perfected as children. Apparently it was just as good at exasperating beady-eyed barmen as workhouse masters.

He stomped heavily outside once more just in case Toller was listening, then quickly tiptoed his way back into the bar, careful to avoid the floorboards he'd mapped out that creaked the most.

Now the only question was, where to go? He hadn't heard the front door open and if Toller's mysterious business took him outside the pub, there was little Alfie could do about it. That left only two options, the cellar or Brine's office. Both lay down the same narrow corridor.

Alfie crept carefully over to it, keeping an eye out for Toller, or Brine, or God forbid, *Murdoch* all the while. At the end of the corridor was a stairwell. If he went down, it would take him to the cellar where the pub stored the many casks, barrels, and bottles required to keep customers happy. It was a damp, dark room with stone walls and a dirt floor. Alfie had already been up and down those splintery boards more times than he could count.

He looked up the stairs instead. He'd been told that way led to Brine's office and was strictly off limits. For a moment he remained on the landing, frozen with indecision. On the one hand, if he went down to the cellar and Toller spotted him, he could claim he forgot to bring up a bottle of something earlier. On the other hand, he'd been all over that cellar; if Toller was hiding something important down there, he'd done too good a job of it.

But Alfie had never been up the stairs before. God knew what he might be walking into if he went that way. However, that just made it more likely that if Toller was up there, he was doing something worth spying on.

Mind made up, Alfie stepped gingerly onto the first step up, wincing as the tread creaked under his weight. Slowly, he leaned forward until his hands rested on the stairs as well. Putting his weight on them caused his injured leg to twitch at the sudden release of pressure, but slowly, step-by-step, hand-over-hand, he made his way up the stairs on all fours like an animal.

There would be no way to explain what he was doing if anyone saw him, but ridiculous as he felt, he was able to make his way up in near perfect silence. When he reached the top, he discovered another unexpected advantage. The stairs led directly up to a closed door, but by lowering his body down to the floor, Alfie could turn his head sideways and peer under it. Grinning at his good fortune, Alfie closed his other eye and focused on what he could see inside the room.

When his eye adjusted, he picked out the unmistakable form of Toller leaning over a desk facing the door. Alfie's breath caught in his throat, but Toller wasn't paying him any attention, instead focusing on something on the desk and grumbling to himself. Then he turned a page and Alfie had just a moment to see a flash of handwritten words in neat columns before it was gone. That glance had been all he needed though. It had to be the ledger that had accompanied the box of coins to the burial club meeting. They hadn't been able to get more of a glance at the last meeting, Alfie too busy with orders and Dominick drinking his growing misery away.

Was Toller just getting everything in order for tonight? But then why the secrecy? It could be that he was only trying to keep the location of the ledger away from prying eyes. That would make sense, especially if it was stored with the box of coins. But Alfie didn't need to be a professional housebreaker to know that the owner's office was the obvious storage place for such things. If he was a thief, it would be the first place he looked. So why had Toller come up here now?

He shifted, uncomfortable with the hard wooden stairs digging into his stomach.

Brine was out, could that be it?

He pressed his eye closer to the door in time to see Toller scratch out something in the ledger out and jot down something else instead.

That had to be it. Whatever Toller was up to, he didn't want Alfie to know about it, but he didn't want Brine to know either. The publican was usually in and out of his office all day, doing whatever it was one did when they ran a pub, burial club, extortion business and whatever other dealings he had on the side.

If whatever Toller was up to needed to be done before tonight's box club meeting, the man must have been growing desperate. Alfie watched a minute more, but all Toller did was mutter to himself and occasionally add something new to the ledger, flipping between pages for reasons Alfie couldn't understand. He was about to slink back down the stairs, when Toller let out an exceptionally loud curse and turned to fetch something from the bookcase behind him. Alfie couldn't see what he was doing, but his attention was swiftly drawn by something else.

At some point while Alfie had been creeping his way up the stairs, Toller had removed his jacket and was down to just his shirtsleeves and waistcoat. When he turned to the bookcase, Alfie was shocked to see that the waistcoat, so plain and forgettable from the front that Alfie had already forgotten what colour it was, looked completely different from the back. The silk—for it was clearly silk—had been dyed a bright purple rarely seen outside of the most exclusive tailors and was heavily embroidered. An oriental dragon wound up Toller's spine, flanked on either side with exotic blooms stitched so carefully that from Alfie's vantage point, they almost looked real. But more striking than the waistcoat was what lay beneath it, for tucked into the back of Toller's trousers, Alfie could clearly see the handle of a knife. It was angled in such a way that the blade lay near-horizontally along the waistband and would be impossible to see with his coat on, but all Toller had to do was reach back and the knife would be immediately to hand.

"What are you doing here?" hissed a voice directly into Alfie's ear as a hand covered his mouth.

CHAPTER 20

Alfie struggled against the hand pinned against his face as his attacker dragged him bodily down the stairs. He threw back an elbow, hitting something soft and hopefully sensitive. He did it again.

"Fucking, ow! Christ!" Hissed his assailant in a voice that sounded familiar.

"Nick?" Alfie mouthed against his hand.

"Of course, it's fucking me. Get your feet under you. Go, go, go!"

Alfie barely had time to follow Dominick's whispered instructions before he was being pulled backwards down the corridor and whisked out into the yard.

"Christ, that was close," Dominick said, releasing Alfie, who stumbled unsteadily. Then Dominick reached out for the wall and doubled over with a groan.

When Alfie stepped over to help him, Dominick shot a hand out to hold him at bay.

"Christ," he said again after several long minutes. "For someone who likes my cock so much, you have a funny way of showing it. Next time I rescue you, keep your elbows to yourself."

"Next time, don't spring yourself on me like a footpad and you won't have to worry about it." Alfie lifted Dominick's outstretched arm over his shoulders and helped him stand upright. "What were you rescuing me from anyway?"

"Murdoch and Brine." Dominick sucked in a deep breath but kept his voice low. Alfie leaned in closer to hear him. "Ran into Brine just as we got back to the pub. They went down to fetch a bottle from the cellar. Lucky for you I was the only one who looked up and saw your feet dangling. Christ, Alfie, what are you up to?"

Glancing back at the doorway of the pub behind them, Alfie whispered, "I think Toller's up to something. I saw him in Brine's office changing things in the ledger."

"Good for him. Brine deserves it."

"Yes, yes, but I want to know what he's doing."

Dominick frowned. "You think it has something to do with the killings? There's a big difference between skimming off the top and murder."

"He carries a knife."

That caused Dominick to pause. "That is... suggestive. But not entirely unexpected considering who he's around day in and day out. Could be for protection, or a quick escape if he is caught stealing."

"*If* that's what he's doing," Alfie admitted with a shrug. "Perhaps he's not stealing at all. Perhaps there's something in the ledger that Brine or Murdoch don't want seen and Toller's trying to find it first. Whatever it is, it's the closest thing we've had to a lead in over a week."

This was enough to brighten Dominick's eyes, but that only made Alfie aware of how dull they'd been a moment before. It wasn't just his eyes either, Alfie could feel the tenseness of Dominick's muscles under his hand, could see the way his shoulders rounded in on themselves. The proud, bold man Alfie loved was being dragged down into a shadow of himself.

I have to get him out of here. Soon.

"What do you want to do?" asked Dominick. "I doubt Toller will tell us what he's up to if we ask nicely."

"I could say I wanted to be cut in?" Alfie offered.

Dominick shook his head. "Too risky. If you had the ledger, could you figure it out?"

Alfie considered this. He was hardly an expert, but he knew what a household accounts book should look like and Gil was teaching him all about running his estate, which involved a truly stunning amount of bookkeeping. Surely running a pub was less complicated than keeping the affairs of an earl in order.

"I think so, but I'd still need to access it first. Some time when I won't get caught, since that was clearly my mistake this time."

Dominick gave him a wink. "How about I cause a distraction and you run up. Give me five minutes. I'll go down the block and shout 'fire'. That'll bring them all running."

Alfie grabbed him around the waist. "No! That is, not yet. I don't know how long I'll need. We know they'll have the ledger for the meeting tonight. If I can get it afterwards, then we might have several days before they even notice it's missing."

"Sounds good." Dominick nodded, leaning in even closer. "If I see a good opportunity for a distraction, I'll give you a sign. Something like—"

"What's going on!"

Alfie jumped as Brine's voice echoed across the yard.

Dominick looked over Alfie's shoulder and nodded. "Mr. Brine. Nothing at all. Just having a word with my friend."

"Having a word is it?" Brine's voice sounded as jocular as ever, but there was a blade of ice underneath his words. "Looks like a bit more than that."

Alfie realised he was clenching his fingers in Dominick's shirt. He risked a look back just in time to hear another voice say, "Conspirin'. That's what it looks like to me."

In the doorway to the pub stood Brine, a bottle in one hand and a couple of empty glasses in the other. Behind him, Alfie could just make out the shape of Murdoch filling up the rest of the doorway. He realised how they must look, off by themselves, whispering in dark corners. In Murdoch's defence, he was right. They were conspiring.

We're discussing how your barman is likely stealing from you. And whether that means he's a murderer or whether either of you are. Anything you wish to contribute?

Before Alfie could say any of that, Brine tutted like a schoolmaster.

"That would be truly disappointing. And after I've been gracious enough to provide employment to you both? Let this be a lesson, Mr. Murdoch, never trust anyone too eager for a job. Now, is it merely the cash box you two are after or the supply of drink as well?"

"Nothing of the sort," said Dominick, much more calmly than Alfie felt. Then to his complete mortification, Dominick released the grip he still had on Alfie's arm and slid his hand down and back, grabbing a handful of Alfie's arse in clear view of both Brine and Murdoch. "We were just discussing terms."

Brine let out a laugh. "Ah, how silly of me to think you'd retired from your previous occupation. Never let it be said I stood in the way of a man earning a little on the side. Or on his knees!"

"Fucking mollies," Alfie heard Murdoch mutter under his breath.

Dominick gave Brine a smile with too many teeth. "Kind of you. If you don't mind then…"

"Oh, go right ahead."

Alfie waited for the Brine and Murdoch to retreat. Neither moved.

"I should probably get back to work," Alfie said. "People will be arriving for the club meeting soon and Toller wanted me to bring in some more firewood."

"Nonsense," said Brine. To Alfie's astonishment, he handed one of his glasses to Murdoch and pulling the cork from the bottle, poured them both a glass of something amber. "There's plenty of time for that. After all, there's time for the two of you to sneak away for a bit of buggery, isn't there? Or were you conspiring after all?"

Surely they couldn't mean…

"Nothing like that, guv," said Dominick, accent thicker than ever. "Just terms, like I said. Charge extra for an audience."

Brine raised the glass before bringing it to his lips. "Then we'll say tonight your drinks are on me. Now, if you're quite ready?"

The brightness that had only so recently returned to Dominick's eyes began to fade.

"You don't have to do this," Alfie whispered desperately.

Dominick nuzzled his neck—not quite a kiss, but

enough to keep their words between the two of them. "You'd rather they suspect why we're really out here?"

"No," Alfie gasped as Dominick began undoing the buttons of his trousers. Despite the circumstances, his body responded instinctively to Dominick's touch, deprived of it for so long. He was already growing hard and dropped his head to Dominick's shoulder, cheeks burning with embarrassment. He couldn't help looking down, but was horrified when he did.

Dominick's hands were shaking, not just fine tremors either, but so badly that he'd only managed one of the buttons on Alfie's fall.

Shame choked Alfie. Good Lord, what was he about to let happen? For all Dominick tried to shrug off his past as a prostitute as just another thing he did to survive—better than some jobs, worse than others—Alfie knew how much it pained him to be thought of that way. He'd seen it in Dominick's eyes when he'd looked at Helen's body, heard it in the way he'd thanked Alfie for paying for her funeral. How much worse would it be for Dominick to be *seen* that way after all he'd done to escape, all his fine clothes, all his horse riding lessons, all the hours of practice Dominick had put into learning the social etiquette and rules of the ton, all to end up back on his knees in the Spitalfields mud.

In that moment, Alfie hated George Brine more than he'd ever hated any man alive. He didn't care if Brine was a killer or merely a petty grasping criminal. If he had his sword cane, Alfie would run the man through without a second thought.

Alfie covered Dominick's hands with his own.

"No," he said again. Clearing his throat, he added. "He

might perform for an audience, but I don't."

Without thinking, he pulled Dominick behind the shed and pushed him up against the wall. From somewhere behind him, he heard one of the men give a bark of laughter. Brine or Murdoch, he didn't care, they could both go to the Devil. The only man who mattered was the one in front of him.

"What—"

"Shh," Alfie hissed. He looked back over his shoulder. The wall of the shed hid them from view, but only just. If Brine and Murdoch took just a few steps forward... "I'm sure they'll leave in a minute."

They didn't. But neither did they get any closer. Murdoch and Brine seemed content to wait out his and Dominick's tryst, but every moment that passed listening to their taunts and jeers, Dominick's eyes grew a little more hunted, a little more *haunted*.

"Ignore them," Alfie whispered. "It's just the two of us, Nick. Just you and me."

He pulled Dominick against him in a fierce hug, trying to will away Dominick's shivering through sheer force of will.

"I could do some moaning if you think that would help," Dominick said in a shaky whisper. "A few groans and what have you."

Alfie pressed his face into Dominick's shoulder to hide his snort. "Don't you dare. I don't think I could keep myself from laughing if you do."

"That wouldn't do my reputation any favours." Dominick sighed. "I suppose we'll just wait it out. You can pretend I'm the most boring fuck you ever had."

Alfie turned his face into Dominick's neck and pressed a soft kiss against his pulse. "I'm not nearly that good of an actor."

They stayed like that for a long while, just taking strength from each other. Eventually, the sound of Murdoch and Brine's voices faded. Whether they were just keeping quiet or had gone back inside the pub, Alfie didn't care. This was the first time in over a week that they'd had a moment together where they were both awake and sober enough to enjoy it. He turned his head to look up at Dominick. He'd stopped trembling, but his eyes were still dull with unhappiness. But as his short beard scraped against Dominick's neck, Alfie couldn't help but notice the way Dominick's breath caught in his throat. Just to be sure, he did it again with the same result.

Well now, isn't that interesting?

Before he could think about it, Alfie dropped to his knees.

Dominick gasped. "What are you doing?"

"They're not paying attention anymore and they can't see us back here anyway. Besides, they already think this is what we're doing. Might as well be hanged for a sheep as for a lamb." Alfie winced. "Perhaps not the best metaphor, but the point stands. I haven't had you in ages, Nick. I miss you."

Dominick spluttered. "But it's filthy out here!"

Alfie couldn't help but smile. "Don't you remember? A little bit of dirt won't hurt me. I'm Lord Alfie of the Mud."

Dominick's eyes were huge, white showing all the way around the blue. His mouth opened and shut, but no words came out. He reached for Alfie, then drew his hands back at the last moment.

"It's all right, Nick. Let me take care of you for once." Alfie rubbed his hands soothingly up Dominick's thighs. His injured leg was already protesting the position, but he'd be damned if he let Dominick know he was in any discomfort.

He moved his hands to Dominick's fall, surprised to find the fabric already tented under his fingers.

"Sorry," Dominick whispered, dropping his chin to his chest.

Alfie winked up at him. "Don't be. You do the same to me."

He gave Dominick's hips a slight push, just enough to get him back against the wall. Unfortunately, this put him out of easy reach. Alfie didn't think he'd be able to stand and kneel again, so he shuffled forward on his knees. When he got close enough, Dominick reached out and cupped Alfie's face in his hands.

Alfie tried to focus on that. On the way Dominick's hands felt against his face, his thumbs smoothing down the grain of Alfie's beard—a proper beard now, if only a short one. Dominick's palms were hot and a little rough, his fingers pressing over Alfie's ears, drowning out the sounds of anything—*anyone*—that wasn't the two of them. Alfie dropped his head to Dominick's hip and stayed there a moment, just enjoying the sensation.

Then he slid his hands up and unbuttoned Dominick's fall, leaving the buttons at the waistband done up so the trousers wouldn't pool awkwardly around Dominick's knees. When he finally revealed Dominick's cock, he couldn't help reaching for it at once. He hadn't realised quite how much he'd missed it until it was literally right in front of his face. He looked up at Dominick with a mischievous grin.

"Hello, again."

Dominick's snort turned into a curse as Alfie's hand moved up and down.

"Sorry," said Alfie, spitting into his palm. "My hands aren't as soft as they used to be."

"Christ, Alfie," breathed Dominick, his breath catching again as Alfie gave the little twist at the end he knew Dominick loved. He spent another few minutes doing just that, listening to Dominick's soft noises of pleasure. Eventually however, despite the quiet, Alfie couldn't help but feel the prickles of being observed creep up his neck. There would be time later to draw things out, to spend hours—all night if he wanted—just touching Dominick, taking him apart slowly, piece by piece. He promised himself that as soon as they were somewhere with thick walls and a sturdy lock, he'd do exactly that, as many times as Dominick would let him.

But for now, it was time to move things along.

At some point, Dominick had let go of Alfie's head, his hands now pressed flat back against the wall. Alfie took them and gently placed them back where they belonged.

"No curls to dig your fingers into," he said apologetically. Dominick's only response was to curl his fingers anyway, dragging his fingernails through Alfie's short hair like he was scratching a cat. Alfie wanted to purr. He pressed his face against Dominick's bare skin and couldn't help but laugh when he felt Dominick shudder again. Apparently he liked the feel of Alfie's beard down here even more.

Rather than torment Dominick further, Alfie took pity on him and instead did the next best thing. Planting a quick kiss to Dominick's hip, he lined up and swallowed as much of his cock as he could manage.

The effect was instantaneous. Dominick shouted loud enough to frighten the birds off the nearest several churches. Alfie paused a moment to let himself adjust before diving down again, a little deeper this time. He stayed there, licking the underside of Dominick's cock as best he could, until the contractions in his chest as his body burned for air became too much. He sat back on his heels, gasping and peppering Dominick's cock with licks and kisses while he caught his breath. He brought his hands up and alternated with mouth and hands, using every trick he knew to bring Dominick to climax as quickly as possible.

Dominick gasped and moaned. Every time he breathed Alfie's name, Alfie would look up only to see Dominick watching him, the look on his face full of awe and something else, something indescribable. Alfie felt the same way.

Finally, the scrabbling of Dominick's fingers against his scalp became increasingly desperate and Alfie knew he was close. Alfie was shocked to realise he was too. He dropped a hand to squeeze himself through his trousers.

"Let me... Let me see," Dominick panted.

Helpless to do anything else, Alfie undid his buttons with one hand. He groaned against Dominick when his cock was freed, the cooling evening air making him shiver deliciously. He wanted to stay there with both of them on the precipice forever, but instead he took a deep breath and took the head of Dominick's cock in his mouth a final time, sucking *hard*. At the same time, he reached further into Dominick trousers, cradling his bollocks for just a moment, before going back even further and running a single finger around his entrance.

That was all Dominick needed. He came with a shout, flooding Alfie's mouth with salty spend. Alfie tried to swallow it all, but could feel some trickling down into his beard. That strange sensation, at once novel and erotic, combined with the hand he had working his own cock, was enough to bring him to his own release.

He watched, floating somewhere far away, as white ropey spurts splattered into the mud, staying distinctly recognisable for several seconds before dissolving into milky puddles. He rested his head on Dominick's hip once more, catching his breath and taking undue delight in the way his beard scratching across Dominick's over-sensitized skin made him shiver.

A sound slowly made its way through the fog of pleasure that surrounded him. It was clapping. Grimacing, Alfie leaned back enough to see around the wall of the shed. Brine and Murdoch were clapping and whistling as if they were at the theatre.

"Now which one of 'em's paying the other for *that* I wonder!"

"From the sound of it, the sod got his money's worth, that's for sure."

Alfie breathed deeply, willing his eyes not to fill with tears. He wouldn't let something so precious between them be marred by those bastards. He carefully tucked Dominick away and set him to rights before working on himself. By the time he'd finished, the taunting jeers had faded, Brine and Murdoch off to find some other soul to torment.

"Here," Dominick said, reaching down his hand. "Let me help you up."

Alfie didn't protest and even let Dominick wipe at his face with a handkerchief pulled from his pocket. There was nothing he could do about Alfie's trousers, no matter what he tried. When they went inside, everyone would be able to see the mud all over them and guess how they'd gotten that way. At least he'd be behind the bar most of the night, and he could put on an apron to cover some of the damage.

He took two deep breaths to calm himself and prepared to enter the lions' den. His hand was tugged back at the last moment.

"Where are you going?" asked Dominick, not letting him go.

"Back inside, where else?"

"No. We're done here," Dominick said. "We'll take the alley. I think I'll fit down it. Damn it, I'll climb over the roof if I have to. There's no way I'm going to make you face those —those *animals* ever again. And I swear to God, if any of them so much as sneezes in a way I don't like before we're out of this fucking cesspit..."

The fierceness in Dominick's voice soothed the bruises on Alfie's heart. He could face anything anyone said to him, because he wouldn't be facing it alone.

He shook his head. "We can't give up now. Not when we finally have something to go on. The ledger, remember?"

Dominick looked unconvinced. Alfie lifted their entwined hands and pressed a brief kiss to his knuckles. He didn't know why that felt so risky considering what he'd just done. Good God, and practically in front of witnesses! What had he been thinking?

You were thinking it was worth the risk to keep them from guessing that you really were conspiring. But it was more than that. He'd been thinking he couldn't bear to see Dominick so beaten down ever again.

"One more night," he said. "We'll stay one more night, just long enough to get through the burial club meeting and see if we can't take a look at that ledger. Then we'll leave, no matter what."

"One more night," Dominick agreed, his words ringing with finality. He glanced at the open doorway to the pub, then reeled Alfie in for a quick kiss, sealing their promise.

Alfie squeezed his hand one last time then dropped it. The sounds of raucous laughter drifted to him as he turned towards the pub, the first drinkers already arriving for the meeting. He squared his shoulders and hoped that if nothing else, the night would pass quickly.

CHAPTER 21

This was the single longest night of Dominick's life.

"I don't know why you're making that face," said Hugh. "If I was getting free drinks, I'd be looking a good deal happier."

Normally Dominick would agree, but every time another round was set before him, it came with Murdoch's heavy hand on his shoulder and Brine's leer from across the pub. At least Dominick's anger kept him from thinking about what Alfie had done to him out in the yard. Had done *for* him. He didn't know how to think about that just yet, so he just focused on drinking his drinks and ignoring as much of Hugh's chatter as possible. It might not have been the wisest course of action, seeing as how Alfie thought there was a good chance Hugh was their killer, but he didn't have it in him to actually pay attention to Hugh. If he ended up missing the man confessing to all his bloody deeds, so be it.

His frustration only grew as he watched Alfie being run ragged by Toller behind the bar. When Toller came by and nearly knocked Hugh out of his seat to reach his empty mug, muttering some very unflattering things all the while, Dominick had to hold onto the last shreds of his restraint by his fingernails.

"I can't wait to leave this fucking place."

"Well, you can't until after you pay your dues," Hugh replied.

That wasn't what Dominick meant, but now it was all he could think about. Once everyone paid their dues, he'd have to come up with a distraction to give Alfie a chance to look at the ledger. He still liked his idea of yelling "fire", although with how many people were in the pub, he didn't want to risk someone getting injured in the panic.

He was still mulling over his options when he noticed Alfie looking pointedly in his direction. Dominick nodded to show he had his attention and Alfie jerked his head towards the corridor just in time for him to see Toller returning with the burial box and ledger balanced on top. It wouldn't be long now.

He twisted impatiently in his chair as Brine gave another speech about brotherhood and Toller began going through the long list of names.

"Hugh O'Donnell!"

"Bit short this week," Hugh called out cheerily. "Add it to my tab, yeah?"

"Why didn't you say you were out of money?" Dominick hissed. He remembered Helen laughing when she couldn't pay and remembered what she'd looked like the next time he saw her, laid out on the table in Jimmy's backroom, her skin pale and the wound in her throat gaping wide.

"I wasn't when I came in," Hugh grinned. "But you looked like you could use the company and *I* wasn't getting my drinks for free!"

Before Dominick could respond, he heard his own name being called. The room spun a bit as he stood.

I must've had more than I thought.

He cursed himself for not keeping a clearer head, but was able to wend his way through the crowd up to where Brine was holding court, Toller and the damned ledger beside him.

"I'll cover Hugh this week too," he said, reaching into his pocket.

"That's generous of you," beamed Brine.

Dominick felt around in his pocket for a moment, then the other, then back to the first in alarm.

"Something wrong?" sneered Toller.

Dominick's pockets were empty. His money was gone.

He searched the floor frantically, but he knew that if he'd dropped the coins, they would've been snatched up before they even hit the ground.

"Dear me," Brine said loudly, "looks as if you can't keep anything in your trousers this evening."

He roared with laughter at his own joke and Dominick wondered what Brine's neck would feel like when it snapped in his hand. Before he could find out, Alfie stepped into his line of sight behind Toller, shaking his head frantically.

Another time then.

"I'll pay next week," he grumbled.

Toller hummed and jotted something down in the ledger. "For Mr. O'Donnell as well?"

Dominick narrowed his eyes. His coins hadn't just disappeared on their own. Had Toller picked his pocket? There'd been that moment when he bumped Hugh, but surely he'd never gotten close enough to Dominick to do anything. Perhaps Hugh himself had pocketed the money.

He was certainly sly enough and Dominick hadn't been paying nearly enough attention to him.

Dominick shook his head to clear the growing fog. Had Murdoch's heavy hand on his shoulder masked a lighter one diving into his pocket? He doubted the thug had enough grace about him to do so without Dominick's notice, but he also hadn't thought he'd drunk enough to feel as tipsy as he was. Perhaps there was more in the free drinks than just Brine's repayment for their "show" earlier.

He couldn't look at Alfie as he turned and slunk his way back to his table. Fuck the burial club, fuck the pub, and fuck all the people in it. If they wanted his damn money so badly they could have it. A year ago, that handful of coins would have meant the difference to him between life and death. Now he'd willingly shower that much on every person here if it meant he never had to see the inside of The Fucking Rose of Fucking Normandy ever again.

He slid the remainder of his drink across to Hugh and watched as the rest of the club came up and paid their dues without incident. Then Toller whisked both ledger and box away again, leaving Alfie to deal with the crowd pushing their way forward, eager to spend the rest of their earnings.

A hand landed on his shoulder.

"Don't fucking touch me," Dominick growled without looking up.

"Brine wants to speak with you," replied Murdoch.

"I'm sure he does."

Murdoch didn't take the hint, just stood waiting behind Dominick, making his skin crawl. Finally, Dominick had enough and pushed back his chair, sending it skittering into Murdoch's legs.

He stalked over to Brine's little corner, the alcohol and anger churning in his stomach. He tripped over someone's outstretched feet and nearly went flying.

This isn't right, a small voice in the back of his mind piped up, but he was too far gone to pay it any attention.

"What?" he snapped.

"Have a seat, Mr. Tripner," said Brine pleasantly.

"I'll stand."

"Suit yourself. I wanted to discuss a business arrangement with you."

"We already have a bis—a bus… that." The room turned in circles and Dominick began to regret not sitting.

"Indeed," continued Brine. "However, I was under the impression you'd be using the wages I paid you wisely. As that seems not to be the case, perhaps the time has come to discuss alternate options. I was thinking, a forgiveness of your debt, as well as future debts up to a certain amount, in exchange for a promissory note?"

Brine's words flashed and darted away like fish in a stream before Dominick could catch them.

"What?"

A shadow fell over Dominick from behind. He turned and looked up into Murdoch's sneer.

"He means, you fucking madge cull," spat Murdoch, "that you'll work off your debt to him or whoever he sells your marker to, since you can't be trusted not to spend all your pay getting your prick sucked by other whores!"

Dominick gave Murdoch a slow look up and down before turning to face the bar. Toller was pouring pint after pint as Alfie, wide-eyed and harried, his limp more pronounced than before, raced to keep up with the unending stream of orders. For a brief second, Alfie caught Dominick's eye and smiled.

Dominick smiled back and mouthed a single word. "Distraction."

Then he spun around and punched Murdoch in the face.

The feeling of teeth cracking under his knuckles was a familiar one, although Dominick had never taken pleasure in the feeling before now. Murdoch roared as blood poured down his face, but recovered quickly. Dominick ducked as a fist the size of his head came sailing towards him, using the momentum to get down under Murdoch's guard and deliver several fast blows to his torso.

The crowd parted around them, chairs and tables overturning as some people tried to get out of the way while others climbed atop them to get a better view.

Dimly, Dominick was aware of shouted bets being placed, but he couldn't focus on that now. He couldn't even check to see if Alfie was using the commotion to retrieve the ledger. All his attention had to be on Murdoch. He struck again, a direct blow to the man's kidney, but Murdoch only grunted before tearing Dominick off him like he was nothing more than a nipping puppy and threw him to the floor.

Dominick rolled as a heavy boot came down inches from his face. He sprang to his feet. Or at least he tried to. He slowly pulled himself upright, using a chair for balance, feeling like he was swimming through molasses. The flickering lights of the pub left trails behind them as he tried to get his body to obey.

This isn't right, insisted that little voice again, but this time Dominick listened. *You're not drunk, you're drugged.*

"The drinks," he slurred.

"Took you long enough," said Murdoch before driving his fist into Dominick's ribs.

Dominick struck back, the fight blurring into a back and forth as they struck and blocked. Even drugged, Dominick was faster than Murdoch, but every blow he landed was like hitting a stone wall and did about as much damage. His fists burned, but Murdoch still kept coming.

Dominick wasn't used to being the smaller combatant in a fight, at least not by this much, and he knew there were tricks, tactics he should be employing, but it was all he could do to stay on his feet and tell his body to keep moving. It was clear that Murdoch was used to his size being all he needed to win. His form lacked training and he obviously spent more time lounging in pubs and throwing his weight around than he did keeping himself in fighting form. Dominick had both the skills Jimmy taught him and long hours in the gymnasium at Balcarres on his side. In a fair fight, he might actually have won. But this was nothing like a fair fight.

A moment of distraction was all it took for Murdoch to land a blow to Dominick's temple. Everything went white, then black. Dominick crumpled to his knees. He tried to get his legs under him.

Up, up! You have to get up!

If only he was sure which way 'up' was.

A hand wrapped around his throat and Dominick was lifted, starlight bursting behind his eyes as he struggled to breathe. His vision cleared just enough to see Murdoch's face inches from his own. Murdoch's eyes were rolling like a mad horse's, one of them bloodshot. Blood dripped from his nose and mouth, thick clots dripping onto his garish neckerchief. He reeled Dominick in until their faces were just inches apart, red spray splattering Dominick's face when he spoke.

"Nick 'The Terror' Tripner, eh?" Murdoch spat. "Is that all you've got? I'm disappointed in you."

"Me too," gasped Dominick as edges closed in once more. Then he used the last of his strength to drive his knee up as hard as he could. It wasn't a move allowed in any boxing ring, but Dominick couldn't bring himself to care. His knee connected with Murdoch's bollocks and the man let out a high-pitched shriek.

The sound cut through Dominick like broken glass. He had a moment to think, *Worth it.* Then they were falling, still entwined.

I hope this was worth it to Alfie and his damned ledger too.

Then Dominick's head struck the floor and everything went dark.

CHAPTER 22

An almighty shriek from the pub below startled Alfie so much he nearly dropped his lamp. Cursing under his breath, he flipped to another page in the ledger. It'd been easy enough to find, the bottom drawer in Brine's desk large enough for the coin box and ledger both.

The drawer hadn't even been locked. He wasn't sure whether that was because Brine hadn't had a chance yet after Toller returned them, or whether he left it that way out of hubris. No one would dare steal from George Brine.

No one except for me. And your barman, you arrogant prick.

Still, Alfie couldn't bring himself to care. He was too busy trying to make sense of the ledger before he was missed downstairs. None of the columns were labelled, and the spiky handwriting that filled most of the book, likely Toller's, made quick reading impossible. Was that number a nine or a seven? That letter an I or an L?

He slowly became aware that the noises from the fight below had ceased. Toller would be missing him any minute and then a minute after that would come looking for him. He couldn't be caught in here.

He looked down at the ledger in his hands. It was too large to hide under his clothes. The window?

He glanced out. The street below was black as pitch, but

enough light poured out of The Rose's windows for Alfie to see a cluster of men smoking and chatting. No, if he tossed the ledger out that way, the men would get ahold of it long before he could. Even if they didn't take it right back to Brine, it wasn't as if they'd politely hand the book from the sky back over to Alfie either.

With a sigh, he opened to a page near the middle and began tearing them out one by one. Hopefully these pages were from far enough back that Toller and Brine wouldn't notice them missing, but not so far back that they wouldn't be useful. He slid the ledger back into the desk and gave the loose pages a quick fold before tucking them down his shirt. He held the lamp up to check. Perfect. The pages would've made a noticeable bulge under the fine linen shirts he wore as an earl, but under the rough canvas they were impossible to make out unless one already knew to look for them. And if he kept his apron on they'd be even harder to notice.

Satisfied, he slunk out of the office and back down the stairs. He'd just reached the main landing when Toller stepped into view.

"Where the fuck were you?" he demanded.

"Cellar," said Alfie, heart pounding. "I figured a fight would make people thirsty."

Then he remembered he wasn't carrying anything bottle-shaped and added. "Took a minute to light the lamp. Was just heading down now."

"Forget about that," Toller barked. "You'd better go take care of your *friend*." Alfie ignored his emphasis on the last word. Clearly either Brine or Murdoch had talked, but he couldn't care about that now. What had happened to

Dominick?

When he entered the main room of the pub, the scene that met him was chaos. Chairs and tables were overturned, arguments were breaking out with money changing hands, patrons yelled at the bar for ale, and in the centre of the room, a knot of people clustered around something Alfie couldn't see. He had a fair guess as to where he'd find Dominick though. Elbowing his way through the crowd, he swore at what he discovered. It was Dominick all right, half-covered in blood and half-covered in the hulking form of Jack Murdoch lying atop him.

Dominick was still, but before Alfie's worst fears could take hold, he groaned and rolled his head to the side.

For God's sake, Dominick! This wasn't what I had in mind when I asked for a distraction.

He knelt painfully at Dominick's side. "Still with us, Nick?"

Dominick groaned again.

Alfie shifted his attention to Murdoch. The man's head was face down on the floor over Dominick's shoulder and Alfie could see blood dripping from a gash in his forehead. His back still rose and fell so he wasn't dead either, a fact Alfie wasn't sure whether or not to be thankful for. He pushed ineffectively at Murdoch's bulk, trying to get him off Dominick so he could breathe properly. The crowd was no help, only laughing as he struggled. Alfie's cheeks grow hot with embarrassment.

" 'Ere, let me help."

Alfie looked over to find Hugh kneeling down across from him. Alfie gave him a nod of thanks and with him pushing and Hugh pulling, they were finally able to roll

Murdoch off Dominick to the cheers of the crowd. By this time, Dominick was slowly coming back around, blinking and trying to push himself up.

Between them, they were able to get a precariously swaying Dominick to his feet, one arm draped over Hugh's shoulders, the other over Alfie's.

"Need help getting him home?" asked Hugh cheerfully.

Alfie considered the odds of Hugh taking advantage of the situation to cut both their throats once they were away from the pub and sell them off as specimens. They'd hardly be able to put up much of a fight. But weighed against the fact there was no fucking way he'd be able to get Dominick back to Jimmy's alone, never mind up the stairs to their room, he found he didn't have much of a choice.

"Thanks," he said as the three of them hobbled towards the door. They were drawn up short by Brine blocking their path.

"Mr. O'Donnell may be free to leave, but I don't believe you've finished your shift. And there's the matter of Mr. Tripner paying for the damages to my establishment."

"Get the fuck out of my way, you bloody lobcock," Alfie snarled.

Brine blinked, clearly unused to being spoken to in such a manner. He should have spent more time in the workhouse then. Alfie knew worse words when he was five. He used Brine's momentary surprise to his advantage, pushing the man aside and dragging Dominick out the door, Hugh laughing all the while.

❄ ❄ ❄

"Ow," said Dominick from his position on their tiny bed.

He tried to push himself upright, but Alfie placed a firm hand on his chest to hold him down. It'd taken the better part of an hour for Hugh and Alfie to wrestle Dominick back to The Barge and into the damned bed; he wasn't leaving it now. Once he was sure Dominick was going to stay put, Alfie went back to scrubbing Dominick's face viciously with a damp towel. Dominick tried to turn his head away from the rough ministrations, but that just gave Alfie access to new areas that needed scrubbing.

"How did you get blood behind your ears?" he muttered. Dominick's cheek was spilt, as were most of his knuckles, but he seemed to have escaped without permanent injury. He was still groggy and uncooperative, but Alfie wasn't sure if that was due to a head injury or just alcohol.

"Do you remember how much you had to drink?"

Dominick squinted at the question. "Not that much. But they were drugged, so…"

That stopped Alfie in his tracks. "You drank drugged ale?"

"Not on purpose." Dominick sounded as petulant as a child. "I didn't realise until… Oh, did I win?"

"The floor won. Stay still."

"It's wearing off a bit." Dominick hummed and this time when he tried to sit up, Alfie let him.

"How can you tell?"

Dominick winced. "Because everything's starting to hurt. Ow."

Alfie huffed despite himself.

Dominick knocked a shoulder against his and winced again. "Did you get the ledger at least?"

"Some of it. Not that it fucking matters. I'm done with this bloody place and this whole bloody city. If they want to keep cutting each other's bloody throats, then I wish them all the best. We're going home to fucking Scotland. Also, fuck you, Nick! By 'distraction' I meant break a window or something, not fight a fucking mountain. Especially not while drunk and drugged!"

"I think I did win," said Dominick, sounding far too pleased with himself. "You're nicer to me when I lose."

Alfie slumped down, all the fear and anger and shame of the night hitting him at once. He let the rag drop to the floor and put his head in his hands.

"It doesn't matter. It doesn't matter and I'm—I'm tired, Nick. I thought I could do this, but you were right. I don't belong in Spitalfields. I can't. I'm not *strong* enough to survive here. I never would've made it through the workhouse without you and if I hadn't taken your place with Lord and Lady Crawford…"

He trailed off. Dominick spent years working, fighting, and selling his body to make ends meet. Alfie had only spent a fortnight working at a pub and had gotten down on his knees in the mud to suck a single cock and he was done. He even liked the cock he'd been sucking and it was still too much.

He couldn't look at Dominick as he spoke. "I don't care anymore if it makes me weak or soft because I have money and live well. I hate this. I hate being itchy and in pain and miserable. And I know, I *know* others have it worse. That I haven't truly had to worry about food or shelter this whole time. But more than everything else, I hate seeing you hurt. I'll never forgive myself for all the years I left you here —"

"That's not your fault," Dominick cut in fiercely. "We've been over this before. None of it was your fault. I've never blamed you for a moment."

Alfie shook his head. "I left you here, but I can get you out now. You were right all those years ago. If you hadn't gotten me out when you had the chance, I would've died. I'm not strong like you are, Nick. I'm weak. But by God, it doesn't even matter anymore. I'd rather be alive and weak than dead."

He didn't fight as Dominick gently pulled his hands away from his face and leaned in for a soft kiss, then another.

"If it makes you feel any better," said Dominick quietly. "I've never thought you were weak. You're fierce and brave and look here, an ogre like Jack Murdoch had to use not only his fists, but drugs and drink and the bloody floor to subdue Nick 'The Terror' Tripner. You've done it with just a kiss."

"Stop being ridiculous," Alfie said, but he gave Dominick another kiss anyway.

"Never," Dominick promised. "Not when the reward is having you with me. Besides, all things considered, I rather like having money too. I'm not going to feel bad about that and neither should you."

Alfie laughed softly. "If you say so. I suppose wringing my hands about it doesn't do anyone any good."

"None in the least. Now, unless you feel like using any of those aristocratic funds to have the whole building lifted up and dropped into Mayfair tonight, I'm going to go to bed and when we wake up we can turn our backs on Spitalfields for good. We'll return to the hotel or merry old Scotland or anywhere else you can dream of. What about America? I hear you can't turn around without bumping into a wealthy heiress out there. You'd fit right in."

Alfie raised an eyebrow, but it didn't stop him from helping Dominick lower himself back down onto the bed. He even gave the meagre pillow a quick plumping before sliding it under Dominick's head.

"I'm not sure if that's meant to insult me or the heiresses. You don't see too many of those with beards."

Dominick sighed. "And you've lost your fine curls as well. I suppose I'll never marry you off now."

"No," said Alfie fondly as Dominick's eyes fluttered closed. "I suppose you're stuck with me."

Dominick's only response was a soft snore. Alfie spent several minutes just watching his lover sleep. He'd imagined before what his life might've been like if he'd never left Spitalfields, if he and Dominick had grown into men together instead of being separated. He'd always thought it would've been similar to this, the two of them sharing some small set of rooms somewhere. Going about their daily work then stumbling home together in the evening after a round at the pub or a visit with friends, then falling into bed before starting all over again the next morning.

In his dreams he'd always managed to forget about the grinding misery of it all. To think, just a few weeks ago his greatest concern had been Janie overcooking the eggs. He shook his head. They'd be back to that soon enough.

Hopefully this time he'd remember to count his blessings. Perhaps he could set up some sort of fund to help the impoverished? Now that was an idea…

He mulled the matter over as he prepared for bed. So caught up in the idea was he, that when he unbuttoned his shirt and a folded wad of papers fell out, he just stared down at them in confusion.

The pages from the ledger. He considered just leaving them on the floor. He and Dominick would be gone in the morning anyway, let Toller keep robbing Brine blind if that's what he was up to. What did it matter?

Alfie squeezed himself into the small slice of bed left by Dominick and closed his eyes. Then he opened them again and sat up with a groan. He snatched the papers off the floor and went to find a candle.

Several hours later, he crawled back into bed.

"Get that all sorted then?" Dominick asked sleepily. He lifted an arm and Alfie tucked himself underneath, draping his own arm carefully across Dominick's middle to avoid any bruises and pillowing his head on his shoulder.

"Maybe. It's odd. Do you have any idea why The Rose would be buying ale in pounds?"

Dominick yawned. "I don't know what's so odd about that. A pub that popular is going to spend a lot on ale."

"I don't mean pounds as in shillings and pounds. I mean ounces and pounds. These orders were by weight."

"That is odd. Shouldn't it be barrels or bottles? Jimmy would know."

"Perhaps we can ask him on our way out tomorrow. And what would you say if I told you Toller was also ordering gin by the stone?"

"I'd say he'd be able to get all of Spitalfields and half of Whitehall drunk as lords," said Dominick.

"That's what I thought too."

"Anything else you don't like?"

"There's a lot of numbers that intentionally could be read as eighteens *or* sixteens," Alfie replied. "But no murder confessions."

"Shame." Dominick pulled Alfie in tighter. "Don't let it keep you up. I plan to be out of here as soon as it's daylight."

"I won't," promised Alfie. But he found himself tracing letters and sums on Dominick's bare chest until the sky pinkened with the dawn.

CHAPTER 23

"Nick? Nick, wake up. Time to leave."

Dominick groaned and pulled the pillow over his face. It stank, but it was better than being awake.

"Nick, the sooner you get up, the sooner you can have a proper bath."

Now that did sound intriguing. Dominick risked lifting the pillow and cracking open an eye. Alfie was already up and dressed, pacing across their tiny room in uneven strides.

"We're going then?" he asked groggily. "Don't know if Maeve will have breakfast ready."

Alfie shook his head. "We'll eat at the hotel. Kippers, toast dripping with butter, buns with clotted cream, jam from every fruit you can imagine and some you can't. You'll need to get your strength up. After all, we need to be at our best before going to a magistrate. I know who the killer is."

"What?" Dominick bolted upright in bed. That turned out to be a terrible idea. His sore head protested the movement and he only had a moment to aim himself away from Alfie's shoes before being violently sick all over the floor.

"I suppose we'll be apologising to Jimmy before we leave," Alfie said. He handed Dominick the rag he'd used last night to clean him off. It was stiff with partially dried blood, but better than nothing.

"You know who killed Larry?" Dominick croaked. "And Helen?"

"I think so." Alfie nodded. "At least, I have enough of an idea to actually get wheels turning this time. I'd like to think about it a bit more before I say anything definite, but I can do that as we walk. Come on, I was ready to leave before everything smelled of vomit and that's hardly changed my mind!"

❋ ❋ ❋

"I suppose it will be a ways before we can find a coach willing to pick us up dressed like this."

Alfie sounded morose as they made their way slowly down street after street. He'd left his walking stick at The Rose the night before, needing both hands to steer Dominick back to their room. Dominick repaid the favour now and Alfie's hand was heavy on his shoulder where he gripped him for support.

"Mrs. Hirkins should have clothes for us," Dominick reminded him. "And we can tell her who the killer is too. Two birds with one stone."

He'd been disappointed not to see Jimmy on their way out, but if he'd gone looking for his old friend, he might've run into Maeve and been forced to tell her about the mess he'd made of her room. Slinking out like a rat was infinitely preferable to that.

To Dominick's surprise, Alfie shook his head. "No, I'd rather not say anything to Mrs. Hirkins just yet. Not until

I'm sure. If I had the rest of the ledger I think I could prove it, but as it is, I'd rather be certain."

"We could go back to The Rose and get it," Dominick offered as he manoeuvred them around a puddle.

Alfie halted suddenly, pulling Dominick to a stop beside him. "Absolutely not! There's no chance I would risk your life on something like that!"

"It'd be quiet enough now," Dominick said. "I'm sure we could sneak in and out in under a minute. Sure, we might not be the most popular blokes there now, but we wouldn't be in that much danger."

Alfie shook his head again. "I'm not worried about us being in danger, I'm worried about *you* being in danger. Nick, I don't want to say too much until I have proof, but if I'm right, the victims were chosen because they were members of the box club who'd fallen behind in their payments."

"Just like me."

"Exactly." The expression on Alfie's face was a strange mixture of anxiety and relief. "That's why I want you out of here as soon as possible."

Dominick nodded, but before he could say anything else, he spotted a coach and waved it down. He got Alfie seated and was about to climb in himself when a thought struck him.

"Dominick? What's wrong?"

"Just like me," Dominick repeated. "And just like Hugh. He didn't pay last night either. If I leave, he'll be the one the killer is after."

The pained look on Alfie's face was all the confirmation he needed.

"That's why I want to get to the magistrate so quickly," Alfie said. "Yes, Hugh may be in danger but—"

The coach's horse stamped its feet impatiently.

"You comin' or goin'?" the driver demanded.

Dominick stepped back from the coach, avoiding Alfie's reaching grasp.

"You go on ahead," he said as visions of bacon and hot baths floated away on the early morning air. "I'll keep an eye on Hugh until you get back. It's better than the blasted fool deserves, but I won't—I *can't*—have another death on my hands."

His voice cracked near the end but it seemed he got his message across. Alfie bit his lip, but eventually gave him a slow nod.

"Be careful," Alfie said as the driver cracked the reins. "And promise me you'll stay away from The Rose!"

The coach was off before Dominick had a chance to promise. As he watched it trundle away through the still empty streets, it occurred to him that it might've been a good idea to ask who the murderer was first.

❋ ❋ ❋

"You're up early." Jimmy was sweeping up when Dominick returned to The Barge. "Maeve has porridge on, won't be but a minute."

"Thanks, Jimmy." Dominick pulled up a stool while Jimmy worked. If he really was leaving Spitalfields for good, this would likely be the last time he saw his friend. He should say something, but how could he explain?

"I..." he started. "I shot the cat all over your spare room.

Sorry."

Jimmy laughed. "It's seen worse. I'll get you the mop after you eat. Is your Alfie going to want a bowl too?"

"My—No, he's already gone. I'll be leaving soon too. I don't know when I'll be back."

Jimmy stopped sweeping and turned to Dominick. He didn't say anything for a long while.

"Let me guess," Jimmy said, stroking his beard. "This has something to do with that job that had you disappearing so suddenly last year?"

"Yes," Dominick admitted.

"And Alfie... He's part of it?"

Dominick smiled. "He's all of it."

Jimmy hummed in thought. The next thing Dominick knew he was wrapped up in the older man's arms. His bruises protested the crushing hug, but Dominick couldn't find it in himself to complain. He hugged back just as fiercely.

"I can't say I understand it," Jimmy said. "But you're happy?"

Dominick nodded, knowing Jimmy could feel the motion.

"Well, that's what counts."

Jimmy stepped back and held Dominick at arm's length. "Keep your guard up."

Dominick shook his head. "Alfie's not like that, he's—"

A swift tap on the side of the head where Murdoch had struck him the night before knocked the rest of his words away.

Jimmy raised his fists. "Keep your guard up. I can tell by the look of you that wherever you go, there's going to be trouble. Keep your guard up, don't lock your knees—"

"—And don't forget to uppercut. I won't." Dominick grinned and swiped at Jimmy playfully. "Get your hands down. If Maeve thinks you're trying to train me again, I'll be the one she blames."

Jimmy laughed, a warm, comforting sound that Dominick was going to miss.

"You know, she's with child again," said a grinning Jimmy. "Maybe if it's a boy we'll name this one after you."

"Don't you dare!"

Jimmy shrugged. "We might have to. We've run out of my relations to name them after and only have a few of hers left. It's that or come up with something original."

"Speaking of her relations, where's Hugh? I need to have a word with him."

Jimmy picked up his broom. "He was out even earlier than you. Said something about checking on the tides to see if anything interesting washed up overnight, then seeing if he could buy up some broken furniture on the cheap to resell for firewood. He certainly knows a way to turn a profit out of anything, that one."

A tendril of icy dread made its way up Dominick's spine.

"What broken furniture?"

Jimmy frowned at a bit of dirt that was refusing to be swept. "I should be the one asking you. He said you broke some tables with your face last night, he's going back to collect them from The Rose of Normandy."

✳ ✳ ✳

Dominick cursed as he ran through the streets of Spitalfields. He'd gone down to the river first, hoping to catch Hugh there, but he'd been nowhere to be seen amongst the mudlarkers and eel men. The sun was rising high in the sky by the time he'd given up and turned back the way he came. He hadn't wanted to go back to The Rose. Even if he hadn't had the chance to promise Alfie he wouldn't, he'd still rather avoid the one place he knew a killer might be hunting. A killer who was after him in particular.

The third time he nearly turned an ankle on the uneven street, he forced himself to slow and draw much-needed air into his burning lungs. He had to be smart about this. There was every chance Hugh had other errands to run first. Maybe he'd found something he could sell—human or otherwise—on the riverbank and wasn't headed to the pub at all. If Dominick came across him in the streets first, all the better, but if he didn't, bursting into Brine's pub by himself would only land him in trouble. Or worse.

He rounded a corner. The Rose of Normandy was at the end of the next street. What he needed was a way to get a look inside the pub without being seen. If Hugh wasn't there yet, he could find somewhere to hole up and keep an eye out for his approach. And if he was already inside, Dominick would have to figure out a way to get him out without them both getting their throats slit.

Another distraction, perhaps? That worked out so well before.

He wished Alfie was there. He'd be giving Dominick all sorts of grief if he was, but he'd always been better at coming up with these sorts of plans, even when they were children.

"All right," he said to himself. "Alfie's not here, so we'll just have to do it one step at a time. First step, see if Hugh's in the pub without being seen yourself."

Dominick closed his eyes and leaned against the nearest building. His fingers touched crumbling brick and old paper, some long forgotten handbill left to weather and rot away. He'd spent years running these streets and knew this part of the city better than he knew himself sometimes. It'd never felt like home, but it was familiar, the first notes of a song he knew by heart.

He tried to envision a way to approach the pub without being seen, but all he could think of was the yard behind it. Christ, had it only been yesterday when Alfie had gotten on his knees for him in that stinking place? He could picture the look in Alfie's eyes, uncertain, but so brave and so full of love. His hands had been sure as he'd unbuttoned Dominick's trousers and when he'd sunk down, Dominick had looked away, unable to stand the impossible beauty of him.

Had looked away and seen the alley at the far side of the yard.

He opened his eyes and tore off down a side street, the map to get to the other end of the alley unfurling in his mind. There were no windows looking into the yard from the pub, but he'd be able to slink in just enough to have a peek if the door was open. If it wasn't, the lock on the door was simple enough, he'd be able to get it open if he could find a bit of wire or a nail.

In no time at all, he'd squeezed through the alley and was facing the back door to The Rose, trying to ignore what had happened only feet from this spot the day before. He gave the handle a gentle turn, ears pricked for any noise from inside, but none came.

Unfortunately, the door didn't open either. He cast about, looking for something he could use as a lock pick. His eyes fell on the shed they'd hidden behind yesterday. Surely there'd be something in there.

He stepped towards it and saw something glinting up at him out of the mud. It was a long pin—the type women wore to keep their hair in place. He couldn't help but think of Helen. Maybe she, or another woman like her, had lost it while plying their trade at some point in the past. Regardless, it was perfect.

He sent up a quick prayer of thanks and knelt to focus on the door. The lock *was* a simple one, but old and rusted from lack of care. He focused all his attention on working the tumblers just enough to get them to click open.

So intent was he that he didn't notice the muffled footsteps coming around the shed, the sound softened by mud. He didn't notice the soft hiss of a knife being drawn. He didn't notice anything at all until the sharp edge of the blade pressed against his throat.

"Well, well. What an unexpected surprise. And a profitable one," said Toller.

Dominick froze.

Toller tapped his knife against the underside of his chin. "On your feet now, slowly."

Dominick did as he was told, his mind racing. *Toller. Toller!* All along, he'd been the one dutifully recording the payments in the ledger, then gone out and hunted those who couldn't pay. And now he had Dominick trapped.

"I can pay," Dominick licked his lips. "I can pay what I owe a thousand times over if you want. I just need to get back to the hotel and—"

"Quiet!" Toller hissed. "You think I haven't heard that before? Been offered silver and fancy snuff boxes too. Have any of those on you?"

All right, that wasn't going to work. Dominick was more than a match for Toller in a fight, but with a knife to his throat and nothing to defend himself with other than a hair pin, he'd be dead before he could throw the first punch. He raised his hands as Toller dragged him back into the middle of the yard. If only he'd listened to Jimmy and kept his guard up.

"Where are we going?" he asked, trying to think of anything he could do to free himself or summon help, but there was nothing.

Toller gave a dark chuckle. "Just a little further back into the yard. The mud will soak up your blood well enough, but I don't want to have to clean the door."

Dominick stopped in his tracks. He might be about to die, but he wasn't going to make it easy for the man. The blade dug in, and Dominick felt a hot trickle of blood run down his neck.

"Move!" Toller demanded. "Or after I'm done with you, I'll go after that little catamite of yours. Won't be any money in that, but I'd do it for the pleasure."

Dominick tensed. If he moved, Toller would slit his throat, but he might have time before he died to hurt the man badly enough he couldn't go after Alfie. He took a deep breath and readied himself to drag Toller down to hell with him.

"I don't think that will be happening," said a clipped voice from the direction of the pub.

Dominick glanced up. A man stood in the now open doorway. He stepped down, his fine Hessian boots sinking into the mud. Above them he wore a suit of sky blue with golden buttons and a starched cravat so blindingly white it hurt Dominick's eyes to look at. He was clean shaven and on his head perched a tall top hat with a curled brim. In his hand he held an ebony cane with a gold handle.

Toller scoffed. "Who the fuck are you?"

The man tilted his head. "Don't you recognise me? I'm the Right Honourable Lord Alfie of the Mud."

CHAPTER 24

Alfie adjusted his grip on his cane while Toller gawked in disbelief. He ran his thumb back and forth over the catch that released the blade within, but he didn't dare make a move while Toller had a knife to Dominick's throat.

He took another step forward but stopped when Dominick's head jerked back, a second rivulet of blood running down his neck.

"Stay where you are!" cried Toller. "Or I'll give him a second smile you won't find so pretty."

Alfie could barely hear him over the pounding of his heart. Terror seized him as it did any time Dominick was in danger, but he had to wait for his moment.

Toller started to laugh, the sound growing shriller the longer it went on. There was more than a hint of madness in the sound.

"Tare An' Hounds!" he cried. "You really are the little sod, aren't you! The bloody hell happened to you?"

"I shaved," said Alfie dryly. "Now why don't you put the knife down and we can discuss what happens next like gentlemen? Dominick already offered you a thousand times what he owes, I think you're smart enough to see I can pay that."

Alfie reached his hand into his pocket and withdrew a handful of money. Not coins, but bills. It was more money than Toller ever would have seen at once. It was more money than he ever would have seen in his lifetime.

"All this is yours if you just let him go."

Toller spat. "A lot of good that'll do me on the gallows! I'm also smart enough to know what'll happen next. You give me the money and before I know it, I'm being dragged out of my bed in shackles. How about this: You come over here and give the blunt, and maybe a judge never has to hear about how an earl sucks cocks like a poxy whore."

"Stay back, Alfie!" Dominick panted, hissing as Toller's blade dug deeper. "He'll kill you too."

Alfie didn't need Dominick's warning to know he was right. The moment Toller was in range he'd attack them both. Even two against one, it wasn't a risk Alfie was willing to take. He had to keep Toller talking. And get that damned knife away from Dominick's throat. He took a step back towards the pub. Toller relaxed fractionally, but not nearly enough.

Alfie hummed. "I don't think that will work either. Who do you think a judge would believe, a murderer or an earl?"

He took another step back, a plan beginning to form. "I have an idea. What if you let Dominick go and you and I settle this ourselves, just the two of us?"

Alfie spread his arms wide, bank notes in one hand, his still-sheathed sword cane in the other.

Toller laughed again. "A fight, you mean?"

"Yes," said Alfie plainly. "I'll even let you keep the knife if you think you need the advantage."

He saw the way Dominick flinched at the very idea.

Hold on, Alfie silently pleaded with him. *Do not do*

anything stupid.

Toller let out a stream of profanity. "I don't need a knife to fight you, you weak, hobbling fop! You think you're strong enough to take me on?"

"No," Alfie admitted. "I realise that I never have been and I never will be a particularly strong man. However, I've been reliably informed that I have other beneficial qualities."

Toller snickered and his hand holding the blade loosened just a little bit more.

Just enough.

"And just what qualities might those be?"

Alfie's eyes met Dominick's and he chose his next words carefully. "For one thing, I'm told I'm very, very good at being a... distraction."

With that Alfie threw the bills in the air. They fluttered like a flock of exotic birds never before seen in such a place, Toller's distracted gaze following their upward arc. At the same time Dominick wheeled in Toller's grip, elbowing the man hard in the stomach and tackling him to the ground. Alfie saw the flash of the blade, but couldn't tell who held it as the two men wrestled in the stinking filth. He ran forward but his injured leg, that had carried him through so many days of torment, finally gave out and he fell to one knee.

He looked up just in time to see Toller roll on top of Dominick, knife raised above his head. Pushing himself to his feet with a strength he didn't know he had, Alfie flailed wildly with the cane, not even trying to unsheathe the blade. One of his swings struck Toller's arm, not hard enough to make him drop the knife but enough to cause him to let out a yelp of pain and turn his attention to Alfie instead.

"I'll gut you for that you fucking sodo—"

The rest of his words were cut off as Dominick twisted violently sideways, thrusting his fist into Toller's stomach. Then he rolled the other way, sinking them both deeper into the mud, but giving himself the leverage he needed to drive his other fist up hard into Toller's jaw.

Alfie heard Toller's teeth clack together violently as his head snapped back. Time slowed to a standstill as he waited breathlessly. Finally, the knife fell from Toller's grasp, dropping like a dart only inches from Dominick's head. Then Toller slumped and fell backwards into the mud. As Dominick scrambled away from him, Alfie slammed his cane against the pub wall in three sharp cracks that echoed across the yard.

At this, the air filled with shouts and the clacking of rattles. Within seconds, the yard was swarming with Bow Street Runners alerted by Alfie's signal, along with thief takers, constables armed with clubs, old watchmen still swinging their rattles and every other able-bodied man the several magistrates he'd visited had been able to throw at him. From inside the pub came more shouts and the sound of breaking glass.

None of that mattered to Alfie now. He half limped, half dragged himself to Dominick's side. Dominick was lying face up, blinking at the sky. The cuts on his throat were still bleeding, although thank God none were too deep. Alfie tugged off his cravat and pressed it to his throat.

"You couldn't have done that earlier?" Dominick panted.

"I was trying to keep you alive long enough to do so," Alfie replied, wiping a bit of mud off Dominick's cheek. "And you say I'm the one always getting into trouble."

"I can't let you have all the fun." Dominick groaned. "But I think I'd like that bath now."

CHAPTER 25

Still damp from washing, Dominick sighed at the simple pleasure of running a comb through clean hair. Repeating the motion released the pleasing scent of orange blossoms from the hair tonic he'd lifted from Alfie. After all, he wouldn't be needing it for a while.

He grinned at the mirror. The silver-backed glass reflected a man as buffed and polished as if he'd spent the entirety of the last few days in the bath, which wasn't far off the mark. He and Alfie had done little since returning to Grillion's other than alternating between bath and bed, taking turns ringing for hot water and food as needed.

In fact, that was where his errant lover was supposed to be now, ordering up one last pitcher of warm water so Dominick could indulge in a shave before they began the long—although hopefully this time less painful—coach ride back to Balcarres. The private carriage, purchased with some of Alfie's funds now that he was free to spend them again, would at least make the ride more pleasant.

He bent his head to the side and examined his reflection more closely. There wasn't much he could do about the scabbed over mess where he'd split his cheek on Murdoch's fist, but the cuts from Toller's knife were healing up nicely. From Alfie's guilty glances every time he saw them, Dominick would be happy to keep the cuts covered until they fully healed. Even if it did mean a return to the blasted cravats. He'd missed the rest of his silky wardrobe, but even if they were softer than rose petals, cravats were still overcomplicated rubbish.

At least he wouldn't have to suffer wearing one through Toller's trial. Those same magistrates who'd ignored Alfie when he came to them for help were all too happy to take the credit when Alfie came to them with a killer all but wrapped up with a bow. Dominick didn't know what all Alfie'd told them to keep from having to testify at the upcoming trial, but while "Disguised Earl Unravels East End Slayings" would have made for gripping headlines, he was glad they could both avoid the whole mess. The headlines about himself would've been far less flattering.

There was a light rap at the bathroom door.

"Nick, are you decent? The maid is here with more water."

In answer Dominick pushed open the door. He blinked with surprise at seeing the old French maid standing slightly behind a grinning Alfie. Alfie raised his eyebrows at him before returning to the sitting room area of their suite. Fat lot of help he was.

Dominick stepped aside to give the woman room to enter. She walked forward with her head held high. Now that he was looking for it though, Dominick could see the slight wobble in her step and the unsteadiness of her hands that gripped the pitcher through protective towels.

She set the pitcher down carefully and glanced back towards the sitting room and Alfie. Dominick waited to see what she wanted to say, but she merely shook her head. To his surprise, she then dropped into a curtsey so deep, he was stepping forward to offer her a hand back up before he even realised what he was doing.

"No, that's really not necessary. Really." As Dominick steadied the woman, an idea occurred to him. "Just wait a moment. Un... moment, yes?"

It didn't take more than a few seconds to find what he was looking for and he returned to the bathroom with a small purse in hand.

"This is for you, for keeping the room nice."

The purse contained the remainders of his and Alfie's pay from The Rose. Precious little in the scheme of things, but an earl and his companion rarely had use for such small coins and they would go further in the maid's hands than in theirs. He couldn't help but wonder who would look after the old woman when she could no longer work, if she'd been able to use her time in England to build a sprawling family like Mrs. Hirkins had to take care of her in her dotage or if she was completely alone. The coins would help a little at least and the bills he'd shoved in the purse as well would help even more.

The woman took the purse with another curtsey—although one thankfully not nearly as deep—and left the suite to carry on the rest of her day's work. Hopefully, she wouldn't examine the contents until they were halfway to Scotland. After the stress of the last few weeks, he wasn't sure he had the strength left to endure another round of Gallic emotion.

"Are you planning on turning up at Mrs. Hirkins' home unshaved or are you just waiting for the water to grow cold?" Alfie called out. "Some of us are fully dressed and waiting, you know!"

"You're just excited to explain to everyone how brilliant you are," Dominick grumbled. "You know, you could have at least told *me* how you worked it all out."

He wasn't sore that Alfie hadn't shared yet. Not much anyway.

Dominick began to whip up a lather in the shaving soap as Alfie's voice drifted in. "We had better things to do. I could still spend a few days getting reacquainted with those pillows. I say, do you think they'd mind terribly if I took them with us?"

Dominick snorted. "You're an earl, they'd have the whole room down to the contents of the chamber pot packed up and sent to Balcarres if you'd like."

He didn't have to see Alfie's nose wrinkle in disgust to know it was happening.

He shaved quickly. Watching the smooth skin be revealed from under the lather made him miss Alfie's beard. Later, he'd have to think up a way to convince him to regrow it. While perhaps not suitable for maintaining the sophisticated air required of an earl in the city, in the rugged wilds of Scotland it might be another matter. But that was something to ponder later. In all honesty, he was as eager to hear Alfie's story of how he solved the murders as his lover was to tell it.

When he reached for the towel the maid had brought with the pitcher, something fluttered to the floor. He picked up the scrap of paper and turned it over. There was writing on it, but none of the letters made any sense together. Beneath the writing was a small drawing. Dominick turned the paper this way and that trying to make it out. A fish with large fins? Possibly a bird?

Alfie's voice came from the bathroom doorway now. "Are you still in here? I told Mrs. Hirkins we'd be there in half an hour! You need to finish dressing so they can pack your trunk."

Dominick handed him the scrap of paper. "Does this make any sense to you?"

Alfie took the paper and squinted down at it. "It's French, I think? Where did you get it?"

"The maid. What does it say? Should I go after her?"

"Put your shoes on at least before you go charging off. And let me see if I can translate. It may be a love letter for all we know."

Dominick followed Alfie into the bedroom and sat on the bench at the foot of the bed, shoe in hand.

"You think I have a chance with her?"

"If she's a woman of any sense, she'll be offended you even asked, you rotten cove. Now let me think. *Ils sont...* they are... in... the bath? I think that's it. It's certainly something about a bath at least, it looks like that word's the same. 'They are in the bath.' Does that mean anything to you?"

"No." Dominick pulled his second shoe on. "That's the same thing she said to me before. If there was anything in there, I suppose we'd have found it days ago."

Alfie hummed in agreement. "All nonsense then. She must be getting doddery, poor thing. What do you think this is supposed to be?"

Dominick looked up to see Alfie pointing at the drawing.

"I'm not sure. A bird?"

Alfie stretched out his arms and looked at the paper

from a distance. "I say, is this the bird from your ring? You didn't drop it in the tub did you?"

Dominick stood up and looked at the drawing again. He pulled the chain from underneath his shirt and turned the ring so he could compare the two side-by-side.

"It could be. Either that or a turnip with wings."

Alfie elbowed him in the side. "Be kind. It's actually quite a good likeness, although I'd like to know when she got a good enough look at your ring to draw it."

"She must have seen it last time she was here. I... was not as dressed as I could have been."

Alfie's gaze went heavenward. "I remember. A good man would chastise you for that. But as I have an interest in keeping you as undressed as possible at all times, I find I'm not a good man. Still, I happen to think the drawing is a good likeness for your bird, especially for such a quick glance. That is, I assume it was a quick glance? I may have only arrived at the end of it."

Now it was Dominick's turn to pray for patience.

"Her eyesight isn't going," said Alfie before Dominick could respond. "Even if her mind is. Poor woman. Speaking of which, I suppose we shouldn't keep the other women waiting any longer. Are you ready to go?"

He passed the paper back. Dominick's hand hesitated over the dustbin before tucking the paper into his pocket instead.

Alfie put a hand on his arm. "Is this really bothering you? We can have the hotel management track her down if you want to ask her more."

"No," Dominick shook his head. "You're right, it's just nonsense. And I'd hate to get her in trouble."

Alfie squeezed his arm, then pulled from his own pocket several bank notes, tucking them under the pillow where the footmen picking up their trunks wouldn't find them, but the maid certainly would.

"I already gave her quite a bit of money." Dominick admitted.

"Good," said Alfie, his voice solemn. "If she's leaving befuddled notes in guests' rooms, it's only a matter of time before someone else gets her in trouble. What's a little for us may mean quite a lot to her."

Dominick loved this man—this smart, caring, reckless, beautiful, ridiculous man—more than he had words to say. Alfie's close-cropped hair was growing in even redder than before, the strands now just long enough to begin to curl in a way that would likely look endearingly awful before it got better. This impossible man, who'd followed Dominick back into the muck even when he'd been told not to, who was wild and fierce and strong, even if he didn't believe it himself. Dominick loved every inch of him. Every time he thought he'd discovered the full shape of his love, Alfie went and did something so thoughtlessly kind that Dominick found himself with whole new acres of affection to explore.

At least some sliver of what he was feeling must have shown on his face, because Alfie gave him a slight, soft smile.

"Come on, Nick. That's enough of that," he said. "If you keep looking at me that way, we're going to be even later getting to Mrs. Hirkins and I'll be damned if I'm explaining to her why!"

* * *

"Master Alfie, what happened to your head?"

Dominick bit back a laugh as Alfie set his hat down on Mrs. Hirkins' table and ran a sheepish hand over his hair.

"It's a long story," said Alfie. "Is Agnes home?"

Mrs. Hirkins gave the two of them a searching look, then her exasperation at Alfie's state shuttered into a protective mask. "You've news."

"We do," said Dominick.

Mrs. Hirkins nodded. "She'll be right down. Sit yourselves at the table, I have things in the oven I need to keep an eye on. Neither of us expected you two to actually be on time."

Once they were all seated around the kitchen table, Dominick couldn't stop himself from repeatedly looking over at Agnes. The poor thing was obviously pregnant now, the outline of her belly pressing against her dress. She gripped her grandmother's hand tightly, but sat as upright as her condition would allow. Her expression made him think of a general who has spotted a messenger from the battle and is not expecting good news.

He looked over at Alfie. He'd been the one to solve the mystery after all. It would've been nice if he could've done so without Dominick getting held at knifepoint, but that was what he got for staying around to protect Hugh of all people.

"All right," said Alfie, twisting his hand nervously on the head of his cane. "The most important thing to know is the man who killed Larry has been caught and will be tried for his crimes."

A loud sob escaped Agnes, causing them all to jump. She buried her face in her hands and it was several minutes before she gave a watery, "Please go on."

Mrs. Hirkins had moved her chair closer and had an arm wrapped around Agnes' shoulders. Her own eyes were suspiciously bright.

"I don't want to trouble you with all the details..." said Alfie haltingly.

Mrs. Hirkins shook her head. "It's better to know everything. Start at the beginning."

Alfie did, glossing over many of the details of their time in Spitalfields and giving Dominick far too much credit for worming his way into The Rose of Normandy in the first place, but it was mostly the truth. When he told them about the other murders, Agnes went alarmingly pale. Dominick was about to tell Alfie to stop, but Mrs. Hirkins caught his eye and gave a firm shake of her head.

"...which was how we discovered the ledger Toller was supposed to be using to keep track of all the money going into and out of The Rose, but it actually contained far more damning information. He'd been stealing from the pub, likely to gamble, and covering his losses from the burial club. You see, each of the members who died had owed the club their dues and were ineligible for a burial. Toller took the money they'd already paid in and moved it to cover his theft. Some of it, at least. The total amount he'd taken out was staggering. He must've been at the end of his tether."

"So, he killed my Larry for the money?" Agnes asked, the confusion clear in her voice. "But he wasn't behind at all, they *did* bury him!"

Dominick couldn't help but think of what Toller had insinuated just before Alfie had burst in with the calvary. *"After I'm done with you, I'll go after that little catamite of yours. Won't be any money in that, but I'd do it for the pleasure."* Had that been why Toller killed Larry? Just for the fun of it?

He softened his voice as much as possible. "Agnes, it's possible your Larry—"

"—Discovered what Toller had been up to and confronted him." Alfie cut in. "We think that's what he was doing the day of Mr. Hirkins' funeral. Larry knew the family would be out and they could have some quiet to discuss things. He thought he was safe here because he never imagined Toller would do anything in the middle of the day in a respectable neighbourhood like this."

"Trusting fool," said Mrs. Hirkins quietly.

Alfie nodded. "A man as nondescript as Toller wouldn't have been remembered by what few witnesses there might have been, but that only made him all the more dangerous. That burnt bit of paper in your fireplace was from the ledger. It was a chilly morning. Likely Larry lit the fire to keep warm while he waited for Toller to arrive and when he confronted Toller with evidence of his misdeeds, Toller killed him and burned whatever proof Larry had.

"I'm so sorry. If it's any comfort, Larry was trying to do the right thing. Your child can know his father died a hero."

His words only set Agnes off on another round of crying.

"Thank you," she whispered finally, both hands resting on her stomach. "It does help, knowing, or I hope it will someday. It's just, I've been so focused on his death, the *not-*

knowing of it all, that now I don't know what to do with myself. That's awful of me, I know. Thinking only of myself when poor Larry is dead."

"Nonsense." Mrs. Hirkins snapped. "Larry's troubles are over, God rest him. He doesn't need to worry, that's for the living."

"What am I going to do, Nan?" Agnes sniffed. "I've no husband, no employer will take me like this. How will I care for the little one when he comes?"

"Can you cook?"

All heads at the table turned to Dominick. He shrugged. "Your Nan said she was teaching you. Napoleon himself would swim all the way from that island of his for one of her dinners."

"Of course, she can cook! And that's Mrs. Hirkins to you, not Nan!" Mrs. Hirkins' wrath was more familiar than her sorrow and it was comforting to know she was as immune to flattery as ever.

Alfie was staring at him wide-eyed. It was possible he should've discussed this with him beforehand, but the idea had only just struck him. Now that it had, it was a perfect solution.

"Janie will be as happy as the rest of us to get her out of the kitchen." He gave Alfie a pointed look. "Besides, it would be better if Agnes was out of town when the trial happens. No need for her to go through all that unpleasantness."

It would be horrible for the poor girl. Even if Alfie's involvement stayed secret, when Toller went to trial, the case of a killer who'd stalked the London streets knife in hand was going to cause a frenzy. Agnes would be hounded by neighbours and journalists alike, never mind the nastier parts of the story she might learn.

"It might be better that way," Alfie admitted. "And a new cook arriving at Balcarres isn't going to make anyone suspicious. You could go up there now to see if you like it. And if you want the job after your… confinement, it would be yours. You wouldn't be obligated, of course."

"Scotland!" Mrs. Hirkins said in a voice that likely carried all the way to the border. "That's your solution, is it? 'You don't want to be in London, girl. How's the arse-end of the Earth instead?' You want to send a woman bouncing all the way to some godforsaken piece of rock in her condition? Alone and unchaperoned? Risking all sorts of injury and highwaymen and, and, and *Scotsmen*?"

"She wouldn't be alone," Alfie offered. "We were preparing to head back to Balcarres ourselves after we saw you two. The carriage is waiting outside."

"Oh, so she'd be alone and unchaperoned except for the two unmarried men with her! Do you think they'll place wagers on which of you is the father or assume it was somehow the both of you at once?"

Alfie looked somewhere between stricken and horrified. Dominick didn't feel much better.

"Is there somewhere else she can go? Maybe one of your other children lives outside of the city? Or we could hire a…" Dominick couldn't remember the word for it.

"A lady's companion," offered Alfie. "To keep her company on the journey."

"Don't be daft," said Mrs. Hirkins, rising from her seat. "I'm going with her."

"Nan!" Agnes exclaimed. Dominick just sat there in

shock.

Alfie found his voice first. "That won't be necessary, Mrs. Hirkins. I promise the best care—"

"Oh shush, Master Alfie. You think I would abandon my granddaughter when she needs me most? Shame on you."

"But your other grandchildren? And children?" Dominick asked softly.

If he didn't know her, Dominick might have missed the way she flinched before straightening her spine, her resolve redoubled.

"I shall miss them. But now that Mr. Hirkins is gone, there's no one keeping me here. They have their own families to care for. They don't need some hoddy doddy like me getting in their way. Now, I don't want to hear another word about it. As I've said before, it's rude to turn down a woman in mourning."

Agnes finally got a chance to speak. "Scotland sounds lovely. Thank you."

"Then that's settled," said Mrs. Hirkins. She went and pulled a tray from the oven. The scent that had already been drifting through the kitchen blossomed in the warm air. Something baked to perfection with just a hint of sweetness. After a quick inspection, she set the tray down on a folded piece of fabric in the middle of the table perfectly sized for such a purpose.

"Now, you two give those a minute to cool while we pack. I suppose there's room on the carriage for our things? Good. And I'll need to send word for one of my children to look after the house, let them fight it out over which one keeps it.

"Up, up Agnes. We've much to do. Don't let me forget

my knitting. That babe of yours will go naked if I have to make all those clothes again. *Scotland,* by God. If Mr. Hirkins could see me now!"

"I'm sorry he can't." Alfie was trying to smile, but his eyes still carried the guilt that he hadn't done enough to save Mrs. Hirkins' husband. Or Agnes' fiancé. Or Helen and Toller's other victims. Never mind that there was nothing he could've done. Never mind that he'd brought a terrible man to justice and saved Dominick's life as well.

Mrs. Hirkins stopped her fussing long enough to lay a hand on Alfie's shoulder. When he wouldn't meet her eye, she grabbed him by the chin in a way no woman her age should be strong enough to do, even if her victim wasn't a peer of the realm.

"It's not your fault," she said frankly. "You hear me? None of this was your fault."

With that, she was off—up the stairs with a much slower and significantly more stunned Agnes trailing in her wake.

Dominick and Alfie were left in the kitchen in silence.

"Should we write ahead to warn them?"

Alfie snorted, then ran a hand over his face. "We probably should. My God, she's going to be named a chieftain in no time. Chieftainess? That is, if all of us survive the carriage journey."

Dominick gritted his teeth. He cared a great deal for Mrs. Hirkins but the idea of being trapped in a carriage with her for untold days?

"I'll buy another one." Dominick grinned. "Do you think the hotel would sell us the one they have?"

Alfie stared at him blankly. "You want to ride across two

countries in that gilt monstrosity?"

"Don't be daft. That's the one we're giving them."

Alfie leaned back in his chair and howled with laughter. Feeling pleased with himself, Dominick lifted two of the buns off the tray, setting one in front of each of them.

"Eat up," he said. "It's the last chance you'll have for some of Mrs. Hirkins' baking until we get there. You know how I can tell she's soft on you? She knew you were coming so she made your favourite, Bath buns."

Alfie's laughter cut off as suddenly as a fiddle separated from its bow.

"What did you just say?"

Dominick tilted his head in confusion. "I said that she made your favourite because she's soft on you? Surely you knew that before?"

"Bath buns," whispered Alfie. "Bath buns. Oh my God, Nick, the note from the maid! The—the French maid! Today! Did you keep it?"

Dominick pulled the note from his pocket and handed it over. "I don't know what that has to do with—"

Alfie snatched it out of his hand, then let out a stream of obscenities that took Dominick back to their days at the workhouse.

"Fuck, Nick!" He finally concluded. "I'm the stupidest fucking sod in England. *Ils sont à Bath!*"

"All right," said Dominick. "What's that make me then? Since I don't have a bleeding clue what you're on about."

"Fucking French. I didn't study it long. Just enough to pretend I'd forgotten it instead of never learned. But what I thought it said, 'They are in the bath,' in French would be, '*Ils sont dans le bain.*' This doesn't say that."

"What does it say?"

"It says, '*Ils sont à Bath.*' In English that's 'They are in Bath.' Like Bath buns! It means they are in the city of Bath, not your tub!"

"All right," said Dominick slowly. "So, the old woman's note said something slightly different that we thought. What's that matter? It's still nonsense."

"Nick, this old woman, this old woman who travelled all over the country with Louis XVIII, she saw the ring on your necklace. The ring left with you at the workhouse in case your family ever wanted to reclaim you. The one with the engraving so worn that only you, me, and someone who'd seen it before could possibly know that it had once been a bird. She saw *that* ring, the ring that belongs to your family, and drew it alongside the message that—"

"They are in Bath."

CHAPTER 26

Alfie settled back into his seat as he watched the city of London slowly vanish outside the carriage window.

"If you want to take a last look, now's your chance."

On the bench opposite him, Dominick let out a yawn. "I think I've had enough of the city to last me a while." He shifted in his seat. "Not that I'm looking forward to being trapped in here for God knows how long."

"Not even with my charming company?" Alfie teased. "And before you answer, it's not too late to catch up to the ladies' carriage. You could ride back with them and leave me to my peace and quiet."

He could almost see the quips forming in Dominick's mind before he wisely decided that discretion was the better part of valour and changed the subject.

"I was joking about buying the hotel's coach, you know."

Alfie chuckled. "I know, but it was worth it for the look on Mrs. Hirkins' face when it pulled up to her house. We can have it repainted when we get back to Balcarres. Besides, it was both quicker and easier to hire a driver and footman this way since they already know the vehicle. I know the footman wasn't strictly necessary, but I feel better knowing the women have some extra protection. Although woe betide the highwayman who tells Mrs.

Hirkins to stand and deliver!"

Dominick laughed. "Frank and Martin handled the crowd at Larry's murder well enough. I imagine they'll be able to protect any ruffians from her wrath."

Alfie stretched his leg out onto Dominick's seat and was pleased to receive little more than an eye roll before Dominick started tugging his boot off for him.

"Do you think we should be concerned at all? Both men leapt at my offer of payment to drive all the way to Scotland. It was a generous offer, but not that generous."

"Too late to worry about it now," Dominick said, removing the boot and motioning for Alfie's other foot. "I was a bit worried too, to be honest, but the way Frank threw his wig into the mud soothed some of my fears. And as for Martin..."

"That's the footman?"

Dominick hummed. "Seems we're to be deviled with troublesome footmen. Did you see how red his cheeks went when he helped Agnes up? He seems a decent enough sort, but it couldn't hurt to keep an eye on him when we get home."

Home.

Yes, Balcarres was already more their home than London had ever been and now with Mrs. Hirkins and her granddaughter there? Dominick's protectiveness of their rapidly expanding household made Alfie's heart do all sorts of gymnastics in his chest, not helped by the way Dominick cradled Alfie's feet so gently in his lap, one thumb rubbing absently over his ankle.

"So, are you going to tell me the truth?" Dominick asked. His tone was bland but his words were enough to jerk Alfie upright. Dominick resisted the pull, keeping Alfie's feet comfortably hostage.

"What do you mean?"

"That whole, 'Larry died a hero' bit. You couldn't lie when you were six and you can't lie now. I know it was a kindness for Agnes' sake, but go on, I know you're itching to show off how clever you were to solve the whole thing."

Alfie huffed. "You did most of the hard work. I just put together the last few pieces."

"Bad at lying *and* modesty, I see."

"All right, all right," Alfie conceded. In truth, he hadn't been sure whether he wanted to tell Dominick. He'd told the magistrates enough of the truth to ensure Toller's conviction, but it felt disloyal to speak ill of the dead, even if it had been Larry's own fault he ended up that way. "Where should I begin?"

"What if I tell you my guess and you let me know if I'm right?" asked Dominick.

Alfie nodded. They did have a long drive ahead of them and a guessing game would help pass the time, even if it was a touch morbid.

Dominick closed his eyes in thought. "First off, Larry wasn't an innocent victim like the others. He was in on whatever it was Toller was up to. I don't know if he was personally involved with the murders themselves, but he certainly knew about them. The ones that happened before his own, of course."

Alfie realised his mouth was hanging open in shock. "How on Earth do you know that?"

"Now I think about it, I don't think he did actually kill anyone himself," Dominick mused. "He'd have been carrying a weapon when he confronted Toller if that was the case. I imagine 'no honour amongst thieves' goes double for murderers."

Alfie didn't know what to say. He'd been so proud to work that out for himself, but here was Dominick, shrugging it off like it was nothing.

Dominick chuckled at his obvious bewilderment and gave him a wink. "Don't look so shocked, love. Toller all but said as much to me right before you came charging in. It seems that Larry got away with a snuff box or two that Lord Sempill's butler didn't catch. If it makes you feel better, I hadn't worked out that they were doing the killings to steal from the burial club. At least, if what you told Agnes was true?"

"It was," Alfie confirmed. "Although I guessed when I said the money was for gambling. I never was able to prove what they were using it for. The only one who knows now is Toller himself and I doubt he'll talk. But based on the doctored amounts in the ledger as well as the items Larry stole from Lord Sempill, that was my best guess. There was a man wearing a waistcoat with a decorated back losing badly at the hell Sempill dragged me to. Toller had a similar one.

"Was it him, you think?" asked an interested Dominick.

"I didn't get a good look," Alfie admitted. "And at that point, I hadn't met Toller yet. But it would explain his changes in mood depending on how his luck ran the night before. In the end, I suppose it doesn't really matter. He wanted money and he killed for it."

"So, why did they meet the day of the funeral?"

Alfie debated the best way to phrase his thoughts. "The

kinder answer is that Larry was confronting Toller like I told Agnes. Perhaps Larry, having learned he was soon to be a father, really did want to start afresh and cut all ties with his criminal past. That would explain why they met at Mrs. Hirkins' house, not The Rose. The bit of ledger in the fireplace might have been him burning some sort of nefarious contract the two of them had signed. A symbol of him destroying his old life for a new."

Dominick snorted. "That's a nice fairy tale. If he was so keen on doing that, why did he run off with Lord Sempill's spoons?"

"The other answer," continued Alfie, "is that Mrs. Hirkins' instincts were correct. Larry never had any interest in an honest day's work. He stole items from Lord Sempill that in a house with a less demanding butler wouldn't have been noticed for quite some time. Long enough to throw suspicion off of him. He either gambled the proceeds away or Toller took the money after killing him.

"But I don't think that was enough. I think he had Toller meet him that day for one simple reason. Blackmail."

Dominick nodded. "The bit of ledger."

"Precisely. Once I was able to get my hands on more pages, it became clear that the two of them were both dipping into the box. I think Larry was going to hold the proof of that over Toller's head, but instead Toller slit his throat and burned the evidence."

"But if they were both stealing, wouldn't this proof show they were both guilty? Not much use getting a man sent up for theft if you're going to be in irons next to him."

An especially large bump in the road sent Alfie nearly

bouncing out of his seat, but he recovered without any damage, except to his pride. Just to be prepared for future jolts, he pulled his feet from Dominick's lap and braced them against the floor of the coach, already missing the warmth of Dominick's hands.

"True," said Alfie. "But I doubt Larry was threatening to go to the regular authorities. And he may have felt it was worth the risk, especially since it was only Toller's handwriting on the ledger, not his own. Larry might be able to plead innocence. Toller could not."

"I feel like this is the part where you reveal how clever you are," said Dominick wryly. "Let me guess, the ledger was never an accounting for The Rose at all. Toller was a French spy and the ledger was his journal. Or no, even better, it appeared to be written in a strange code and you were the only one who realised that when held up to the mirror, it was actually a confession of all his wicked deeds."

"You're closer than you think. It was just a standard ledger, albeit a heavily embellished one. If Brine had spent a fraction of the attention on his pub that he should, he'd have caught on almost immediately that the numbers didn't add up, but I'll come back to him. As it was, it fell to me to crack the cunning, yet simple, code."

Dominick made an inelegant noise at that, but Alfie ignored it.

"You see, my suspicions were aroused when I noticed that there were multiple orders for a certain ale, totalling several pounds in weight each."

"I remember you mentioning that, even if I was half-dead at the time. Weren't they ordering gin by the stone too?"

"Indeed they were."

"All right, so I see how you worked out someone was stealing. There was something funny about those orders. But Brine had access to the ledger as well. He could've been nudging his own figures to hide the money. Or it's possible even Murdoch could've done it, although honest intimidation to get money out of people is more his line than messing about with figures."

"Ah, you see, that's where I was truly brilliant," admitted Alfie. "I knew it was neither Brine nor Murdoch, because the abbreviations didn't work."

He savoured the look of confusion on Dominick's face.

"Abbreviations?"

"Indeed. Jack Murdoch and George Brine. J.M. and G.B. What are the abbreviations for stones and pounds?"

Dominick hesitated. "Stones is st. and pounds is…"

"Lb. Simon Toller and Larry Brennan. S.T. and L.B." Alfie finished, barely able to keep back a crow of triumph. "When I added the amounts with either abbreviation against each other, they came out equal. They'd been smart enough to steal in odd amounts so as to be less noticable, but kept track of whose turn it was for the next payment.

Dominick looked as if he'd been run over by their carriage, then the fancy gilt one as well for good measure.

"Christ," he breathed. "You worked that all out from some snatched bits of paper? I'm buggering the smartest man alive."

Alfie tossed his head back and laughed. "Not anytime soon you're not. These benches may be more padded than that damned mail coach, but the walls of coaching inns are still going to be far too thin for that."

Even that bad news wasn't enough to knock the sense of wonder off Dominick's face. "You're... I don't even know what you are to work all that out."

"Astonishing? Incredible? Phenomenal? Spectacular?"

"All those things, you pompous little git. And you told the magistrates all this?"

"I did," Alfie said. "I showed them the pages I had and told them to make sure they got the rest of the ledger in the raid. But there's more than just that, Nick."

Dominick slumped back in his seat and Alfie risked propping his bad leg up in his lap again, if only so Dominick had something to tether himself to while basking in Alfie's genius.

"Of course, there's more. Were the royal jewels stashed in the box fund?"

"Not quite, although do you remember when I told Agnes and Mrs. Hirkins there was damning evidence in the ledger? Well, it damned more than just Larry and Toller. Why was The Rose of Normandy seemingly doing so well when most pubs in the area, your friend Jimmy's included, are just as good or better, but taking in much more modest earnings?"

"Because he was having Murdoch scare protection money out of the whole block?"

"Yes, which Toller dutifully accounted for in the ledger. And not only that, we both saw Brine ply his patrons with more drink than they could afford, then go have private chats with them. It turns out he was accepting notes of hand in lieu of payment, then selling those on to others. Essentially, selling his customers into indentured servitude for a cut of the profits."

"Buying carcasses," Dominick said with a noticeable shiver. "That's what it's called."

"Now who's the clever one? I imagine he helped the process along with a bit of whatever was in your drink the night of the fight."

Dominick squeezed his foot tightly. "Christ, Alfie. No more of this damned crime solving. Do you realise how lucky we were not to get tangled up in any of this ourselves?"

In fact, Alfie had been doing his best to not think about that at all. He continued on. "Unfortunately, Brine can claim the intimidation was all Murdoch on his own and the rest isn't *technically* illegal. But between not collecting prompt payment on all those drinks and the money Toller and Larry stole, I believe that close inspection will show he's in debt. Considering the damage caused by the raid on the pub and the looting I 'm sure happened after, Brine won't be able to pay what he owes to his suppliers."

Dominick grinned. "After the raid, I may have sent word to Hugh to bring a cart around. With any luck, Jimmy won't need to pay for alcohol for several months, although he'll have more furniture and mugs now than he'll ever know what to do with."

"I'm sure Hugh will figure something out. He's resourceful that way," said Alfie confidently. "And Brine won't be able to pilfer the burial club box for funds either. Toller was at least accurate in his accounting of who actually made payments, so returning the dues to their rightful owners shouldn't be too difficult. Brine will be in debtor's gaol for the rest of his life. It isn't exactly Newgate Prison, but it's better than filth like him deserves."

"Alfie!"

"What? That man is the worst sort of scum for preying on the unfortunate like that. Luring them in with his burial club, giving them hope for a bit of peace in the eternal life, all the while doing his best to squeeze every ounce of suffering out of their mortal lives for his own profit. At least Toller killed quickly."

Alfie took a deep breath to bank his anger. "I just kept thinking it could've been you, Nick. This whole time. If things had gone just slightly differently in our lives, you might've been the one he plied into servitude with drugged drink. You almost were! Or been forced to work for him as a thug for real, another Murdoch in the making. Or been another one of Toller's victims, left to bleed out alone in the dark."

His voice caught in his throat, the horrible possibilities overwhelming him only now that they were safe. He fought to get any more words out, but before he could, Dominick was pushing his leg aside and throwing himself across the carriage.

He grabbed Alfie's face with both hands and pulled him in for a searing kiss that was part heat, part comfort, and part the same overwhelming fear that was already choking Alfie.

He gasped into the kiss, unable to breathe for long, terrifying seconds. But Dominick was there. They *were* safe. None of those terrible things had actually happened. And somehow, feeling Dominick's own fear, knowing that he worried for Alfie as much as Alfie worried for him, didn't feel suffocating anymore. It was a balance. Dominick could be strong for him when he needed it, and in his own way, Alfie could be strong for him too. They looked out for each other, because that was what you did when you loved someone. Because it was easier to take the risks yourself than to put the person you loved in danger, but it was even better to face that danger together.

When they pulled apart, both their faces were wet with tears.

"I'm not sure if these are yours or mine," Dominick said, wiping at his eyes.

Alfie laughed wetly. "We can share."

He rubbed his hands over his face. At least that awful, scratchy beard was gone. Although Dominick clearly liked it. Perhaps he'd regrow it later, when he knew he'd be able to wash the damn thing every day if he felt like it. Because that was part of love too. It wasn't just the terrifying, life-and-death gestures, but the small ones. Little things like pouring a second cup of tea, or badgering someone into doing their exercises, or growing uncomfortable facial hair just for the feeling of the man you loved running his fingers against it.

Dominick sat back down, this time on the seat beside him. Alfie took the opportunity to lean against him. He smiled when the pressure against his shoulder increased, Dominick leaning on him in turn.

"Any other villains you brought to justice while my back was turned?" Dominick asked. "What about Murdoch?"

Alfie sighed. "There wasn't much I could do about him. I rather exhausted the extent of my goodwill with the courts getting us out of having to testify at the trial. There's no proof he knew anything about the killings. Like you said before, that's not really his style. If anyone is willing to come forward about his intimidation, something might be done, but I doubt it."

"Don't worry about him. He's a cur with no master now. Spitalfields will take care of him."

They rode in silence for some minutes before Dominick spoke again.

"It's true then. On top of everything else he did, Toller killed to steal from the burial box. Christ, Alfie. Handfuls of pennies! That's what those lives were worth to him. And if I'd given Helen my money that night—"

"No." Alfie cut him off, his voice quiet but fierce. "No one is responsible for her death other than a greedy man who's awaiting his turn at the gallows now. Any time you start to think otherwise, you just remember that when no one else would or could do anything, you threw yourself into harm's way to find out the truth, even when you knew I would hate it. It was the right thing to do. Who knows how many lives you saved by stopping this monster."

"I thought you were the genius who solved everything?"

"Only because I had a brave, strong partner who'd done most of the work for me. Now stop fishing for compliments and pass me that basket. I never got a chance to have any of Mrs. Hirkins' Bath buns earlier and I'll be damned if I let them sit there uneaten a moment longer.

Dominick laughed, but opened the basket, taking a bun for himself and passing another to Alfie. "Don't you think you'll be able to get more once we arrive? How long will it take to reach Bath anyway?"

Alfie chewed as he considered, the bun's sticky glaze

dissolving into sweet nothingness in his mouth. "Too long to leave these uneaten. Besides, I doubt real Bath buns are as good as hers. Although I do look forward to testing this assertion."

"It's a good thing that we're headed there to find out." Dominick said, passing Alfie another bun just as he was savouring the last bite of the first. "Thank you, by the way. I know that sending Mrs. Hirkins to Balcarres while we go to Bath isn't ideal. We'll be lucky if the entire house hasn't been rearranged by the time we get there. And it's likely a fool's errand besides. There's such a small chance we'll find out anything about my family in Bath. It's not like the French are known for being reliable, even at their best, which that maid certainly wasn't. But I have to try."

When they'd gone back to Grillion's to ask the maid what else she knew, it was to find she'd left the hotel without further word, taking only the money they'd left her and her spare pair of shoes. Wherever she was, Alfie hoped she was happy.

"It's a small chance but a worthwhile one," Alfie said. He'd said something similar when he'd paid for Helen's funeral.

A few coins for a burial, a single sentence on a scrap of paper, a second helping of a favourite treat. Sometimes the small things were the most meaningful of them all.

He closed his eyes as the carriage trundled along. With every mile, the air grew sweeter as they left London behind and the countryside unspooled before them. With any luck, they'd reach their destination in a day or two, but Alfie knew it would only be another stop on their long and happy journey together.

He hummed in question as his hand was lifted. The sound turned into a groan as the sinuous, wet heat of Dominick's tongue curled against his fingertips, licking and sucking until every trace of sticky glaze was gone.

Cheeky devil, thought Alfie. *Perhaps we'll be testing the thickness of the coaching inn walls after all!*

The End

AUTHOR'S NOTE

I delved into a lot of fascinating research for this book and just wanted to mention a few quick points of interest.

First of all, if the system of thief takers, constables, magistrates, etc. mentioned in this novel confuses you, don't worry! The system of policing (such as it was) in London at the time was extremely complicated and decentralised. The question of "Who do you call when you find a dead body?" wasn't nearly as straightforward back then as it is now and "What do they do about the dead body after you show it to them?" was even more complicated.

Secondly, the Grillion's Hotel really was one of the most luxurious hotels in London and Louis XVIII really did stay there. It unfortunately no longer exists and I had to rely on descriptions of other hotels for the interior as very little information about it remains. Indeed, in several of my sources, it was spelled "Grillon's", sometimes even changing spellings within the same document! I've gone for the spelling with the extra "i" as that's the way the parliamentary club which once met at the hotel most consistently spells its name.

One of the things that interests me most about writing historical novels is learning which words and phrases are much newer or older than I would've expected. For example, in this book I describe Jack Murdoch as having a "crumpled pair of boxer's ears". The term I'd planned on using was "cauliflower ears" but after far more extensive research than was probably warranted, I learned that phrase only started being used around 1905 and that earlier terms were generally either too scientific, too bizarre, or too offensive for me to use.

I want to thank Emily for her keen eye and many helpful (and poetic) suggestions that improved my early drafts immensely. And thanks also to Veruska for catching all of the last fiddly little things that I'd missed.

Also, a final thanks to my dear friend Margot, who first started me on my journey to becoming a professional author. Her support and humour when I needed them most will never be forgotten.

ABOUT THE AUTHOR

Samantha SoRelle

Samantha SoRelle grew up all over the world and finally settled in Georgia, USA where the humidity does all sorts of things to her hair.

When she's not writing, she's doing everything possible to keep from writing. This has led to some unusual pastimes including perfecting fake blood recipes, designing her own cross-stitch patterns, and wrapping presents for tigers.

She also enjoys collecting paintings of tall ships and has one pest of a cat who would love to sharpen his claws on them.

She can be found online at **www.samanthasorelle.com**, which has the latest information on upcoming projects, free reads, the mailing list, and all her social media accounts. She can also be contacted by email at samanthasorelle@gmail.com, which she is much better about checking than social media!

BY SAMANTHA SORELLE

His Lordship's Mysteries:

His Lordship's Secret
His Lordship's Master
His Lordship's Return
His Lordship's Blood
Lord Alfie of the Mud (Short Story)
His Lordship's Gift (Short Story)

Other Works:

Cairo Malachi and the Adventure of the Silver Whistle
Suspiciously Sweet
The Pantomime Prince (Short Story)

HIS LORDSHIP'S BLOOD

Even after a year of having an earl for a lover, Dominick still isn't prepared for the dazzling high society of Bath with its ruinous gossip and scandalous fashions. All he wants is to uncover who his parents were so he and Alfie can return to their quiet life in Scotland. But as long-buried secrets come to light, Dominick finds himself trapped in a web of intrigue that may prove impossible to escape.

When an old acquaintance winds up dead, it's almost a relief. With a murder to solve, Alfie and Dominick have something to distract them from the jaws of fate slowly closing around them. Assuming, of course, that they can avoid being murdered themselves.

Alfie knows how much learning the truth about his family means to Dominick, but as events begin to spin out of control, it soon becomes clear that knowledge may come with a terrible cost--their happiness, their relationship, and even their lives.

His Lordship's Blood is the fourth novel in the His Lordship's Mysteries series.